Missy
Whynaught

Missy Whynaught

Elizabeth Ball

Baraka Books
Montréal

ISBN Paper 978-1-77186-435-0
ISBN Epub 978-1-77186-448-0
ISBN PDF 978-1-77186-449-7

Cover artwork by Oona Ode (oonaode.com, @oonaode)
Cover design by Leila Marshy
Book Design by Folio infographie

Editing: Leila Marshy
Proofreading: Elise Moser

Legal Deposit, 4th quarter 2026
Bibliothéque et Archives nationales du Québec
Library and Archives Canada

Published by Baraka Books of Montreal
Printed and bound in Quebec

TRADE DISTRIBUTION & RETURNS
Canada: UTPdistribution.com

United States and World: Independent Publishers Group
IPGbook.com

We acknowledge the support from the Société de développement des entreprises culturelles (SODEC) and the Government of Quebec tax credit for book publishing administered by SODEC.

Société de développement des entreprises culturelles Québec

Financé par le gouvernement du Canada
Funded by the Government of Canada | Canada

PUBLISHED & PRINTED IN CANADA

For my father and muse, David Ball.
May he roam in peace.

Dangerous Man

Father and daughter took to the sky
On a frightfully bright white plane,
They drank some rye, and waved goodbye,
And hoped they'd feel no pain.
The daughter looked out to the great skyline,
And prayed to a shining star,
"Oh charming father! Oh father of mine,
What a dangerous man you are,
            You are,
            You are!
What a dangerous man you are!"

Father said to his child, "Don't act so riled!
You seriously ruin my mood!
We are taking this trip, don't give me that lip!
I suggest you learn to delude."
They flew away, for a week plus a day,
To the island of sugar and cheer.
And there by her hut, a young lass strut
Dressed whorish to mask her fear,
            Her fear,
            Her fear,
Dressed whorish to mask her fear.

"Young miss, are you willing, to sell for a shilling
Your youth?" Said the maiden, "I must.
To feed my large clan, I will lie with you man
And disguise my furious disgust."
The daughter recoiled and silently boiled,
Which she regrets for all of her days;
But hand over glass, at the edge of the shore,
She joined in his lecherous ways,
            His ways,
            His ways,
She joined in his lecherous ways.

1
Dog Song

The night before my father, Pup Whynaught, was found dead in a hole on the beach, there was torrential rain. It was late October in Cuba, monsoon season. Everything was wet, wet, wet. The unpaved streets were giant mud puddles. The laundry wouldn't dry. Mould grew on the birds' feathers right under their beady birdy eyes. The leaves on the palm trees couldn't rise to their regular perky attention but instead hung heavy like exhausted arms.

Pup had been wearing filthy beige cargo shorts and a Hawaiian shirt. He'd lost his threadbare sandals and was barefoot. He said he couldn't buy new sandals because the shops were closed due to the monsoon flooding—but he'd run out of money, so he couldn't buy new ones anyway. He'd also lost a front tooth, and it hurt; he wasn't sure how it had happened.

He knew he had to find shelter. Hurricanes were on their way.

Earlier in the day, he asked one of his expat buddies, the one he'd helped buy a laptop to keep in touch with his wife and kids back home, if he could crash at his place for a night or two. "Sorry, Pup," the buddy said. "My girlfriend's sick."

He asked another expat buddy, the one he'd helped install a solar panel for his Cuban-home-away-from-Canada home. "Sorry, Pup, I'm washing my hair tonight."

He went to Alonzo, the bartender at his favourite watering hole. "I'll sleep on the floor," Pup pleaded. "Please. Just for a few nights until the hurricanes pass."

"Sorry," Alonzo said. "Your tab's unpaid. Your visa expired. Big fine for us if immigration finds you here, *hombre*. Big fine." Before Pup could ask again, Alonzo snapped a warning: "How's your son?" Pup didn't respond, or remind the bartender that he'd paid for his mother's gastric bypass surgery the year before.

Head down, he made his way back to his hole in the beach. It was his best bet. It was where he belonged. A dozen stray dogs followed behind like a funeral parade.

The day before that, Pup had brought his five-year-old son, my half-brother, Juan-Howard, to the beach without telling anybody.

After racking up a tab he couldn't pay at Alonzo's bar and drinking copious amounts of rum he knew he shouldn't drink, he went to pick Juan-Howard up from school. My brother was surprised to see him. A little nervous, too. But Pup expected it and, despite being smashed, came prepared. It wasn't the little guy's fault he'd been poisoned against his own father. With a pocket full of candy, Pup performed magic tricks, pulling the sweets out of Juan-Howard's ear. Juan-Howard's frown turned upside down. He took our Pup's hand and skipped towards the bike and the trailer hitched to the back of it. Pup had made the trailer himself with scrap metal and a baby stroller.

He'd decorated it with fairy lights and drawings of Juan-Howard's favourite things: planes, trains, dinosaurs. If he could attach an engine to it, they'd fly off the island one day. As he pedaled to the beach, Pup and Juan-Howard sang "Row, row, row your boat."

The two of them built a sandcastle. A huge, marvelous sandcastle. The best sandcastle in the world! With a moat and a drawbridge and two dozen soldiers made out of shells guarding against a seaweed-pebble dragon. They played in the waves. They shared a mango the size of a rugby ball and wiped its juice from their faces with their sticky, sandy hands. They sang "Row, row, row your boat" another hundred times.

After a while, Pup was tired. It was muggy and the sun was slowly setting. He looked at my half-brother and said, "I'm going to rest my eyes for a moment before we head back, okay, darlin'? Just for a moment."

The week before that, Pup had been on a bender. He spent his days sitting at the bar crying to Alonzo. "Can you believe I wasn't invited to Juan-Howard's birthday party? A birthday party that *I* paid for! The pig roast, the birthday cake, the stupid fucking earsore of a band they hired. All *my* money for *my* kid! I brought up three perfectly fine and healthy children in Canada already. How dare Yolanda tell me how to parent! She's just a kid herself! A few beers never hurt no one. It takes the edge off. It's her fault I started drinking again, anyway. Always on my case for this, for that. Coming up with our "arrangement," which isn't an arrangement at all, just her telling me how and when and where I can spend time with *my* son! How long did she think I would keep up that kind of arrangement? I can't even take a shit without her or The Marias having something to say about it. I'll teach her a lesson or two about what happens when you tell Pup Whynaught what to do!"

Six months. That was exactly how long he put up with the "arrangement." Twice a week he was allowed to spend the afternoon with Juan-Howard on the condition that he remain sober. Three hours at a time, with one of Yolanda's sisters or cousins or aunties (who he called The Marias, as he couldn't tell one from another and all their names seemed to have Maria in them) there to supervise.

Also in the arrangement was that Pup could move back into the house he'd built with his two hands and his life savings. It was three stories high, the biggest house in town. Juan-Howard, Yolanda and Yolanda's boyfriend lived on the top floor. The Marias lived on the main floor. And Pup lived downstairs with Juan-Howard's grandmother, Marisol. Marisol was in her fifties, like Pup, with kind, tired eyes and tiny hands. She cooked all his favourite foods: fried *patatas*, deviled *huevos*, roast *pollo*, black beans mixed with salsa and mayonnaise. She did his laundry once a week: sheets, cargo shorts, three pairs of underwear, and three Hawaiian shirts. Every morning, she made grapefruit juice the way he liked it: sour, no sugar, with a touch of mint; he spiked it with rum when her back was turned. Unlike Yolanda, her teenage daughter he'd knocked up, Pup trusted Marisol. "Yolanda will spend it all on nail polish and her boyfriend," he complained to Marisol whenever Yolanda asked him for money. "She's as slippery as deer guts on a doorknob! You're the only one I trust to spend it wisely." Having his grapefruit juice with Marisol in the morning was Pup's favourite part of the day. He told me that before she turned against him like "the rest of 'em." He sometimes wished it had been her he'd knocked up rather than Yolanda. "But who am I kidding?" he said. "It works because I'm not banging her."

Marisol liked Pup, too. She liked his sparkly eyes; they reminded her of the ocean. She liked his cheeky smile; it reminded her of her beloved grandson, Juan-Howard. She even liked how he needed her. It made her feel important to go out early every morning with money in her pocket to buy him grapefruits and the best hunks of *cerdo*. It made her feel good to give him a second chance at living with them. Before they met Pup, her family lived in a small shack without running water or electricity. Prior to Pup, they lived off government rations of rice and beans, only eating meat on the holidays, Christmas and Easter. The only extra money they'd had coming in was from Yolanda's hooking with tourists. If Pup hadn't knocked Yolanda up, Marisol would have considered marrying him herself. If Pup hadn't kept breaking the rules of the arrangement with Juan-Howard, she might have been able to look past his pissing the bed and waking her up every night screaming in a blacked-out stupor. "But who am I kidding?" she said. "I'm much too old to put up with this. We've given him more than he paid for."

A week before his bender, Pup woke up on the floor beside his bed; he was naked, covered in piss and vomit. His heart was beating so fast and loud that he thought it was the construction outside. When he remembered it was monsoon season and construction was halted, he was sure he was dying. He was scared of dying, always had been. He began screaming in his broken Spanish: "Help! Help! Ayuda! Yo muriendo!"

Four men, relatives of the mother of Juan-Howard, came into the bedroom and told him he had to leave. Now. *Ahora.* Though they knew Pup to be a gentle soul who wouldn't fight with anything but words, one of them had a bat just in case. They gave him ten minutes to clean up and get dressed. They gave him another five minutes to pack up his stuff. His only possessions were several items of clothing and a Ziploc bag for his passport, address book and photographs of his four children, me included. He'd recently lost his passport, however, so the only things he took were the photographs and address book, tucking them in the deep front pocket of his cargo shorts. He left without the clothes or a fight, not even a fighting word.

"Dios mío," whispered Marisol, as she watched the father of her grandson make his way towards the ocean. "Perdónanos."

Three months before he took Juan-Howard to the beach, Pup had been calling me in Saint John every night. Always around three a.m. Even without the phone calls, I wasn't sleeping: my two-month-old son was sucking my breasts on one end and my boyfriend was poking me with his hard-on on the other. Sometimes I answered the phone; sometimes I didn't. Sometimes I could make out what he was saying over the rum and the lousy reception; sometimes I couldn't. "When will you visit me, Missy? When can I visit you?"

"I just gave birth."

"How wonderful! When can I meet him?"

"Soon, Pup. I promise."

If I told my boyfriend about the phone calls, those conversations were all the same, too.

"There's no way in hell he's coming here," he said. "And there's no way in hell I'll allow you and the baby to go over there."

"He's not well."

"All the more reason for you not to see him."

"But he needs me!"

"We need you more."

The sun was shining when the security guard found my father dead in the hole on the beach. Back at the house he'd built with his two hands and life savings, Marisol and Yolanda and The Marias and all the neighbours, even the grapefruit vendor, fussed over Juan-Howard. "What would you like to do today? Are you hungry? Here, have some cake for breakfast. You deserve it for being so brave!" They were going to have a little fiesta in the evening to thank the fisherman who'd found Juan-Howard two days earlier wandering the beach alone and brought him safely home. There was a lot to celebrate.

Dozens of stray dogs gathered in front of the house. One by one, they began to howl until all you could hear for miles and miles was dog song. Yolanda opened the door and threw a shoe at them. Marisol suddenly felt a little weak in the knees, so she sat down in a kitchen chair to rest and pray. Juan-Howard tilted his head to the sky and howled, too.

I know this to be true because I heard it. From that village in Cuba, across the ocean, through the sun and the cold, slushy, late October rain that had started to fall because November was right around the corner in Saint John. I heard it in our apartment where only a second earlier, I lay awake in bed, sandwiched between my baby's hungry lips and my boyfriend's dick. I sat up and howled along with them.

2

Ode to Pup

My father was born in a doghouse. That's the story.

One morning, my Grampy Whynaught found him sleeping in the backyard doghouse, curled against his dog Daisy like a big pink growth. At first, Grampy thought it was a pesky rat causing trouble. He wanted to hit him over the head with the pail of scraps he'd brought for Daisy. But then it cooed and opened his big eyes, and Grampy could see right away that it was no rat. It was a baby. His own baby Jesus. Arriving exactly four years to the day of their six-year-old son's death from meningitis. Grampy's cries of joy woke up the whole town and put everyone in the best mood they'd ever known.

Grampy and Grammy Whynaught loved that baby like nobody's business. Sure, they tried to find his parents. They put up signs. They put an announcement in the paper. They even offered a hundred-dollar reward, money they didn't have, just in case someone was missing him. The story of the baby found in the doghouse traveled far and wide, from their hometown, Milton, Nova Scotia, to the snow-capped mountains of BC. It even made the *Toronto Sun*, which was a big thing for a Maritimer. For a moment, the Whynaughts and the boy pup were celebrities.

They named him Philbert, Pup for short, and no one ever did come to claim him. For the first time in years, Grampy stopped thinking about jumping in front of a train, and Grammy got up from bed more than once a day. He dumped his whiskey down the sink; she opened the curtains. He brushed his teeth; she washed her hair. They even went back to church. They were going to be parents again.

But though my father was a good boy, an otherwise normal boy, the bigger he got, the more dog-like behaviours he assumed. He crawled until he was two years old, his bum wiggling high when he was proud of himself. When he'd done something naughty, he put his hands over his face and hid in the corner. He refused to use a spoon, preferring to shove his face straight into the bowl. He howled wildly during thunderstorms.

His doggiest trait of all was that he hated being inside. When he wasn't sniffing around the backyard, the only walls he tolerated were those of the doghouse, and he only went there to take his meals and naps. To keep him happy, his parents painted the doghouse like a human house. They carved out a window so he could wave if he wanted biscuits, and laid down decorative pillows to keep him comfy. Old Daisy was dead by then, so Pup had the whole place to himself. When winter came, they added insulation.

By the time Pup was old enough to go to school, he'd outgrown both his naps and the doghouse. His parents got another dog, a scruffy, black mutt named Terry, to encourage him to sleep in his big boy bed. And he did, as long as Terry was by his side. At six years old, he finally walked on two legs and used utensils. And, boy, was he handsome! He had shaggy dark hair like Terry, and big, forget-me-not-blue eyes with long lashes. He wasn't tall, but he wasn't short either, and he was the fastest runner at school. All the girls were in love with him, and some of the boys, too.

Despite his charm and athleticism, Pup did terribly at school. He had a hard time keeping still and fell so behind that he could barely read and write his name. According to Grammy, he was always up to trouble, like bringing frogs to class or stealing milk from the cafeteria. Whenever he could, he'd slip out of school, where Terry waited for him desperately. The boy and his dog would then spend the day wandering the woods, daydreaming, looking for small animals, climbing trees, digging holes. Their favourite spot was the Deep Hole, an old quarry turned popular swimming spot for Miltonians. They'd swing off the huge pine tree everyone called the Wishing Tree, and splash into the water. Followed by an afternoon siesta under the tree, after which they may or may not have slipped back into school before the last bell. The teachers tried to scold him, but they couldn't help but smile. Pup was everyone's favourite. Plus, it wasn't like he was headed to college. "He'll be lucky to finish high school," they told his parents. "It'll be a small miracle if he doesn't drop out before he's sixteen."

Pup wandered during the night, too. Unless there was a thunderstorm, which still got him riled up like a werewolf. In the morning, his parents would find him curled up on the porch with that carefree smile of his, like he was dreaming of chasing rabbits, utterly unbothered by the cold floor. Oh, how they begged him to stay put! "What if you get lost in the woods? What if a coyote attacks you? We've already lost one child; we can't lose another!" But his father was too soft-hearted to follow through on any punishment, and his mother was too fat to chase after him. So, Pup continued as he pleased. He wanted to make his parents happy, but he wanted his freedom more.

Whatever control my grandparents had over my father when he was a child went out the window when he became a teenager. As predicted, he dropped out of school at fifteen and hung out on the rough edges of town, preferring the company of drifters and loners, making money running lobsters for the fisherman to the rich tourists on their way to and from Lunenburg. He took up with Sexy Suzie, a scruffy redhead with a big bum and puffy eyes that made her look like she'd been crying her whole life. Sexy Suzie lived with her alcoholic parents in an old hunting shack. The relationship between her and Pup ran hot and cold, and no one was ever sure if they were together, but they weren't surprised when he knocked her up.

When his parents heard about the pregnancy, they decided to approach Pup about his future. In those days and parts of the world, unless nature had other plans, a baby was sure to arrive, like a thunderstorm or a rainbow, however you wanted to look at it. The thought of a new baby made them happy. So, one evening when they knew Pup would be home, his mother cooked up his favourite dinner—corned beef and cabbage—and his father opened a bottle of cider. Over blueberry cobbler, they announced their decision to remortgage the house.

"So you and Suzie can build a home of your own," they said, their eyes cast down, worried they might spook him. "We can buy the plot next door, if you like. That way, we can help with the baby."

Pup cocked his head and chuckled. He loved his parents and wanted to do right by them. "I want to do right by everyone," he told them. "But I have plans of my own. I'm going to become a welder. I leave next month to start my training in Halifax. I'll get a job, and with the big bucks, I'll be back to buy a house in no time."

And that's what he did. Almost. When he was seventeen and Suzie was four months pregnant, he packed a change of clothes and a dozen tins of sardines, left Milton and went to Halifax. After his training, he got a job on an oil rig off the coast of Newfoundland. And he did make big bucks that he sent to Sexy Suzie—which she used to move to Texas to become a cowgirl-turned-pole dancer.

But he didn't come home. Not for the birth. Not after he learned that Sexy Suzie had left my baby half-sister, Jemima, with her pickled brained parents like a sack of rotten potatoes. Not for almost a year. And when he finally did come back, it was as if the carnival had come to town. Everywhere you looked, my father brought cheer to someone or another with the money he'd made offshore. He bought a houseboat for Sexy Suzie's parents. He paid off my grandparents' mortgage. He bought a tractor for a down-and-out buddy and paid a year's rent for another. The local watering hole, the Cuckoo Nest, tacked a bronze plaque with his name on it above the bar for the large donation he'd made to fix their roof. All the women in the town were in love with him, and some of the men, too.

His visit only lasted six weeks before he up and left again with the same backpack and an empty bank account, this time for a job in Tuktoyaktuk. "There's no work here. And we can't afford to turn down the money," he told everyone, which was true. But it was also true that no matter what he did, he couldn't shake the itch to travel. He loved his baby girl, but he loved his freedom more.

Over the next five years, Pup came home three times. Once for Jemima's confirmation. Once for Grampy's funeral. And once to help put his 750-pound couch-ridden mother in a nursing home. Pup howled until his throat was hoarse as he watched Grammy being driven away in the back of a flatbed truck. Even though he promised he'd come back to take care of her, he knew he wouldn't. Instead, he paid for a nurse to wait on her full time at the nursing home and to walk the chihuahua he'd bought to keep her company. He called every Sunday and sent pink carnations once a month. Grammy commissioned his portrait and hung it on the wall next to her super-sized hospital bed. A table beside her displayed her favourite things of his: Terry's old leash, a tin of sardines, his baby chew toy. Every time she survived another heart attack, she said it was her son, her own baby Jesus, that had saved her.

When Jemima was old enough, Pup sent for her to visit him wherever he was working. She spent her seventh birthday in Boston, her ninth in Calgary, and they went to Disney every March break. The attractive, dark-haired, blue-eyed daddy-daughter duo celebrated Jemima's tenth birthday at Pizza Hut on Rothesay Avenue in Saint John. Pup had work at the Irving Refinery shutdown. That's when Pup met my mama, Wendy, a busty blonde waitress who gave them free garlic fingers.

"What a striking pair!" she said.

"Back atcha, doll," Pup replied. "Why don't you join us for drinks at the motel after your shift?"

Of course, she did.

She spent the next day at Mispec beach with them, eating pickled mackerel straight out of the jar. And she offered to look after Jemima while Pup worked so the girl didn't have to watch TV all day at the motel. She quit Pizza Hut a few weeks later to follow him to his next job in Denmark. "What've I got to lose?" she said.

At twenty-one years old, my mama didn't have anything to lose by leaving Saint John. The eldest of five, she was still living in the trailer she'd grown up in, helping her single mother put food on the table. She'd had enough of achy feet and smelling like she bathed in tomato sauce. She'd had enough of the trailer park boys, with their ATVs and gas huffing, who only wanted to get down her pants then toss her away like an empty box of Timbits.

Mama followed Pup everywhere. While he worked in Belgium, she walked around in high heels, gorging on chocolate all day. In Italy, they got drunk and fell out of a gondola. In Egypt, they took pictures of themselves groping the tits of an Egyptian queen statue. It was the happiest time of her life. Shortly after Pup got a job in Algeria, where they lived in a construction camp in the desert, Mama announced she was pregnant.

"A construction camp is no place for a pregnant woman," he told her. "You have to go back home."

My mama got down on her knees. "Oh, please, Pup. Please let me stay," she cried. "What if the plane crashes? What if the baby dies? I can't bear doing this without you!"

Pup hated her tears and her pleas. It gave him visions of his mother crying out from the flatbed truck, begging him not to let them take her to the nursing home. It reminded him of the promises he'd made to come back and look after her; of his overwhelming urge to run as far away from her and Milton as his hairy legs could take him.

He put his hands over his face, hoping my mama would disappear.

When that didn't work, he looked for a corner to hide.

When that didn't work, he reached into his pocket and pulled out his chequebook.

"It hurts me as much as it hurts you to say goodbye," he said. "But I couldn't live with myself if something happened to you here. I'll stay here and finish up the job while you buy the best home you can find in Saint John, okay? Make it perfect for us. I'll be back in no time. I promise."

So that's what happened. Almost. When she was five months pregnant with my brother, Randall, my mama flew back to Saint John. And she chose the best home she could find: a ground-floor apartment next to the City Market, two blocks from the liquor store, four blocks from the bowling alley. She made it perfect by painting the walls the same shade as Pup's baby blues and cultivating the cutest little garden that was so magical the local fairies were always flying about.

But Pup didn't come back soon. Not for my brother's birth; not after he learned Mama was as sad as a foggy Saint John day; not after she threatened to hire a hit man. Instead, he took a detour to Spain and spent a few weeks swimming with dolphins and mastering the Spanish omelette. When he finally did come back, he only stayed long enough to buy her a spunky, blonde puppy they called Madonna and get her knocked up again. With me. After that, he continued as he pleased. Chasing tail elsewhere, I suppose, as dogs all over the world are known to do.

3
Poverty Hill

Madonna was buried alive. But that's top secret. No one knows about it except for me, my brother, Randall, Mama and, well, half of Saint John. But it was a secret from Pup, who thought she died peacefully of old age in her sleep. Everyone knew Pup could never find out. It would've killed him. I wished it had killed me instead. Here's why.

When I was eight, me, Randall, Mama, and our big, yellow dog, Madonna, moved from our downtown apartment in Saint John to a little cottage on Poverty Hill, a dirt road off the highway on the way out to the wealthy Rothesay suburbs. Mama said the cottage would be cheaper than our downtown rent. She said the country air would be good for us triplets, which she called us because me, Randall and Madonna were all born within eleven months of each other. "You triplets won't have to worry about the fuckin' bible-thumping neighbours or their screaming babies no more," she said. "The country air will taste better, and you can go to school where the rich brats from the suburbs go. I can sell Avon anywhere. The rich brats will be better friends than your poor friends downtown," she assured us, "because they have fuckin' money and stuff."

I was good at making friends and always up for an adventure, so I didn't mind moving. I liked the bible-thumping neighbour kids well enough, even though they were always on my case about being a girl with short hair and calling myself Michael Jackson. On the day we moved, me and Madonna hopped into the back seat of our brown station wagon and, with all the neighbours waving, I squished my lips against the window into hideous shapes as we pulled away. By the time the smears faded, it felt like we had lived on Poverty Hill forever.

Ours was the first house after the train tracks. A little white one with black window frames and a crooked deck and peeling paint. Being part hound, Madonna howled every time she heard the train whistle. On the hour, sometimes all night. That drove Mama crazy, and she didn't know what to do because she loved Madonna but she also loved the cottage and a good night's sleep. Eventually the howling and the train became white noise and she got used to it. It became a joke for us to howl along with Madonna. Anyone would have thought we were a pack of feral mutts that had busted out of the SPCA. I still can't hear a train whistle without tilting my chin toward the moon and letting out my inner dog.

The first thing I did at the new house was climb the most enormous pine tree on the lot. While Mama was unloading the car, Randall was playing on his Gameboy, and Madonna was sniffing out rabbits, I reached my Michael Jackson-gloved hand over the bare one until I was at the seventy-five-foot peak of the tree.

"Hey, Mama!" I hollered down, "Look at me!"

That sure scared her! But, like Madonna's howling, she got used to that too because once we found out I had squirrel genes, there was nothing she could do to keep me out of the trees. That pine had a perfect fat branch three-quarters of the way up where I could spend hours reading my Archie comics and spying on the neighbours. A woodpecker had drilled a deep hole where I hid all my secret stuff, like my diary and letters from Pup.

The second thing I did after I went up that tree was burst into tears, weeping and wailing as if I'd been stung by a swarm of hornets and was about to fall to my death. All of a sudden, way up in that tree far from our old apartment, it hit me that Pup would never be able to find us. We hadn't called to tell him we were moving because he didn't have a phone. We hadn't written because he didn't have an address. We hadn't spoken to him for months because he was on some oil rig in the middle of the ocean making loads of money so we could afford this new house, and weren't we the most selfish people in the world? What would happen if he showed up at our old place and found us gone? He would think we'd abandoned him. Like that stray black cat we used to feed sometimes. I named him Jackson. Mama wouldn't let us adopt Jackson because she said adopting a black cat was just asking for trouble. We hadn't said a proper goodbye to Jackson either because he was also MIA in the days leading up to our move.

But I think my crying scared Mama too.

"Unless you're stuck, you better get your fuckin' arse down here immediately, Missy Whynaught! And if you are stuck, well, you're shit outta luck cause the fuckin' phone ain't connected yet, so I can't call the fire department! And don't think I'm climbing up there after ya. I just got my fuckin' nails done!"

When I finally climbed down, I told her why I was so upset.

"Nonsense!" she said. "Jackson's got his paw out to every other fuckin' family on that street. He doesn't give a cat's meow who leaves him food as long as he's fuckin' fed. That's what cats are like. Only in it for themselves. As for your father, don't you worry about him. That man can sniff us out from the other side of the fuckin' world. He'd find us even if we covered ourselves in tomato juice to mask our smell and lived underground like moles. He's like that fuckin' hobo dog on TV. Believe me; he'll show up when we least expect it. Plus, you know he can't go without seeing Madonna for too long."

I wasn't convinced that black cats were any more trouble than any other cats. But Mama was right about me and the bible-thumping neighbours being the same to Jackson. Cats, I've learned over the years, are about as fickle as they come. She was also right about Pup being like that hobo dog on TV. The one that showed up out of nowhere and saved the day. It'd be raining or snowing or hailing, no one would be around for miles, and then—*poof*—the dog would appear all calm and smiling that happy hobo smile, pull the dying guy out of the hole, lick him clean, and then—*poof*—disappear again. Everyone wishing he would stay forever but knowing he wouldn't because it was in the hobo dog's nature to wander alone.

That was Pup.

Except Pup rarely saved the day. In fact, he was often either the guy stuck in the hole or the guy who pushed the other guy into the hole. And only some of us wanted him to stay forever. But he was calm, and he smiled a lot, and spent most of his life wandering around until he decided to show up in the middle of an ice storm or Mama's thirtieth birthday party. Plus, he loved dogs—Madonna most of all.

I clung to the idea of Pup being a hobo dog. I was proud of it. The hobo dog on TV, after all, was a hero. And so, so cute. In school, whenever we had to write about our summer vacation or Christmas holiday, I'd write about Pup as a hobo dog. Some of my stories had elements of truth; others were bullshit. Most were combinations of both. It's hard for me to decipher the truth from bullshit. I'm a bit like Mama that way.

I caught Hobo Dog coming down the chimney dressed up just like Santa! He left a pogo ball for me, just like I wanted. Randall got a Nintendo, and Madonna got a vanilla cake with red and green icing! Hobo Dog's some smart, knowing dogs are allergic to chocolate! I didn't let him know I'd seen him, though. I didn't want to spook him. He's really sensitive, and I wanted to make sure he comes back next year. I hope he liked the rum and eggnog we left him. The End.

Five percent true. I was nine. It was our first Christmas on Poverty Hill, and Pup hadn't smelled us out yet. I was sure it was because I'd eaten too many tomatoes that year. We'd bathe Madonna in tomato juice after a run-in with a skunk or rolling in something dead. I figured if that works to get rid of Madonna's smell, maybe it was masking my scent, too. It felt like a reasonable explanation. SpaghettiOs, goulash, tomato soup. I removed anything with tomatoes from my diet. I even tore the tomato plants out of the garden. Just to rile me up, Mama and Randall poured ketchup on everything—even Christmas dinner. I blamed them that it took Pup almost the whole year to find us. The 5 percent truth was in the presents. I did get a pogo ball, and Randall did get his Nintendo, just like we'd asked. And Madonna did get a vanilla cake with green and red icing that she puked up under the Christmas tree. The tags written in Mama's handwriting said the presents were from Pup.

Hobo Dog took us to Disney for March break! We drove all the way to Florida and slept in the car. We saw flamingos and ate oranges and ice cream for every meal! I got so sunburned that Hobo Dog rented us a motel so I could soak in the cold bathtub. My skin had so many blisters it looked like bubble wrap. At first, he was mad that I made us lose two days' vacation, but it ended up raining so hard that we couldn't do much anyway. So we watched movies and ordered take-away. We ended up having a blast! Even Madonna had fun. She didn't get carsick and puke in the car like she usually does. The End.

Twenty percent true. I was ten. Pup had finally sniffed us out. He showed up at the schoolyard driving Mama's station wagon with Madonna riding shotgun. He'd gone to see Mama on Poverty Hill but she told him he had another thing coming if he thought he was staying with us after taking a month's vacation in Thailand doing God only knows what with God only knows who, and this after a four-month gig on an oil rig off the coast of Scotland. She threw our suitcases at him along with her car keys. "Take the fuckin' dog, too!" She said, "I need a break!" We begged him to take us to Disney, but because of some dodgy business involving a hitchhiker and a stolen passport, we went to visit Jemima and Grammy Whynaught down in Milton. When we got there, Jemima was on a holiday of her own and we didn't have a key, so we slept in the car for a night. It was so cold Randall got frostbite and had to have part of his left ear amputated. After he was discharged from the hospital, we spent the rest of the week visiting

Grammy during the day at her nursing home. It was pretty boring. It was me who got car sick because I couldn't stop reading *Flowers in the Attic*. I always wondered why Mama let him use her car.

Hobo Dog built us a pool with his bare hands! It's so big all the other Poverty Hill kids swam with us every day. He'd just come back from Africa where he rode on an elephant so he made the slide in the shape of an elephant's trunk! Hobo Dog said he'd never seen such a good swimmer and that I must be part mermaid. I even outswam him sometimes, and hobo dogs are excellent swimmers. I got it from his side of the family, he said. The End.

Thirty percent true. I was eleven. Pup showed up after working six months in a construction camp in Nigeria. He brought me a little ivory elephant. He was devastated to find Madonna so decrepit. Her hips were all bony, and she had difficulty getting up the stairs. Her eyes were milky-blue blind. She spent most of her time sleeping, and she'd gotten really fat. At eleven-and-a-half years old, she was an old woman. Pup only had a three-week leave, and he spent most of it trying to rehabilitate Madonna. He took her to the vet. He put her on a diet. Then he dug a grave for her in the middle of the yard. He was sure she was going to croak while he was away. He thought he was doing Mama a favour, so she wouldn't have to dig it herself. But he was dead wrong. When Mama saw the hole, her face turned gravel grey. I was sure she would faint or run for the hills, but she didn't do either because Pup was so busy crying that she had to console him. We all did. Even Madonna hauled herself up from where she was sleeping and hobbled over to cuddle him. She was a very intuitive dog. On the day before Pup left, we went to the beach. I spent hours in the water flippin' and dippin' while Randall, who hates the water, sulked under a tree. Pup did say I was part mermaid. And he did say I must've gotten it from his side of the family. It's true; I am an excellent swimmer. As for other kids on Poverty Hill: bullshit. The Whynaught triplets were the only kids for miles and miles.

Mama wasn't worried when my fifth-grade teacher, Mrs. Walker, called to talk about the Hobo Dog stories. I overheard their conversation while waiting in the hallway outside the classroom. "I think Missy's confused about her father," Mrs. Walker said.

"Nah, she adores her father! She's just creative," Mama answered.

"I worry Missy might find herself in trouble one day."

"Really?" said Mama. "I foresee that she'll be in the circus one day. And I have a sixth sense about these things."

"So, let me get this clear, Mrs. Whynaught, you're not worried about Missy? You don't want her to see the guidance counselor?"

"Mrs. Walker, I like to live in the here and now. What's the point of worrying about troubles that haven't happened yet? Shrinks are for crazy folks. Missy's a free spirit. Like her father. You should see how fast she can climb trees! But I appreciate your concern."

What Mama worried about was the grave in the middle of our yard. Not because it was one hell of an eyesore—she was used to Pup's holes. He was known all over the county for them, notorious for showing up and offering to dig holes for things he rarely finished. We had a partially built septic tank in the backyard that we used as a hideout. Pup borrowed a buddy's bulldozer once and dug out half a basement for us. We had a six-foot pile of dirt for a whole year until one of the neighbors offered to drag it away. Pup started on a goldfish pond for Jemima once, but when he abandoned it halfway through for a job out West, her boyfriend turned it into a marijuana garden.

No, it wasn't the hole per se that was a problem. It was the hole's purpose. Mama was convinced that, by digging Madonna's grave before she croaked, Pup had put a curse on our family. "It's worse than naming a baby before it's born," she said. "Worse than adopting a black cat. Worse than complimenting a beautiful child. Did you know that in India, parents ask the person who gave the compliment to spit in the child's face immediately? Did you know that in Russia, if you change your underwear between Christmas and New Year's, you'll get boils? Did you know that in the Philippines, you can't go straight home from a funeral? You need to make a pit stop somewhere to shake off the bad spirits first, like McDonald's."

She took a bunch of books on witchcraft out from the library and painted so many evil eyes all over our property that it felt like we were in a Big Brother movie. She racked up a huge phone bill calling a psychic named Pinky.

Pinky said you should never have a mirror facing your bed. Spirits from the other side are just waiting to suck your soul out through it. Pinky said not to refill the grave because it might tempt the devil even more. Pinky said we should beware of the letter D, the number seven, mysterious rashes, and the colour purple. But good fortune would come to us from someone else's misfortune when we least expected it.

Randall and I would tease her.

"But, Mama, we're not Indian or Filipino or Russian."

"Hey, Mama, did you see that lonesome crow staring at you from the kitchen window this morning? I'm sure it had a purple bow around its neck."

Once, we moved all the mirrors in the house to her bedroom. When she woke up in the morning, she was sure she'd died and gone to hell. "Laugh all you fuckin' like, kids," she cried as she rubbed the Avon lucky horseshoe pendant she wore around her neck, "but believe me, bad luck is on the horizon."

Outside, Madonna dozed next to her grave, content as a well-nursed baby.

Mama could also be surprisingly wise sometimes (and maybe Pinky really did have a knack for divination). When my face broke out so bad that I stopped keeping my hair short so I could use it to cover my face, Mama took me to the doctor.

The doctor said, "This is acne, ma'am, it's genetic, not a mysterious rash."

"Genetics, my ass," Mama said, "nobody on either side of the family ever had skin like that." When our neighbor, Mr. Duncan, got run over by the train, and everyone said it was an accident, Mama said, "No accident there. That old soul knew the train schedule like I know when I'm about to get on the rag. Timed right down to the minute. D for danger; D for death. D for Mr. Duncan." We got a thousand-dollar compensation when the neighbour's oil spill contaminated our water supply. Mama used it to pay off her enormous phone bill. "See?" she said. "Just as Pinky predicted."

Eventually, I stopped sharing my Hobo Dog stories at school. I was too old for that. They ended up in my diary, which I hid in the woodpecker hole in my pine tree.

Hobo Dog took me and Madonna camping for a week. We had a great time. We slept in a tent with Madonna smack dab between us to keep us warm. We went snorkeling in the ocean and ate periwinkles with safety pins that we picked off the rocks ourselves. Delicious! We met other campers and had a party around the bonfire. We sang and roasted marshmallows and told ghost stories with flashlights under our chins. At the end of the party, Hobo Dog was worried about the bears getting at our leftover food. One of the guys said, "Hang it up in the tree!"

So Hobo Dog said, "Of course, great idea, buddy! Go on, Missy, you do it. Show 'em how tree climbing's done." So I took the garbage bag and climbed the highest tree on the campsite. On my way down, I tried showing off by doing it one-handed, but my leg got caught in a branch and I fell, getting a nasty cut on my thigh on the way down. The next day we went snorkeling again. Boy, did the salt water ever sting my cut! But I didn't let it stop me. The minute of pain was worth the hours of fun I had in the ocean. I can't wait to go again next year. The End.

Seventy percent true. I was twelve. Pup began to spend more and more of his time in the tropics, mostly Cuba, between jobs. He promised to send for me to visit soon. "We'll go on bike rides to the beach and go snorkeling," he said. "I know this woman who will braid your hair for a buck. And a guy who will drive us around on his motorbike for two bucks. And another who will cook us anything we want for three bucks. Come to think of it, you can pay just about anyone to do just about anything for under five bucks over here. You can even buy yourself a boyfriend, Pet! You'll love it!"

Meanwhile, Mama had changed the locks so he couldn't show up whenever he wanted even though, to keep his New Brunswick residency, he had to come home every six months. That summer, he rented a trailer by the ocean with a bunch of other construction guys. Randall was too busy being thirteen to hang out with us, but me and Madonna spent the week with Pup. We did have campfires with marshmallows and ghost stories and ate buckets full of periwinkles that we picked ourselves and ate with safety pins. And one night, some guy did suggest that we hang our garbage from a tree, which I did, but then fell and hit my head so hard on my way down that I was knocked unconscious for a few minutes. Apparently, Madonna wouldn't stop howling, and everyone thought it was amazing how concerned she was. But I didn't fall because I was showing off. It was because Pup gave me a few beers, and I could barely walk a straight line, never mind climb. We didn't go to the hospital right away because he was worried they'd smell the beer on me. We didn't go until the next day when my head wouldn't stop bleeding, and I kept having this scary-weird feeling that I wasn't real anymore, that nothing was real anymore. I had a hard time calming down. My heart was beating really fast, and my mouth was dry. I was sure I had brain damage, but when I asked the doctors, they said, "No, you just need some rest." When it didn't go away a few weeks later, I asked Mama if I should get checked out again, but she was only concerned about the number of stitches to my head. "Of course, you needed seven. Pinky was right again. It's all downhill from here, Missy. It's all downhill from here."

Hobo Dog bought Randall an electric guitar for his first big show. His band is the coolest in town! They played at the school dance, and it was the biggest turnout ever. I danced so much I got blisters on both feet! During a slow song, the most popular boy at school asked me to dance. I couldn't believe my luck. At the end of the night, he kissed me and asked for my phone number. Everyone crowded around us and cheered. I think he might ask me to go out with him, but I'm not sure because he seems kinda shy. I won't write down his name because I don't want to jinx it. The End.

Thirty percent true. I was thirteen. Randall was fourteen and in a band. Every day after school, his band rehearsed at one of his buddy's houses. Randall didn't have his own guitar, so he borrowed one from said buddy whose family had lots of money. Once, buddy's mother called Mama and offered to buy Randall a guitar and pay for lessons. "Your son's got natural talent," she said. "A real Jimi Hendrix."

But Mama wouldn't take any charity. "I got my pride," she told Randall. "Plus, if your father can afford to gallivant around the fuckin' tropics on his time off, he can afford a fuckin' guitar. Go ask him."

The next time Pup called, Randall did just that, and supposedly Pup agreed. The next week, however, Pup said he didn't remember the conversation. "Another blackout," he said. "Sorry 'bout that, son, but money's tight at the moment. How about a ukulele instead?"

Randall vowed never to speak with Pup again. Then he went and stole money from the school cafeteria to buy a guitar for himself and got caught. He got suspended and wasn't allowed to play with his band at the dance. I went to the dance, though. With a bunch of kids I'd been trying to impress for months. I brought some peach schnapps I stole from Mama so we could drink it in the woods. I got so drunk that I didn't care that nothing felt real, and ended up giving my first blow job to the most popular boy in school. His name was Dirk. When we eventually went inside, Dirk's friends saw the mud on the knees of my white jeans and formed a circle around me, chanting *Miss Piggy! Miss Piggy!* One of the teachers came over and called Mama to come to pick me up. I got suspended for two days. When Mama saw that the guitar Randall had bought was purple, she sighed. "Of course, it's purple. The writing's been on the wall all along." I didn't dare tell her the boy's name started with D. I didn't dare.

Madonna was buried alive. I wish it was me instead. Hobo Dog can never find out what happened. It would kill him. The End.

Here's what I know to be true:

I was fourteen. Mama was so fed up with my lip that she told Pup he better take me or she'd put me in a group home.

"Sure," Pup said. "I'll send you some money, and she can live with me in Cuba for the summer. A little fun in the sun is exactly what she needs."

Also true: I was so excited, I told everyone I was moving to Cuba. I planned a going-away party when I knew Mama was gonna be on one of her Avon training weekends.

Also true: Pup changed his mind. "I got a last-minute job in Berlin," he said. "Money's too good to pass up. Maybe next year."

Also true: I had the party anyway. There were supposed to be ten kids: five girls, five boys. We had a couple of two-fours and a pill bottle full of blotter acid someone stole from their brother's friend visiting from Halifax. We sat around the kitchen listening to

Pup's Black Sabbath records. The boys took turns doing their best Ozzy impersonations, and the girls got Madonna howling in exchange for Cheetos. I told them about the grave Pup dug for Madonna, and we laughed and laughed. I was so stoned my voice sounded squeaky and echoey like a cave bat. Maybe I really was a cave bat, I thought. Everyone around me sounded like cave bats, too.

Also true: Suddenly, a crazy train pulled up and let loose fifty suburban teenagers on our front lawn. They were everywhere. Stomping through the house in muddy Doc Martens. Putting out cigarettes on the floor. Raiding the fridge. Making out in Mama's bed, right under the evil eyes. Outside, cars were parked all the way down Poverty Hill, right to the highway. One guy was pissing on the front door, and another was smashing the deck with a baseball bat. At one point, I found myself lying under our big old pine tree with Dirk's hand down my pants. Up above, cave bats flew in and out of the branches in an air show. Any doubts I had about my brain damage went out the window.

Also true: Madonna died that night.

When Mama got back from her Avon thing, she refused to believe the truth about Madonna. Accepting our beloved family member had succumbed to the most tortuous form of death was just too painful. "It's true, Mama, the boys threw her in the grave," I said.

"No, Missy, that's fuckin' impossible, she must have fallen in."

"Seriously, Mama, that's what happened. She must have broken her back because she couldn't get up, so they all freaked out and started throwing dirt over her until she couldn't breathe."

"Shut your fuckin' hole, Missy!" She slammed her fist on the table. "I'm glad your friends were there to help you put her out of her misery. I don't know if I would have had the strength to do the same. But if I hear one more word about it, you're the one who's gonna be fuckin' buried alive."

I cried and cried and cried and said, "Fine. But it *was* all my fault. And I'm pretty sure I really *do* have brain damage because everything still feels so unreal, and every time I speak, it sounds like I'm in a cave. I wonder if maybe I've gone crazy or that actually I'm dead and this is just an afterlife kind of dream state? But, if not, like, maybe I should get some help because it's really scary."

"For fuck's sake, Missy! All teenagers have brain damage," she said. "Madonna had a good life. That's the only thing worth remembering. And there wasn't a fuckin' thing you could've done differently to change her fate. Fate is fate. But if you have to blame someone, blame your fuckin' father."

"But, Mama, Pup wasn't even here."

She looked at me long and hard, with more conviction than I'd ever seen. "Exactly," she said.

When Pup came home and found out about her death three months later, he was devastated. Telling him the truth wasn't an option. He particularly lost it when Mama told him the vet disposed of her remains because she couldn't bear to use the grave and cremation was too expensive. He didn't know what to do with himself. He kept crying and going on long walks that made him miserable because Madonna wasn't with him, but still, he wouldn't let anyone join him. He'd stay out for hours then complain about the cold weather. "Why on earth people live in Canada is a mystery to me!" For the first time, I wanted him to hurry up and leave already.

He left soon enough, but organized a funeral first, inviting his buddies and the neighbours and some of me and Randall's friends from school. He made a big pot of seafood chowder and sang a sad, sad song about a man and his son who fought all the time and the son only realized how much he actually loved his father after the father died and it was too late. I don't know why he chose that song. It was really inappropriate. Randall kept rolling his eyes, and Mama tapped her feet the way she did when she was waiting in line and the person in front of her was taking forever to count their change.

Near the end of the funeral, the train went by and whistled. Me and Randall and Mama snapped our heads as if an invisible Pavlovian button had been pushed by the God of the Canines. Looking at each other, the three of us knew we were the only ones who heard Madonna's ghost howl and wasn't that the weirdest, most magical moment ever? As one, we howled, then burst out laughing. Then we howled again, and laughed some more. At one point, I wondered if it was another one of my unreal moments, but then Pup yelled, "Show some respect!" so I knew it was real. Rolling around on the ground, holding our chowder-filled bellies, tears streaming down our faces, we bonded in a way we'd never bonded before and might never do again because that furry, blonde glue that held us together was gone gone gone. It was hysterical, and we knew Madonna wouldn't have wanted it any other way.

4

Beloved

I've always hated my name. Missy. It's such a stupid name. It's not short for Melissa. Or Marissa. Or something glamorous, like Amaryllis. Just Missy. It's an ugly name. A dog's name. Similar to Miss Piggy's name, which even the stupid boys at school figured out. When I was old enough, I used to say that I'd change it to Betty. As in Boop. That's what Andy and Ethel, who moved onto Poverty Hill the summer after Madonna died, had called me. Because of my bob haircut that I dyed jet black to look more like half-sister, Jemima's, and to make my blue eyes pop like Liz Taylor's, even though Mama said it only exaggerated my pale, pimply skin. Andy and Ethel said my butt and hips were nice and curvy like Betty Boop's, too. But I didn't believe them. Those disgusting hips and butt of mine that grew bigger and bigger every day, that, along with my pimply pizza face, made me stick out like a baboon in a fluffle of bunnies. That's what I overheard my teacher tell the guidance counselor: *That Whynaught girl sticks out like a baboon in a fluffle of bunnies.* Even though I came to hate them, I liked it when Andy and Ethel called me Betty. They were the only ones who ever called me anything close to pretty.

I also hated being alone. It's just not in my nature. But I didn't have much control over that either. I didn't have my driver's license and we lived in the middle of nowhere. Other than Randall, there wasn't anyone my age who lived on Poverty Hill. Pup was too busy chasing Caribbean tail to come home anymore, and, in her sadness, Mama pretty much gave up on being a parent. She sold Avon products during the day, and at night she drank. Sometimes she hosted Avon parties and got really drunk. Mama was the prettiest drunk for miles around. I knew it blew her mind that she had such an ugly daughter. Andy and Ethel said she was only pretty on the outside. "On the inside, you mama's rotten to the core."

To get to the school bus stop, I had to walk along the railway tracks for twenty minutes. The bus ride was another forty minutes, where I had to put up with chants of *Miss Piggy!* That's why I started to skip school. Mama threatened to ground me if I didn't stop, but there was nothing to ground me from, and she couldn't follow through on anything anyway.

I stayed home and spied on the neighbours instead. I'd been spying on them since I was eight and still cute enough to pass as part of a fluffle. I'd climb up into the treehouse or sneak through the woods and squat in the bushes for hours with my binoculars and write down everyone's secrets in my diary.

I think Mrs. McPherson's got someone captive in her basement. That's why the curtains are always pulled, I'm sure of it.

Mr. Bennet is washing his ATV again. What evidence is he trying to wash off?

Mrs. Leblanc has an awful lot of visitors this week. I wonder what she's up to? What's she planning? Is it the Russians?

I started breaking into their homes when I was eleven, around the same time my butt, hips and acne started to pop. I never stole anything; I just liked to hang out, take baths, read magazines, etc. Sometimes the neighbours left things out for me, like cookies and shampoo. One time, the McPhersons left me a little card with five bucks inside. *Dear Missy, buy yourself something that makes you happy*. I used the money to order a porcelain poodle from Mama's Avon catalogue. I had elephants and tigers and pandas lined up along my dresser like a poacher's wet dream. Even though my grades were terrible, I wanted to be a vet one day.

When Andy and Ethel moved into the abandoned house that late spring, I spied on them from my treehouse. Big fat Andy with his bushy mustache and Raiders cap. And teeny-weeny Ethel with her thick, Coke-bottle glasses, pigeon toes and jean shorts that barely covered her perfect bubble butt. They didn't do much. They mostly spent their time rolling cigarettes, drinking Diet Pepsi, and watching pirated Van Damme movies. But they had the most beautiful Rottweiler I'd ever seen.

I would have given anything to have that Rottweiler in my life, so one day I risked getting my face chewed off and broke into Andy and Ethel's place. I spoke softly, threw bologna through the window, and next thing I knew, the dog was curled up next to me. I didn't know her name yet, but she was as ripped and glossy as a female superhero, so I called her Hero. Hero had a swollen tummy and ten teats. I didn't need to be a vet to know Hero was pregnant.

After that, I broke in to visit Hero every chance I had. I'd lie down on the floor beside her and make squeaky noises, pretending to be her puppy, and she'd lick me all over. When I told Hero about the bullies at school, her black eyes got all teary. I joked that I'd bring her to school one day so she could kill them all, even though I knew she didn't have it in her, and neither did I.

Then, one day, after falling asleep in Hero's paws on their kitchen floor, I woke up to Andy and Ethel standing over us.

"Who the hell are you, and what the hell are you doing in our house?"

"I-I-I'm Missy. Your neighbour, I'm sorry. I—"

"Oh, shit, Andy, she's that weird girl who watches us all the time!" Ethel sat down on the floor to tickle Hero's ears and light up a cigarette. "Want a smoke, kid?"

"Missy?" The big guy let out a belly laugh then looked at me a little closer. "That hair of yours makes ya look like Betty Boop! I'm gonna call ya Betty from now on!"

And that was that. The next thing I knew, I was practically living at their place. Drinking their Diet Pepsi, watching their movies, rolling and smoking their cigarettes, sleeping on their pull-out couch and taking Hero—whose real name was Roxy, but they were cool with me renaming her—for walks every day. They didn't care if I skipped school, especially since the year was almost over anyway. Andy hadn't finished high school, and he hosted his own late-night country rock show on the local radio, while Ethel said waiting until her thirties to get her GED was the best thing she ever did. The bullies had had their way with her in school, too. "If I hadn't dropped out," she told me, "I'd a thrown myself off the Reversing Falls Bridge long before I found my Andy Candy." One day, she promised me, especially with an ass like mine, I'd find an Andy Candy of my own.

Hero's puppies were born on the night of June 15. I remembered the date because it was my fifteenth birthday. The week before, Ethel had excitedly announced, "We've got an early birthday surprise for ya, Betts! We're throwing you a party next Friday! I'm gonna bake hash brownies and order pizza and rent *Animal Farm*! We'll have a blast!"

I was too happily surprised by the announcement to mention I'd also been surprised they'd chosen *Animal Farm* out of all the movies in the world. We were reading that in English class, and it seemed a bit too fancy for the likes of such diehard Van Damme fans. Plus, I didn't want them to think I was a snob. The opposite was true. I adored them and was so grateful to have them in my life. Who cared what movie they chose and why? I forgot about it as quickly as my homework. I sure didn't forget about the party, though. Boy, was I excited! They'd also invited some of their CB radio friends to come, and I was looking forward to meeting the apparently cute nineteen-year-old guy they thought I'd hit it off with.

"Who knows, Betts?" Ethel said, winking. "Kermit might give you a kiss as a birthday present. Your very own frog prince!"

"Ha, ha, very funny, guys," I said. "Kermit the Frog and Miss Piggy? Come on, you can do better than that."

"No, seriously," said Andy. "Kermit, or Froggy as we call him, is his real name. You'll understand as soon as he opens his mouth."

The week leading up to the party was full of exciting unknowns: Hero was ready to pop any day; the party; the potential kiss that I wanted more than anything else. Even though me and Dirk from the school dance, who I secretly called Dirk the Jerk, still fooled around sometimes, we'd never kissed. I hoped Ethel was right. If so, Kermit's kiss would be my first. I bought myself a red sundress with cherries all over it at Value Village and red platform sandals to match. I wanted to rock the Betty Boop look as much as possible. I added gold hoop earrings, bright red lips, and thick black eyeliner. I hoped Kermit liked it!

When the day finally came, I'd forgotten Andy's comment about what came out of Kermit's mouth. But the second he spoke, it was impossible to forget. This can't be real, I thought. He must be one of those people who are really good at impersonating voices, Kermitt the Frog in particular. Andy and Ethel were planning to use this party trick to play a Miss Piggy and Kermit the Frog joke on me after all, right? But it was no joke. I instantly felt sorry for him. And disappointed. What a turnoff.

But I knew how terrible it felt to be rejected. So, I squeezed between Andy and Kermit on the couch when it was time to watch the movie anyway. The other guests sat on the floor. Directly in front of us on the coffee table were everyone's drinks. Ethel had used their crystal wine glasses, which they'd been given as a wedding present by her great auntie. Second to Andy and Hero, she'd told me, they were her most valued possession.

Worrying about knocking over the glasses if I moved was partly why it took a good five minutes for me to clue in that it wasn't the *Animal Farm* movie I'd expected. Kermit's thigh against my bare leg was the other reason I couldn't focus, plus the hash brownies were kicking in, which made me feel a little dizzy and nauseous. I wasn't sure if I should leave my leg touching his, or find an excuse to move it. Ethel had been right, he was really cute. At least when he was silent. So I was thinking: maybe I can ask him to whisper, or we can develop our own sign language. A secret love sign language, just for us. How romantic.

But those thoughts shut down the second he croaked, "Holy fuck, take a look at that!" My eyes snapped to the screen where a lady was having sex with a horse. These animals were not planning a revolution at all! All of a sudden, my mild waves of nausea became a level five tornado. Trapped by two big men, a coffee table, a dozen wineglasses, and a couch, I couldn't stop the carnage. Without standing, I projectile-vomited hash brownies, Diet Pepsi, and pizza all over the coffee table.

Fortunately, none of the puke got on any humans, or my pretty red dress. The glasses, yes, but they were washable and, most importantly, none broke. So, no one got upset. They just laughed and called me cute as I stood and wobbled off to get cleaning supplies. The movie was paused mid-scene of a lady riding a horse in a way I'd never seen before and hoped I never would again.

I was wiping down the table when Hero came whimpering in the room. Little legs were sticking out of her beaver like some kind of alien parasite.

"Is that—is that—?"

"It sure is," Andy exclaimed. "Okay, y'all, party's over. Everyone but Betty has to go on home now! Go on, get! You, too, Froggy!"

Even in her own hour of need, Hero rescued me. From the porno and the frog man.

From ten p.m. through to the next morning, we stayed up helping Hero with the birth. We gave her treats, rubbed her belly, and told her how brave and strong she was, even though she behaved as if absolutely nothing out of the ordinary was happening to her beaver. It was so trippy. I kept asking Andy and Ethel if I was hallucinating from the hash brownies, or maybe it was a symptom of my brain damage. Another unreal moment? But, "No, Betts," they said. "This is about as real as it gets."

The puppies kept popping out like kernels in a popcorn bag. Just when we were sure the popping was over, another one popped out. I even made up a little song about it: *Three, four, pop, pop, pop. Eight, nine, pop, pop, pop.* Which Andy quickly changed to: *Keep 'em coming, girl, pop, pop, pop. We're gettin' two hundred bucks for each, so don't stop, stop, stop.*

To pass the time, I did the math. At 8:30 a.m., when it seemed Hero was finally done popping, I announced, "That's, um, $2,100 in one night, right? You're rich!"

"Good try, Betts," Andy chuckled. "Twenty-four hundred, to be exact. But we'll only be getting twenty-two."

"Huh?"

"Stick to dogs, Betts, not math," Ethel said. "But we *are* rich. In cash *and* in good neighbours. Now, go on, choose whichever one you want."

"Huh?" I said again.

"You can choose your very own puppy to keep," Andy said.

"Seriously?"

"Seriously, Betts, pop, pop, pop," they sang. "Happy friggin' birthday, Betts, pop, pop, pop!"

As if on cue, Hero popped one more time. Her grand finale. Her thirteenth puppy. My puppy. It was the best birthday gift in the whole world. Better, even, than a first kiss.

I called my puppy Bee, short for Beloved. I didn't think I could love another dog more than Madonna and Hero, but I did. And I didn't think life on Poverty Hill could be so fun, but it was. The next seven weeks were some of the best of my life. Not only did Hero keep treating me as if she were my own, but she let me help with her puppies. I spent the rest of June and all of July playing with them, keeping watch while they slept, and making sure the big ones didn't hog all the milk from the little ones. I gave them names to suit their personalities: Sneaky, Snoozy, Biggly, Sir Poops-a-lot and Shy Baby.

I was feeling so good I wasn't even fighting with Mama and Randall anymore. I wasn't getting those tummy pains that harassed me in the middle of the night when I thought about the boys at school. I wasn't even having nightmares where I was frantically trying to dig Madonna out of her grave, but could never reach her on time. My unreal moments, cut down by half, no longer made me wish I'd never wake up. I was even considering asking Andy and Ethel to invite Kermit over again so I could give him another chance. I was so happy that I felt I could take on any challenge. Creepy voices included.

But on August 15, eight weeks to the day since the birth, while I was out walking Hero, the same afternoon Andy and Ethel were selling the last of the twelve puppies, everything returned to shit.

"Where's Bee?" I said, when I brought Hero back.

"Oh, sorry, Betts." Ethel avoided eye contact. "You're not gonna like this—"

I looked around for Bee. Under the table, under the bed, in the closet, in the fridge.

"—but we really needed the cash, so—"

I started throwing empty bottles of Diet Pepsi and dog food and full ashtrays against the walls as if that would help Bee magically appear. When she didn't, I grabbed Ethel's bony shoulders and growled into her face: "Tell me you didn't! Tell me you didn't sell Bee!"

I couldn't stop screaming and throwing stuff around, and if Andy hadn't pulled me off Ethel, I think I might have killed that cross-eyed toad. That's what I called her. "You cross-eyed toad!"

I don't remember much of what happened next. I punched a window and Andy had to hold me in a grizzly bear hug in the back seat of the car while Ethel drove me to the hospital. Five stitches to my hand later, Mama showed up to take me home. "After all those people did for you," she said. "You can be such a fuckin' ungrateful brat sometimes, ya know?"

I lived in the treehouse for the rest of the summer. The only person I saw was Dirk the Jerk, who showed up a few times with junk food and a hard-on. At least I managed to get my first kiss out of the way. It wasn't anything to write home about, though. His saliva tasted like moth balls. But I was happy for the company and grateful for the treats.

Meanwhile, Andy and Ethel put bars on their windows and kept their curtains closed. Whenever I struggled to fall asleep, I pretended to be a puppy again, wrapped in Hero's strong, warm arms. I was back to wishing I'd never wake up.

I pulled out my stitches early one morning and drew pictures of Hero and Bee and Madonna on the wall with my blood. I signed one as *Betty*. One as *Miss Piggy.* And the other as *That Fucking Ungrateful Brat*.

I hated Andy and Ethel, but I missed them something fierce.

5
Milton, Ho!

Pup showed up two weeks before school started and announced he was taking me and Randall to Milton to visit Grammy Whynaught and our half-sister, Jemima. He'd flown in from Honduras at two a.m. and I found him stuck in the dog flap in the kitchen when I went to make my breakfast. Only his head and right arm were visible. The rest of his body was splayed out on the front deck like a beached walrus, covered in piss. Randall pulled him out by the legs while Mama fired off a list of his most recent broken promises. It took a good hour, but Mama could have kept going. His house key, he told us, along with his pants, had been stolen by a prostitute.

Despite this, his smile was sunshine.

"I got a surprise for ya, kids! We're going on a road trip! And, Missy, you better not fuck it up again!"

Surprised, I was. But more by the invitation than his arrival. The fuckup had happened the previous summer when he'd taken us across the US border to Calais for the weekend. On our last night at the motel, I snuck out of our room to check out the gang of Hells Angels who'd pulled up. I couldn't help myself. I was so curious. They were in the parking lot, and I was drawn to their music and laughter like a pig to a newly dumped slop. Plus, we'd run out of smokes, which I used as an excuse to crash their party, where I lectured them about not wearing helmets and shamelessly flirted with an unimpressed Thor look-alike. It was just as they were circling me, making jokes about all the ways they could get rid of me, that Pup showed up. He was furious. He apologized for my existence. Then he dragged me away, vowing to "Never. Ever. Over my dead body, Missy Whynaught, will I take you on a road trip again!"

I didn't really understand why Pup got so angry. Something about poking a hornet's nest and ending up in a barrel at the bottom of the sea. In any case, he barely spoke to me for the rest of the trip. Just a few hours after dropping us off, he left for a job in Calgary. That was the last time I'd seen him before the dog flap. Thank God for Pup's broken promises, I thought. His return couldn't have come at a better time. I was still licking my wounded hand from punching Andy and Ethel's window. The scar looked like an upside-down smile. It made me want to slap myself. Sometimes I did. But now I had something to look forward to again. And over my dead body would I screw it up. Milton, Ho!

Mama pretended not to care that she wasn't invited. "You couldn't pay me to visit that fuckin' shithole," she said. While Randall whined, "You're gonna have to pay me to visit that shithole," which earned him an updated Gameboy for the seven-hour drive. But there was no bribery or pretending for me. Milton was my happy place that, along with Madonna, Hero and Beloved, I thought about when I was feeling shitty. When anyone asked where I wanted to live when I got older, I'd say, "Milton, 100 percent." Milton beat any place in the world. "Oh, you think Alaskan whales are big?" I'd say. "You should see them in Milton." "France has the best food? I guess you've never had Milton's boiled cabbage and tongue." "Italian women are the most beautiful? No way! Look at her," and hold up a Polaroid of an ebony-haired beauty in a sparkly blue ball gown to match her sparkly blue eyes.

"Did you go to Disney? Is that Snow White?"

"Even better. That's my half-sister, Jemima Whynaught."

Also in that picture is ten-year-old me, wearing a hot-pink tracksuit two sizes too small, exposing my triple tummy roll. My arms are wrapped around the twenty-three-year-old Snow White doppelganger's hourglass waist, and I'm looking up at her with the adoration that little girls all over the world give a princess. Side by side, the two of us were as different as a Chia Pet and a long-stemmed rose. The only things we had in common were our blue eyes and devotion to Pup. I look like her pimple. And because Randall had mono—or pretended to—so he didn't come, and Pup had disappeared on a bender with his buddies shortly after we arrived, she was stuck with me that week, like a pimple too.

But girls like Jemima don't get pimples. She took me everywhere, introducing me as her "little sister." To her work, where she was an orderly at Grammy's nursing home and regularly dressed up to sing golden oldies with a karaoke machine. On dates with her dreamy boyfriend, Bobby, who was Brad Pitt to her Snow White. To Milton's one and only watering hole, the Cuckoo Nest, where she bought me Shirley Temples and pickled eggs.

Back at Grammy's old house where Jemima lived since Grammy moved to the nursing home, she let me sleep with her. We lay side by side in her bed looking at the pop star posters plastered on her walls, pretending what it would be like to date them. Patrick Swayze, Kirk Cameron, NKOTB. She talked about her relationship with Bobby and got me to imagine boyfriends of my own.

"Like, he acts all macho, but he's really a big softy. He likes to brush my hair and run me baths. He cries a lot, too. Like, when we have a fight and after sex."

"Why? Does sex hurt him?"

"No, sweetie. The opposite. He says sex with me is like talking to God. *That's* how much he loves me. It can be a bit too much, though."

"How come?"

"Well, he can get paranoid. Thinking I'm cheating on him or don't love him enough. Which makes him do stupid shit like flirt with other girls, or get really drunk and pick fights with me, accusing me of stuff I didn't do then calling me late at night to apologize. But I know it's just because he's afraid of losing me. He always snaps out of it."

"Wow, he really does love you."

"What about you, Missy? What kind of guy do you want?"

"Definitely someone just like Bobby."

"Good. And don't settle for anything less. You're gonna be a real heartbreaker one day, ya know? Afterall, you're a Whynaught."

Even though we both knew I had more chance of sprouting a mermaid tail than catching the eye of someone like Bobby, never mind Patrick Swayze, she made me believe it. Deserved it, even.

Jemima made me feel as much an important part of her as the beauty mark between her perfectly plump lips and cute button nose. The opposite of a pimple. I wanted to be just like her. She's the reason I dyed my hair black. She's the reason I tried out (unsuccessfully) for the school choir. In this way, Jemima *was* Milton. I couldn't wait to see her again.

This trip, Pup spent a good part of the drive ranting about how much he hated cars.

"Whoever invented the fucking automobile should be shot in the head because they're destroying the earth and making everyone fat. I'm only driving one because Canadians are too fucking fat and lazy to take the train like they do in Europe. The Cubans got it figured out, too. They get thrown in jail if they're caught driving alone. It's written in their constitution and their DNA. It's the same as why they're all born good dancers. It's called evolution, kids. A Cuban doctor explained it to me and Cuban doctors are the best in the world which is more proof that their DNA is superior. I once saw ten people and a couple of goats on one moped!»

He got himself so riled up that we went off the road. No damage done, but it was the perfect excuse to stop and buy a six-pack of Moosehead to calm his nerves. It was close to three p.m. anyway, way past his usual eleven a.m. whistle wetting. By the second beer, his mood started to mellow. By his third, right on cue with Black Sabbath's "Mama I'm Coming Home," he was singing along like a kindergartener. And by his last, he didn't need more. He was riding high on the *Welcome Home Pup!* posters we saw tacked up on the road signs as of twenty kilometres outside of Milton, guiding us to its strip mall that also housed Grammy's nursing home and the Cuckoo Nest. Even more intoxicating were the people waiting for our arrival as if at a parade and we were the main attraction. There was a band of fiddlers, a bubble machine, a cotton candy stand, enough booze to pickle several tons of herring, and children riding a one-of-a-kind talking llama decked out in a Milton blue and green tartan. In the middle of it all was what I thought was a kind of float made to look like a giant bed with a giant old lady tucked in it. I thought it was supposed to be the Little Red Riding Hood scene when the wolf was chatting away with the grandmother before gobbling her up. Except there was no Little Red Riding Hood. Or wolf.

"Holy fuck," Randall said. "Is that…is that Grammy?"

"Sure is!" Pup jumped out of the car.

As he ran towards the colossal hospital bed and jumped into her colossal arms, the crowd erupted in a cheer. Fireworks went off that scared the llama, who kicked a child, who fell into the cotton candy machine, which knocked over a fiddler and broke his fiddling hand. Mama's boy was finally home.

The welcome party went on until the early evening rain flushed out the old, the young and the feeble, including Grammy, who we promised to visit bright and early the following morning. The diehards moved to the Cuckoo Nest. Before joining them, we dropped off our stuff at Grammy's. Jemima followed behind in Bobby's silver jeep. There was a heat wave, and Pup was itching to transfer the pig we'd brought down for a roast into the fridge before it started to smell like ass. Randall didn't want to leave his precious guitar in the car either, plus he'd recently discovered the importance of hygiene, and wanted a shower before going out. He'd won the coin toss over who got Grammy's room with its ensuite bathroom with a shower—one hell of a treat considering we didn't have a shower on Poverty Hill.

I didn't partake in the coin toss; I prefer baths. And my heart was set on using Jemima's room. She wasn't going to be there, since she lived with Bobby, now her fiancé, but I was still excited to sleep in it again. Pup joked during the drive that my alternative sleeping arrangement would be the backyard doghouse where he'd been found as a baby. Or, worse, the couch Grammy was unable to get up out of once she topped the scale at 750 pounds. The one she managed to live in for ten years while Grampy brought her food and sponge bathed her until he died and she was moved to the nursing home. The couch that was still infused with her bodily fluids, but no one would get rid of it for sentimental reasons.

But what began as a fun talk soon became reality.

"You know what?" Jemima announced, shortly after we arrived. "I think I'm gonna stay here after all. I wanna see yas as much as possible. Missy, you cool on the couch?"

Jemima stood between Pup and Bobby, holding their hands. Pup threw his arm around her shoulder and kissed her cheek. Bobby dropped her hand as if she'd given him an electric shock and looked at her as if she'd done it on purpose. Meanwhile she looked at me in that pleading, wide-eyed "Just follow my lead I'll explain later," way. The one Randall gives me when Mama asks if I've seen her smokes right after I just saw him steal them.

"Sure, Jemima! I'm happy to take the couch!"

Despite my disappointment that she hadn't invited me to sleep with her again, I wasn't lying. It was another happy surprise. I would have gladly slept on the couch even without the plastic covering to spend more time with Jemima. I'd have done it naked without the plastic. And from the way she included me in whatever problems she was having with Bobby, I knew she wanted to spend more time with me, too. Maybe she'll let me sleep with her after all, I thought. 'Cause that's what good sisters do.

But it was Randall who won the prize of good siblinghood. It was Randall who asked to ride along in the Jeep to the Cuckoo Nest, so Jemima wasn't alone with Bobby. It was Randall who found a quiet table to talk, instead of making a beeline for the bar like Bobby. And it was Randall who insisted Jemima sit next to him, with their backs to Bobby, unlike me and Pup, who sat in his line of vision. Even though Bobby was with his buddies, he barely took his eyes off Jemima. I watched him watch her while I drank the half Sprite-half beer shandy Pup convinced the bartender to serve Randall and me, because "That's how it's done in England. And fifteen and sixteen are close enough to seventeen, which is basically the same as eighteen, which is legal in Quebec, which borders New Brunswick, which borders Nova Scotia, and borders are just a white supremacy conspiracy, so good for you for being so progressive, buddy!" Bobby was like a hungry cat watching a pretty bird in a cage. I found it so romantic. How Jemima could turn down sleeping with Bobby, who was even dreamier than I remembered, was a mystery. They must have had one hell of a fight, I thought. I would've given anything for someone to look at me like that. A little wave of jealousy hit me. But that was quickly extinguished by a tidal wave of heat when the beefy guy with long brown hair standing next to Bobby winked at me. It was even stronger than the shot of tequila we'd had before leaving Grammy's. I couldn't believe it. Did that just happen? But then he winked again. It was real, alright. Just as I was about to wink back, Randall kicked me under the table.

"So," Randall said to Jemima, "why don't you want to sleep at Bobby's?"

"Well, as you know..." She took a few deep breaths then started crying. "We're getting married next month. But I just found out he cheated. Again. He says it meant nothing. That it's only because—"

She looked at Pup to see if he was paying attention. But like me, his eyes were on the bar. Randall must have kicked him, too, because then he gently patted Jemima's hand.

"Go on, darling. We're listening."

"Because I'm pregnant." She pulled her baggy sweater tight to expose her small but obviously pregnant belly. "He says he only cheated because he's so scared about it. The money, the responsibility, that I'll love the baby more than him. He even says he's scared to touch me because he's afraid to hurt me. As if I'm a leper or something. But I'm not a leper, Dad! And now I don't know what I'm gonna do—"

Like a bingo winner, Pup jumped up, threw his arms in the air and whooped in elation. "What do you mean, what are ya gonna do? You're gonna have a baby! I'm gonna be a grandpa!"

"But what about the cheating?" Her tears spilled while Randall rubbed her back.

"Don't you worry your pretty little head about that," Pup said. "I'm with Bobby on this one, it's just stress. It's totally normal. He just needs to let off some steam. A wedding and a bun in the oven, that's a lot for a young buck. Take it from your old man, it's not you, it's him. He'll soon come round."

Before Jemima could respond, Pup was up on the table hollering. "Next round on me! I'm gonna be a grandpa!"

The crowd erupted into cheers. All of a sudden, the fiddlers were back fiddling. The llama reappeared for a second shift of rides and good conversation. Folks lined up to congratulate Pup and were throwing pickled eggs at each other like rubber balls, a Milton baby-announcement tradition. The party was exploding, and being a good sister was not on my mind. It had turned into a chore I'd do tomorrow, like studying or making my bed, which I never did. My only thought was asking Jemima about Bobby's cute friend. But when I looked for her, she and Randall were on their way out. Randall had one arm linked with hers and used the other like a shield to push through the crowd. Like a good bodyguard, he wasn't going to leave her vulnerable to a predator, even if that predator was the father of her baby, who, I was thrilled to notice, was at the bar with Beefy Guy and Pup. It was one happy surprise after another.

On my way to the bar, I looked back at the door and caught Jemima's eye. It was hard to tell whether her expression was concern or disappointment, but I chose concern. "Don't worry," I mouthed, pointing to Pup. "I'm with Pup."

Seconds later, the cuckoo bird in the bar's enormous grandfather clock poked its little head in and out eleven times. Everyone paused and cuckooed along, like concert fans singing to their favourite song.

Shortly after joining the men, Bobby went outside to do some blow, and Pup took off with Carrie, a Dolly Parton look-alike old flame. This left me and Beefy

Guy, a.k.a. Rudy, alone. My jean shorts kept riding up my butt, and my black tube top kept rolling up my tummy. We stood so close that my bare shoulder touched his bare arm. He smelled like cigarettes and aftershave. This was the closest I'd come to a slow dance. I wanted to put my head under his Metallica shirt and lay my cheek against his beefy chest. I wanted him to pick me up and sit me on the bar and kiss me, slowly and passionately, like a soldier returning to the love of his life. And I could tell he wanted me too by the way he stared at my lips and kept closing his eyes and shaking his head. The way he drew out my name like a sexy snake turned my body on like a tap.

"So, Missssssssy? Are all Saint John girls as cute as you?"

"You're just saying that. You're lying."

"Never! I've never told a lie in my life. What kinda things ya good at, Missssssy?"

"I'm a really strong swimmer. I can go for hours and hours."

"Oh, I bet you can go all night. Maybe I should take ya to the Deep Hole for a midnight swim. But you probably didn't bring your bathing suit, did ya, Misssssy?"

"Let's do it! I can go in my undies. I do it all the time back home!"

"Oh, God. Stop. You're giving me bad thoughts! You're gonna get me in trouble. How old are ya anyway? Your old man would kill me if we went swimming. You'd probably drown anyway. How many of those shandies ya drink?"

"Sixteen," I lied.

"Sixteen? You'd better slow down, baby girl!"

"I mean, I'm sixteen. Seventeen soon." I lied again.

"Well, at least you're not jailbait! My twenty-two-year-old cousin just married his sixteen-year-old girlfriend. That means you, Missssssssy, are as legal as my Mama's special church cookies."

But to my great disappointment, whatever plans we might have made were shut down by the cuckoo bird's midnight set, followed by Pup's sudden appearance, which made Rudy jump away from me like I was contagious. Much to Rudy's relief, however, Pup didn't give a shit, if he'd noticed anything at all. Pup was in fantastic spirits, especially with Carrie hanging off his arm.

"Okay, Pet, party's over! Bobby's gonna give you a lift home. Me and this hot mama wanna catch up somewhere where no kids are allowed." He shot Rudy a man-to-man wink. "Missy, you can use my room tonight."

"And you, son," he said to Rudy. "Thanks for keeping my Missy here outta trouble. I hope she didn't talk your ear off. Takes after her mother, this one! Not in looks, mind you. But, man, can they ever chatter! Worse than being woken up by a flock of fucking starlings on a hangover! Ha! Anyway, your tab's taken care of. And give your folks my regards, eh?"

With that, Pup escorted me to the parking lot where a scowling Bobby waited in his Jeep. He didn't speak the whole way. Instead, he blasted Garth Brooks and aggressively revved the engine as if to say, "Fuck you, Missy. I'm only driving you home to stay in your father's good books and the hopes of catching Jemima alone. Otherwise, I wouldn't even pick you up if I saw you hitchhiking with one leg."

But Bobby's hopes were dashed when we found Jemima and Randall jamming on Grammy's porch. The lights were on, and Jemima was more beautiful than ever singing to the moon in a pink nightie, rocking her little tummy with both hands. Randall, who kept strumming his guitar, saw us first. Even from that distance, I could read his back-the-fuck-off expression directed at Bobby. He might have been sixteen, but he was the more buff of the two. Bobby saw Randall's warning loud and clear, too; the second I closed the car door, he sped away. But the tire tracks left their own warning that this wasn't the last of him.

There wasn't room for me in Jemima and Randall's singalong, so I went straight to Pup's childhood dog-themed bedroom. There were basset hound bookends, a Dalmatian lamp, posters like Lady and the Tramp and Benji, and a life-size Goofy doll stood in the corner dressed as a waiter, holding a platter of dog figurines. Not counting the hundreds, maybe thousands, of dogs on the curtains and wallpaper, I counted sixty-one, over and over again, to stop obsessing over Rudy and get some sleep.

When I finally slept, I dreamt that me and Rudy were sharing a plate of spaghetti, like the epic scene in *Lady and the Tramp*. The one where they sucked up opposite ends of the same piece of spaghetti until their lips collided for their first kiss. Except we weren't dogs. And the spaghetti was worms. I ate them because he said it turned him on. They tasted fishy, not at all like I imagined a worm would taste like. It must have turned me on too because when Jemima woke me at 7:30 a.m. to join her on the nine o'clock shift, I felt like I did when I straddled my pillow pretending it was River Phoenix.

She was wearing a long, flowy yellow dress with a daisy crown pinned in her hair. She and Randall were doing a sixties set for the old farts that afternoon, she said. She opened the curtains and sat on the bed. "Ya have fun last night?"

"I had a great time!" I said. "Mostly talked to Bobby's friend, Rudy. Ya know him?"

"Everybody knows Rudy Tickler, Missy. He's a drug dealer and nothing but trouble. Like all the Ticklers."

"But he seems so sweet!"

"Sweet people do bad things. And bad people do sweet things. Seriously, take it from me. I've known Rudy Tickler my whole life. He's rotten to the core. I hate it when Bobby hangs out with him down at the Deep Hole. But, Bobby, I can't stop. You, I can. So get him out of your head and promise me you'll stay away from him. Okay?"

"Okay, Jemima, I promise."

Despite her concern, Jemima didn't want much to do with me after that. When she wasn't working, she and Randall were glued at the hip. Still, I tried.

"Hey, Jemima. Anything I can help you with?"

"Maybe go ask if they need help in the kitchen."

"Up for a movie tonight?"

"Sorry. Me and Randall are working on an eighties set."

"Wanna have lunch together?"

"Nah. Gonna nap through lunch again. The thought of food makes me sick. Pregnancy is exhausting."

When I tried bonding over Pup, things got messy. "Hey Jemima, you pissed Dad's barely around? My mama says he's the most selfish bastard in the world. That all he cares about is himself. She says he spends all his money on other people, so it's his fault we're broke. Maybe she's right—"

"Missy!" she snapped. "You don't know how good you've had it. You think it was fun being raised by my alkie grandparents? That I liked growing up on a filthy houseboat, being slapped around, working overnights at the bakery so I could buy my own food and clothes? You think I wanted to spend summers in Texas with my hooker mother, who made me hook for her just so she could put her feet up? Because Pup couldn't afford to send her anything 'cause he sent it all to your entitled princess mother? I know it hurts, but it's time you learned the truth, Missy. My childhood sucked after you two came along. I know it's not your fault, but Randall seems to get it. You don't. There's more to life than boys and partying. You haven't even asked about the baby."

"Randall? Caring? You should hear the way he talks about Pup! He hates him! He just uses him for money! He doesn't speak to him when he calls. He never makes time for him when he's home. It's me—"

"See? Just listen to yourself. It's always 'Me, me, me.'"

"But—"

"I don't have time for this right now. I need to nap. Let's talk later."

But later never came. Not after I cleaned her room (which she said was an invasion of her privacy). Not after I bought the baby a teddy bear (which she said was bad luck before the birth). Not even after I left an apology note on her pillow:

Dear Jemima, I am so sorry that I hurt you. I didn't mean to. I love you and wish your childhood had been better. I wish more than anything in the world that it had happened to me instead. I can't wait to meet my little nephew or niece. I'm so happy for you! Please forgive me. Love, your sister, Missy.

But I couldn't convince her that I cared. She finally saw me as a pimple. It was like Andy and

Ethel saying I used them for the puppy, or the time I made pancakes at a friend's sleepover and her parents called me selfish for leaving a mess. They were wrong; all I wanted to do was make them happy. And like me. But once they saw me as a pimple, they kept their distance. It's the only surefire way to make pimples go away.

Unlike Jemima, Grammy couldn't get enough of me hanging out in her room. It stung that she kept forgetting who I was, but once I reminded her, she'd light up like a Canadian Tire Christmas tree. Everything about her was Christmas. With her puffy white hair, red velour muumuu, and roly-poly body in the gigantic custom-made hospital bed, she was an oversized Mrs. Claus. The stacks of glossy TV Guides and shiny wrapped candies on the side table looked like Christmas presents. She had a collection of snow globes and angel figurines among her many pictures of Pup. She even had pine air freshener that smelled like Christmas trees that she'd spritz spritz spritz all the time. She said it made her feel connected to the woods. And helped mask the smell of her sea coochie.

"'Cause Lord only knows I won't see the woods no more! But, oh I miss it! Especially the Deep Hole. I'd trade whatever life I have left for one more day at the Deep Hole," she said. "But everyone's too busy farting around in mittens to take me nowhere. I keep asking the staff, but, no, no, they're too busy. Busy my fat, rosy ass! They're not too busy to be friggin' around with my room spray! One minute it's full, the next it's empty. One minute it's on my table, the next it's gone. 'Magine that! The right sneaky bunch! Don't trust 'em further than I can throw 'em! But what do ya expect from foreigners, eh? Typical!

When I was a girl, I thought coloured people were just make-believe. Now we might as well rename Milton Little Africa!"

Grammy watched too much TV. The only foreigners in Milton were American tourists on their way to Lunenburg to see the ships. Milton was white as toilet paper. But I was too busy steering the conversation to challenge her.

"Hey, Grammy," I said. "Do you know the Ticklers?"

"Do I know the Ticklers? Does a reindeer have a butthole? They're my third cousins," she told me. "Just thinking about Bud Tickler gets my sea coochie excited. A right dreamboat he was. What a tragedy his Skidoo went through the ice. Or was that Shifty Tickler? Anyways, don't you go telling nobody, but Bud Tickler was my first. I never told no one that. Your Grampy, bless his pointy little head, went to his deathbed thinking he popped my cherry. But it was Bud Tickler. Or was it Shifty? Anyways, whoever Tickler it was, I was sixteen. And it happened at the Deep Hole. That's where all the Milton girls get their cherries popped! It was about as pleasurable as a Pap smear. That he was hung like a horse didn't help either. Ha! Word around town is it's a family trait. Makes up for the Ticklers' small brains. Personally, I like my peckers small."

"Where is this Deep Hole?"

"'Bout twenty minutes on foot. Just follow the path behind the parking lot. Through the woods, up the cliff. Walk any further, and you'll fall into the water. Bring me back a souvenir, will ya? Maybe a sprig from the old Wishing Tree. The huge pine with the tire swing. Make a wish for me while you're at it. Tell the old gal that Shirlette Whynaught is ready to go and wants to come back as a Canada goose so

I can winter down in Florida. Always wanted to be a snowbird. Ha! 'Magine that!"

"But don't go wishing for nothin' else. You can only make one wish a day, else it's bad luck. That's how Clem Fermentog lost his pecker. He wished for a motorcycle and a handsaw on the same day. Can't remember which one took his pecker. Pass me my spray, will ya? Who are ya, again, dear?"

"I'm Missy. Pup's kid. And of course I will."

Over the next couple of days, I visited Deep Hole multiple times, morning and evening. Because of the heat wave, it was crowded, but there was never a hint of Rudy. Kids swung from the rope into the water all day long, while at sundown, teenagers got drunk around the fire pit. I tried chatting with them, but all they were really interested in were my smokes. I spent most of the time swimming and floating on my back, silently begging the Wishing Tree to grant my wish to see Rudy. Although I lied to Grammy about making her wish, I always brought her back a sprig of pine. By the fifth visit, the bouquet looked like a mini Christmas tree. It was the closest thing she'd get to the real deal, and that made us both happy.

On my sixth trip to the Deephole, I was all dressed up for Pup's pig roast scheduled for 6 pm in the Cuckoo Nest's parking lot. I was wearing the red cherry-print sundress I'd bought for my fifteenth birthday party at Andy and Ethel's. Underneath I wore my zebra-print bathing suit, but I'd decided not to go in the water after all in case I messed up my hair and makeup. As usual, my lipstick matched both my dress and sandals, and my thick black eyeliner matched my blow-dried bob and purse. I had the song "Lady in Red," in my head, and was fantasising Rudy would feel that way about me when we finally laid eyes on each other.

I've never seen you looking so gorgeous as you did tonight

I've never seen you shine so bright, you're amazing

I spotted him just after I'd reapplied my lipstick. As I stood up, a branch from the Wishing Tree got caught in my hair. Instead of untangling, I clung to it, feeling shaky from the sight of Rudy and Bobby walking towards me. They were bare-chested. Rudy carried a two-four of beer and Bobby had brought along a boombox. Rudy looked so sexy in his skull-print swimming trunks.

"Missy! What a happy surprise!" he exclaimed. "What in the hell did the poor Wishing Tree do to you?"

He set his stuff down and gently tried to untangle my hair. "I'm happy to see you, Missssy," he whispered in my ear.

Once again, his words turned my body on like a tap. He kept untangling. It was impossible that he didn't feel my breath against his bare arm. Here was my chance to lay my head on his chest. And I might have if Bobby, already drunk and wobbling, hadn't been standing beside us huffing and puffing like the wolf in "The Three Little Pigs." Instead, I tried reading the *God is Greater than my Highs and Lows* tattoo on his bicep. Except I went cross-eyed and got it wrong.

"God is Greater than my... thighs...?"

Rudy looked down at my thighs. Panicking that maybe I actually was dripping, I bent down to tuck my dress between my legs. The branch followed, yanking hard on my hair.

But Bobby had had enough of our threesome. He lunged and ripped the branch from my hair. "Hurry the fuck up, dickwad, and help me start the fire!" he screamed at Rudy. "And you," he said to me once he was done, "can now fuck right off outta here."

The pain was fast and humiliating, like walking into a lamppost on a busy street. Best pretend it didn't happen. Avoiding eye contact with Bobby, I picked up my purse and smoothed out my hair. Then I took the risk of silently throwing a second wish at the Wishing Tree: *I wish to stay here with them.*

"Oh, you guys aren't coming to the pig roast?" I said, trying my best to channel Randall's natural coolness.

Bobby cracked open a bottle and flicked the cap at me. It hit the corner of my eye.

"Fuck your daddy's pig roast and fuck your cunt of a sister," he said. "Oh, wait, I already fucked her, didn't I? And what a shitty lay she is! Like fucking a dead fish. And she wonders why I look for better pussy! But now that I'm stuck with the pregnant bitch, she won't even look at me. Glued to that goon brother of yours. What the fuck's wrong with your family? Ya'll are fucking parasites."

Rudy rolled his eyes. "Don't mind him," he said. "Bobby's a bit sensitive today. Lady problems. He'll get over it. Always does. Why don't ya stay a bit and keep me company? This bozo's useless. Here, have a beer."

I accepted the beer. My second wish was granted. Before taking a sip, I discreetly tipped my bottle in appreciation in the direction of the Wishing Tree and tried my luck at a third: *I wish to be alone with Rudy.* Then, pouring beer on my hand, I washed the blood from my face where the cap had cut me.

The next two hours went by kind of like the last leg of our drive to Milton. After my first beer, I stopped babbling and pulling my hair over my face. With my third, I sang along to their mixtape, oblivious that I sounded like the starling Pup claimed I was. I finished my fourth floating on my back like an otter sucking on a baby bottle. Concerns over my hair and makeup disappeared along with my sadness about Jemima. When the men started firing off dares and cheering me on from the cliff like swim coaches, I was drunk on their attention as much as the beer.

"Do a backflip, Missy!"

"Swing upside down from the rope!"

"See how long you can hold your head underwater!"

"Pick up a rock from the bottom!"

I did them all. I was a notorious dare champion. When I was nine, I put my underwear in a neighbour's mailbox. When I was eleven, I hung my friend's baby sister by her ankles off the balcony. When I was twelve, I climbed onto the school bus roof while it was moving. I held on for three minutes until the driver clued in. I was suspended for a week. "Your daughter," my teacher told Mama, "is going to seriously hurt herself or someone else if she doesn't learn to control her impulses. You might want to consider redirecting her fearlessness into something healthier. Like rock climbing or break dancing."

The dares got wilder once I got out of the water to fetch my fifth beer.

"Run through the fire, Missy."

"Pretend to give your beer bottle a BJ."

"Show us your tits."

"Give Bobby a lap dance."

Only the Wishing Tree knows how far it would have gone if Bobby and Rudy hadn't gotten into a fight during the lap dance.

"Looks like you chose the wrong Whynaught girl!" Rudy said. "This one's nothing like her tight-ass sister."

Bobby pushed me off his lap. I was facing the fire with my back to him. I landed on a rock, leaving a scratch the size of a cheese slice on my right knee and black soot all over my palms that ended up on my face.

"What the fuck did you say?" Bobby screamed. "I didn't quite hear ya, buddy, come closer and say it again. So I can punch your ugly face in!"

Bobby smashed his beer bottle against the Wishing Tree and waved the neck of the broken bottle at Rudy. It was dark now, and the shadows on his face from the fire made him look like the devil I knew he was. But instead of attacking him he burst into tears.

Rudy rolled his eyes again. "Ya okay, buddy? I was just messing with ya."

Bobby threw the broken bottle into the woods. "I'm outta here," he said.

With Bobby gone, my third wish came true. Grammy didn't know shit about the tree's rules.

"Looks like it's just us now," Rudy said. He sat on a log and patted the spot beside him. "Come sit. I promise I won't bite. Unless you want me to."

I grabbed what might have been my sixth or ninth beer and sat down. I was wearing only my bathing suit. Sitting so close to the fire made the burns on the soles of my feet sting something nasty. But I wasn't going to risk him suggesting we leave by telling him. Especially since he'd just scooched in closer. I closed my eyes, sure the kiss was coming. But instead of kissing me, he buried his face in my hair and inhaled loudly, like it was a pair of underwear he'd just picked off his bedroom floor.

"Your hair's still wet," he said. "And smells like Deep Hole."

"Err, is that a compliment?"

"That it smells like Deep Hole, or it's wet?"

"Both?"

"Well, I certainly like wet things."

"Oh, yeah? Like what?"

"Like this."

He put his hand between my legs, pushed aside the crotch of my bathing suit and slipped a finger inside me. I didn't see it coming. It happened as quickly as a sneeze.

"Shit, girl!" he said, laughing. "You're soaked! And I only just got started. I've never seen anything like it! You're amazing! Another?"

I didn't know what to say, so I didn't say much at all. My body did all the talking. I guess it told him more, more, more. Like my deep gasps. And the fact that every time he asked to put in another finger, I nodded yes.

Even for his fist.

Even when he said, "You're wild, Missssy. You're like a natural phenomenon. You should cash in on this. Bottle?"

The whole time, I kept wondering if this was normal. I kept laughing along with him. I kept wishing he'd kiss me instead of playing with my body as if it were some cool but useless toy. Like a slinky or a Magic Eight Ball. The ones you use once, then throw away. Which is exactly what he did with the beer bottle when he was finished, whipping it at the poor Wishing Tree, where it smashed to pieces. In the firelight it looked like mini fireworks. I imagined all the wild animals, watching from the woods, oohing and ahhing over the show, hoping for an encore.

"Score!" he yelled, wiping his hands on his swimming trunks. "Ya ready to get going?"

"Sure," I lied.

Leaving was the last thing I wanted to do. I was still waiting for that kiss. I would have done anything for that kiss. But it never happened.

On our way out, I wondered how many bottle pieces had blood on them from my burst cherry. While Rudy took a piss, I bent down, picked up a shard, and slipped it into my purse. I pricked my index finger. More blood. As I sucked my finger, I rested my other hand on the Wishing Tree and whispered, "I'm so sorry for making such a mess."

The mosquitoes feasted on my body the whole walk back. But like the earworm from "Lady in Red" that had settled in my brain earlier that day, they wouldn't take no for an answer.

There's nobody here
It's just you and me
It's where I want to be
But I hardly know this beauty by my side
I'll never forget the way you look tonight.

Rudy, on the other hand, couldn't get rid of me fast enough. He walked a good five feet ahead of me on the path through the woods, then left me standing alone to find his buddies the second we arrived at the party-concert-vibe pig roast. Still, I took the only three words he said to me, "See ya later," as proof he'd eventually find his way back.

In preparation for his return, I went to clean myself up in the Cuckoo Nest's bathroom. On the way, I found Jemima arm in arm with Bobby. I was happy to see them back together. I figured it meant she was in a good mood.

"Hey!" I said cheerfully. "How's it going?"

She looked at me as if I'd just thrown grape juice all over her white sundress.

"We need to talk. Now!" she snapped. "Also, you look like death."

After she gave Bobby the kind of passionate kiss I'd been wanting all night, I followed her to the parking lot. It was still littered with pink- and blue-stained cotton candy cones, popcorn, paper cups, and bottle caps. The little pen that housed the chatty llama hadn't been taken down yet either, and I wondered where the strange creature was. A few fold-up chairs were exactly where they'd been left, along with the bubble machine. For a second, I thought I saw bubbles floating by my face. When I tried to pop one, Jemima looked at me like the staff at Grammy's nursing home looked at the demented patients.

"What the hell are you doing? Are you crazy?"

"I was trying to pop that bubble. You didn't see it?"

"All I see, Missy, is a backstabbing slut who wants to ruin my life."

"I'm sorry," I said quickly, trying to scratch an unreachable mosquito bite in the middle of my back. I was sure she was talking about the broken promise. Or the way I spoke about Pup. Or the cursed teddy bear.

"You really think Bobby likes you? You really think you stand a chance—"

"Bobby?" I cut in. He was the last person I thought she'd mention. I'd erased him from the night. "What are you—"

"Let me finish! Seriously, Missy. Let's forget for a second that he's my fiancé and the father of my unborn child. Do ya really think he's into you?"

Of course, I didn't. But I knew anything I said would come out wrong. Another bubble floated by.

I watched it drift towards the llama pen where it hovered, spinning round and round like a mini spaceship. Maybe it is a mini spaceship, I thought. With mini aliens inside researching Miltoners' behaviour. Stranger things had happened that night.

Jemima broke my trance.

"Answer me, Missy! What's going through your mind? I really wanna know. I mean, I knew you had a crush on Bobby when you were little, but actually making a move on him? A fucking lap dance? Who does that? He said he was so shocked he couldn't move. He's totally traumatized."

"They dared me," I whispered.

"They what you?"

"They dared me," I repeated, louder. "We played Truth or Dare, and I guess it got out of hand. It was stupid. I'm stupid. It meant nothing. I'm not into Bobby. I swear. It's Rudy I like."

"For Christ's sake, Missy. I don't even know what to say. I warned you to stay away from Rudy Tickler, but maybe yas are perfect for each other. How could you do this to me? I actually believed what you wrote in that note."

"I—"

"What did the little troublemaker do this time?" A booming but familiar voice was suddenly behind me.

I turned around to see Randall and Pup standing together. I had no idea how long they'd been there or how much they'd heard. Pup shook his head slowly and pursed his lips in disappointment. Randall smirked.

"She made a move on Bobby," Jemima said with tears in her eyes.

"Aww, sweetheart. Come here," Pup said, inviting Jemima into a hug. "You just can't catch a break, can ya?"

I left the parking lot while Randall and Pup sandwiched Jemima in a bear hug. Plan A was to find Rudy and see if he wanted to hang out again. I circled the lot a few times until I caught his eye. But when he looked away, I moved on to Plan B: sleep it off in the dog house before hitchhiking home at dawn. I didn't want to face my family, especially Jemima, ever again. Thoughts of what happened with the bottle were popping up in my brain like the mosquito bites all over my body. I didn't know how to get rid of them. I knew scratching them would make them worse but the torment was there no matter what I did. I had to find a way to ignore them. That meant running away from Milton as fast as possible. I wished I had Grammy's bad memory. I wished I was old and on my way out like her. But not even the Wishing Tree could grant me that. Not that she'd ever trust me again. But if she did, I'd ask to come back as a mermaid and swim off to a faraway land where no one knew me. The Wishing Tree could take my voice in return if she wanted it. All it did was get me in trouble anyway.

The sudden need to see Grammy was almost as strong as my need to kiss Rudy. I turned toward the nursing home and saw that her window was open due to the heat. I climbed in, tiptoed to her bed, and gently shook her big doughy shoulder. She opened her eyes.

"Jesus Murphy! Is it breakfast? I hope it's blood sausage day!"

"Shhh," I whispered. "It's not morning. It's almost midnight."

Her eyes adjusted to the dark. "What the hell happened to you? Ya look like something the cat wouldn't drag in. Ya hurt? You get in an accident or something?"

"I'm fine, Grammy. I was partying at the Deep Hole with some friends and tripped on my way back. I'll shower later. I wanted to say goodbye first."

"Oh, no. You're not leaving already, are ya? Who are you again, dear?"

"I'm Missy, Grammy. Pup's daughter."

"Pup's here?" she exclaimed. "Where is he?"

"Shhh, Grammy, please, you'll wake everyone up. Pup will come and see you at breakfast time, I promise. I just need to talk with you about something first," I said softly.

"I hope it's juicy. Lord knows my life ain't juicy no more. Dry as a fucking popcorn fart it is. Go on, then. Spit it out. I'm all ears."

"I made out with Rudy Tickler tonight," I said. "Well, kinda."

"Good for you! Ya get your cherry popped, did ya?"

"That's the thing, Grammy. I'm not sure. I'm not sure it's supposed to be done that way."

"What on God's green earth ya talkin' about? There's only one way to get your cherry popped. It's not rocket science. Believe me. If it were, I'd have failed."

"Yeah, but. He used a…"

Knowing she'd forget everything I said within thirty minutes was the only reason I was able to spit it out.

"He used a what, hun?"

"A beer bottle," I whispered.

I vowed to never say those words again.

"A beer bottle?" She frowned. "Well, that's a new one, even for me! I hope ya smacked him over the head with it!"

"I didn't."

"Ya liked it then?"

"No," I lied.

"But I guess *he* thought I liked it," I continued. "He must have, right?"

I didn't get my answer.

"That fucker! Ya want me to send Bronko Knickle to punch him in the balls? Good ole Bronko owes me a favour or two and, man, can he throw a punch. He wins Milton's strongman potato sack throwin' contest every year!"

"Please don't, Grammy," I whispered. "I'm not mad at him. I told him it was okay. I just don't get why I let him. Or why he didn't kiss me. That's all I wanted."

Grammy sighed deeply and shook her mop of white curls. "Kisses take time, hun. Men can be weird about kisses. Don't you worry about that. You're young and got lots of time still. Believe me, there's plenty of kissy fish in the sea."

"And, hey," she continued, perking up again. "Maybe you'll be one of the lucky few who catches a fish who actually knows how to give a good bonkin'. I sure did. My Howard was a right magician in bed. Wouldn't have known it to see him, but holy smokes! Made up for his small pecker, I tell ya that. Ha! Now, pass me my room spray, will ya, umm, who are ya again, sweetie?"

"I'm Missy, Grammy. Pup's daughter."

"Of course! What a happy surprise! Is Pup here too? I sure miss my beautiful son. He's such a good boy. My pride and joy, he is."

"He'll be here for breakfast. Soon, Grammy."

I stayed with her for only a few more minutes. Then I gave her a long hug that felt as real and special as Christmas morning before lying that I'd be back to visit soon. If she didn't live in Milton, I'd have visited her all the time. I loved Grammy's jolly, memory-free world. Her forgetting who I was all the time was kind of a blessing. But, over my dead body would I ever return to Milton.

Before leaving through the window, I went to the bathroom to pee and finally clean myself up. Jemima had been right, I looked like death. More like near-death. A perfect image to put in a fire safety pamphlet. A warning example of one of the lucky few who managed to get out of the burning house by the skin of their teeth. *Just imagine the ones who didn't make it,* the caption would read.

I used up a whole roll of paper towel to wash myself, filling the garbage can to the brim with dirt, soot and bloodstained crumpled-up sheets. Somewhere in there was the bloodied shard from my popped cherry. Whoever emptied it wouldn't have a clue what Grammy had been up to, and Grammy wouldn't remember a clue to share. To add to the mystery, I took out my red lipstick and wrote *Milton Ho* on the mirror. Another nickname to add to the list of many. Looking down at my hands as I did, I saw the upside smile scar I'd managed to forget about until then. I slapped my cheeks hard enough to match my red dress. And the scratch on my knee. And the cut on my eye. And the burns on the soles of my feet. And the mosquito bites all over my body. And the tiny prick mark on my finger.

Never forget the way you look tonight.

The lady in red.

6
Big Red

A few months after Andy and Ethel moved out, Big Red moved in. Big Red wasn't his real name, of course. It was Seamus. Seamus Gunn. But everyone called him Big Red because of his bright red hair and how big he was. He was also known by his CB radio handle, "Red Fox," and he dyed the tips of his long greasy hair white to make it look like a fox's tail to fit the part. Being big was the biggest thing about him so I stuck to calling him Big Red. In fact, he had such a big freckled forehead and was so tall and muscly that I wondered if he had that rare disease where your bones keep growing and growing and growing until one day you die. Like Andre the Giant, the one with the German accent who side-gigged in *The Princess Bride.*

After the first time I shook his hand, I thought I'd caught the giant disease, too, because my hips and ass had another growth spurt. But I never got any taller, which really messed with my proportions. Still, the giant disease became a bit of a preoccupation. I measured myself every night for reassurance. I once tried binding my hips and ass like I'd read they'd done to Chinese girls' feet back in the day. I even asked Mama if I could go to the doctor to get checked out, just in case.

"Missy, you're no fuckin' giant! You'll be lucky to reach five foot two! And you're gonna live as long as Grammy Whynaught even though you're not blood related, no doubt about that," she laughed at me.

But she didn't think it was so funny when I asked her if Big Red had it. "Maybe he does, maybe he don't," she said. "But you keep that fuckin' tongue of yours in your mouth and leave the poor gentle giant be. The last thing he needs is you poking and prodding about his personal life."

I stopped measuring and binding myself soon enough. And I never asked Big Red whether he was dying of the giant disease; I left that up to him to tell me. But I did struggle to keep my tongue to myself, which you'd think I would have mastered after the Milton trip disaster. But I hadn't. Just like I hadn't given up on spying on my neighbours after the Beloved disaster. I was like a weed that just kept growing in the same direction no matter how many times I'd been chopped down. Now, instead of pointing my binoculars at Andy and Ethel, I pointed them at Big Red. Every day after school, I'd sit in the tree house and wait for him to come outside to tinker on one of his motors. Then I'd pretend I was going for a walk down to the Irving gas station for some milk or a Mr. Freeze, stop all casual-like in front of his place, and ask if I could buy a smoke.

"Oh, hey, Red. How's it hanging?" I acted surprised to see him, as if I hadn't just seen him the day before, and the day before that, in the exact same place at the exact same time. Big Red, I'd learned, was a stickler for routine. "Can I buy a smoke?"

He stopped tinkering, reached into his plastic Mötley Crüe cigarette case he kept in his back pocket, and handed me a smoke. "Nah, you're good," he'd say with a half-smile, waving away my outstretched hand and the shiny quarter I held between my fingers as if I were a little kid offering him a bite out of my half-eaten, slobbered-over ice cream cone.

And that was about the extent of our conversation over the next hour or so as we hung out in his driveway. Despite his flash hair and name, Big Red hardly said boo, which was fine by me because I was such a chatterbox. "That Missy Whynaught can talk the ear off a rock," my teachers were always saying. As if rocks had ears. But it was true. And Big Red being a good listener was true, too. Which was a pleasant surprise because the only guys I had contact with those days were Randall, who just grunted, or Dirk the Jerk. He just grunted, too.

Sometimes, if it rained, we'd stay inside his place and watch movies or play around with his CB radio. But mostly, our ritual played out in his driveway. Big Red leaning up against his rusty green pickup truck, chainsmoking. Me, in a tank top and jean shorts, straddling his ATV like the world's scruffiest, chubbiest porn star, yakking about whatever struck my fancy that day. The rom-com or horror paperback I was reading. My dream of visiting Pup in Cuba. How I got panic attacks when I looked at the stars or how I'd found Mama's stash of lesbian porn mags hidden behind the fridge.

The more I talked at Big Red, the more he fed me smokes, which I could suck back like the best of 'em. Smoking felt as good as scoffing down a dozen donuts in one sitting but kept my ass from moving from the disproportionate-but-still-acceptable size to Grammy Whynaught's can't-move-no-more size. At least that's what I'd read in the health section of Mama's lezzie magazines. As for Mama saying Big Red didn't want me hanging around down there all the time, I could tell by a little sparkle in his eye that she was wrong. Sometimes, a wave of pink travelled up his thick neck to his giant face and ears like a spray-on sunburn. That's when I knew Mama was really wrong.

Things carried on like this for a few weeks until one day, Big Red asked me if I'd clean his place every Monday afternoon while he did his groceries. In exchange, he'd give me a pack of smokes. I was surprised at first, and even a bit hurt. I started wondering if all that time Mama had been right. Maybe he did find me a nuisance and was looking for a way to get me out of his flaming hair that was reminding me more and more of that creepy serial killer doll. Maybe he was fed up with me bumming smokes from him all the time. But then I came around to liking the idea. It would be like a part-time job, I decided. Maybe he wanted to see if I'd still hang out with him if I had my own smokes? In the end, it seemed like a pretty sweet deal.

Until I found the Polaroid.

Tacked to his bathroom mirror, the first time I went in to clean his place, I found a colour Polaroid of Big Red. Naked. His blank face looked straight at the camera. His tall, giant body stood in profile, emphasizing his gargantuan erect penis. My first thought was how red his pubic hair was. I started thinking about all the people I knew and their pubes. Did everyone's pubes match what we saw on the outside? Had Grammy's turned grey along with the hair on her head? I'd never be able to look at another redhead the same.

My second thought was, surely Big Red hadn't left it out on purpose. Maybe Randal had found it while he was playing video games and snuck it there for me to find as a joke? Maybe Big Red had a lover I didn't know about, and she'd left it there, unaware I was coming to clean that day? The shy Big Red I knew would have been mortified if he knew I'd seen it. Yes, it was definitely a mistake. I quickly finished cleaning, hoping to get out before he returned, deciding not to mention it when I saw him next. I was equally kind of excited and repulsed. But mostly, I was embarrassed. For us both.

I was hesitant to go and see Big Red the next day. But I didn't want to hurt his feelings. So what if he had a nudie pic of himself? I'd seen racier things looking through Mama's magazines—those women didn't even have pubes! At fifteen and three-quarters, I was sure I was mature enough to handle it at all. So off I trotted down the road, nerves in check with an already lit smoke from the pack I'd proudly earned from my new part-time job.

I found Big Red lying under his truck, only his long legs and humongous yellow work boots visible. For a moment, I thought he was dead; run over, suffocated, or the giant disease finally got him. But then his leg twitched, and I knew he was just tinkering.

The ritual began.

"Oh, hey, Red. How's it hanging?" I said to his legs, cringing over my word choice. It was my turn to be shy, but he didn't notice because it took a few minutes for him to slide out from under the truck. Once he was back on his elephantine feet, I offered him a smoke.

"Nah, keep yours. Ya worked hard for them," he said. Same half-smile. Same waving away of my offering with that big, freckled hand of his that I still wondered might be contagious but managed not to flinch, so I didn't offend him. Same reaching into his back pocket for his cigarette case as he did every afternoon. Same everything, which I thought was pretty strange because for sure he knew I'd seen the Polaroid, right? I kept watching his face to see if it got any pinker than usual, but nothing was out of the ordinary. In the end, I decided he must have practiced really hard to keep things normal between us. That it was his way of saying, "Nope, that pic wasn't for you to find, Missy. Sorry 'bout that."

By the time I was ready to clean up his place again, I'd begun to think I'd made the whole thing up.

Until I found the second Polaroid.

The next Monday, as I was vacuuming the bedroom carpet, I found another Polaroid. This time it was on his nightstand. Frontal pose. Mouth slightly open as if he were about to say something dirty. He wore a cock ring. At least, I think that's what it was. At the time, I figured it was some kind of brace like the ones used to keep your finger straight if you've sprained it. A penis brace. Which was a very odd thing to wear. Whatever it was, Big Red's freckled member stood as straight and thick as a tree trunk. It looked as if it had been collared like some wild, speckled beast. An exotic lizard, maybe. Or a giraffe. Suddenly, I felt as if someone was watching to catch my reaction. I tried to act as normal as possible in case I got it all wrong. *Keep cleaning, Missy. Just keep cleaning.* I began to fuss over the dust on the nightstand. I couldn't decide whether to lift the Polaroid to clean the whole surface or just dust around it. Either way, he'd know I saw it, and that scared me more than being watched. In the end, I left the whole thing dusty. My hands were too shaky to do it anyway. I hoped I'd still get my smokes.

That evening, over supper, I didn't say or eat much of anything. Mama wondered if I really was coming down with something.

"Maybe we should take ya to the doctor and get ya checked out, Missy," she said as Randall snickered into his plate of beans and wieners. "What's got your tongue all tied up, eh? Since when don't ya like weiners?"

"Just feeling a little sick. That's all." I'd always liked weiners, but every time I tried to take a bite, an image of Big Red's penis brace came to mind, and I wanted to hurl. How could I tell Mama? She would've either laughed into her plate, or burst into heaving tears that made me feel like the worst daughter in the world. Ever since Big Red moved to Poverty Hill, she'd had him do all kinds of things around the house that Pup was never home long enough to do. Chopping firewood, putting up a deer fence. He even fixed our septic tank, so we didn't have to shit in the woods anymore when the water supply was low. In exchange, Mama made him pies and sewed up his shirts and gave him a five dollar bill here and there if she could. Mama depended on Big Red as much as her peach schnapps. Same for Randall. They had become great buddies because they were both into video games and smoking pot. In exchange for selling the pot Big Red grew in his backyard to the kids at school, he gave Randall 15 percent of the deals and let him use his fire pit for parties. They all had too much to lose if I spilled the beans.

The next week, I still wasn't sure the Polaroids were for me. Though I'd surprisingly begun to feel a little jealous if they weren't. Our hangouts hadn't changed a bit, but I'd started having erotic nightmares. In them, Big Red was a giant woodpecker. I was a bird creature, too, but my wings weren't as big and strong, so I couldn't get away. In the end, he always caught me between his jumbo feet, carried me to his jumbo nest, and pecked away at me with his jumbo beak. I'd wake up excited and petrified, checking myself all over for the spots.

I found the third Polaroid lying on his pillow, waiting to be discovered like a surprise birthday card. He held a red rose in one hand and his spotty knob in the other. He knew my favorite color was red. I'd told him. It scared me that he had remembered, almost as much as it lit me up the way Rudy had said my name. *Missssssy.* It was then that I decided it was my turn to act. That I needed to hurt him or make him mine forever. There was no other way to make the nightmares go away.

It poured the next day. Like, raining cats and rats poured. I kept looking out the classroom window to see if it would let up, but it never did. I was sure that was a sign. I remembered that sometimes when it was rainy, Big Red would invite me to watch a movie with him. So as soon as I got home, I put on Mama's lingerie, a red lacy one-piece with a bow stitched onto the bum like a bunny tail. It was tight and uncomfortable because Mama was skinnier than me. I squirted on some of her Avon perfume, slipped on a clean pair of jean shorts and a tank top, and grabbed one of Randall's Terminator movies. As I skipped down the hill in the pouring rain, my tummy flip-flopped as though I'd just swallowed Lucky, our giant goldfish-turned-carp. The one who had jumped out of the tank in an attempt to escape but got stuck behind the washing machine. We'd found him a week later shrivelled up, covered in dryer lint.

I knocked on Big Red's door to the tune of one of Pup's favourite little ditty: *Shave and a haircut, two bits, I gotta girl with, two tits.* "Hey!" I said, holding out the VHS like a box of Girl Guide cookies. "Movie?"

I went straight to his living room and sat down on the end of his brown velour couch. There was a pot full of stale Rice-a-Roni and a wooden spoon on the coffee table. Beside it was a glass ashtray with a chipped joint lying on its side and a lighter in the shape of a busty blonde wearing a blue bikini. Big Red was in the next room fetching me a towel, so I lit the joint. The flame shot out of the plastic woman's mouth like she was an angry fire Goddess.

When Big Red came back, he handed me the towel. Then he popped the movie into the VCR and sat down at the other end of the couch.

"Ya ready?" he said.

"Ready." I had a buzz on. I was still cold from the rain. I don't know why, but I was having visions of Grammy all alone at the nursing home, sitting in her own shit, looking for her room-spray, which made me want to cry. Still, I scooched up beside him and wrapped my chubby legs around his waist as I'd planned. I started rubbing his shoulders and stuck my tongue in his ear. The bitter taste made me gag, but I lapped it up anyway. I'd read in one of Mama's lezzy mags that it was a surefire turn-on.

"What the fuck, Missy!" he yelled, and leapt off the couch.

"Huh? I—the photos. I—"

I didn't wait to hear what he said next. My ears were ringing, and my inner Missy was flogging the hell out of me. All I remember is grabbing the pot on the coffee table and throwing it at him, but I missed and it hit the wall. Rice-A-Roni showered us both like a dirt-bag wedding ceremony.

I ran out of his place and went straight to my treehouse. I stripped off my wet clothes and scratched at my hands and arms that had abruptly doubled in size until they bled. That's when I knew I really had caught the giant disease. Mama was dead wrong. It was real, alright. I *was* dying. Any minute, I was sure I'd start growing so fast my limbs would pop out of the sides of the treehouse. I was like Alice in Wonderland. But there wasn't a potion on Poverty Hill, not in the whole world, that could save me. My old Barbie dolls, lined up along one wall like a bunch of silent bridesmaids, were no help at all.

7

Puppy Love

A few months after Big Red, Pup bought me a ticket to visit him in Cuba over March break, just like he'd been promising for years. Mama and Randall had been sure it'd never happen. "That man throws away promises like he throws American dollar bills around the Caribbean!" Mama said. But they were wrong. The ticket arrived, like all the other letters he sent me, in an envelope with my name, *MISS MISSY WHYNAUGHT*, in capital letters and a heart drawn around it. On the back, he did the same with *MR. PUP WHYNAUGHT*.

Pup had been sending me more and more letters since he'd chosen Cuba to be his home away from work. I treasured them. I'd been worried he'd stop sending them after I'd upset Jemima so much in Milton, but he didn't. Sometimes he drew stuff like dolphins and squiggly palm trees in the margins, which was a pleasant surprise because I had no idea he liked to draw. He often tucked something cool inside, too, like sand or dried hibiscus flowers or a Bucanero beer tab folded in three like a shiny quarter moon. The postmark was always from some random Canadian town.

Got my buddy, Doug, from Bonnyville, Alberta, to send this one for me. Can't trust the Cuban post.

Real nice guy, Doug. Retired RCMP. His wife's got MS or something. He looks after her. Real sad story. He comes down here to decompress every few months. Got himself a nice Cuban girlfriend.

I wasn't sure if he meant it was sad that Doug's wife had MS or that he had to look after her.

I hope my friend, Tommy, from Berri, Ontario, don't forget to send you this letter. Not too bright and ugly as sin, but a nice kid. He's a few years older than Randall. He lives with his parents and works at Tim Hortons. He comes down here every six months for a few weeks or so. Ain't got no girlfriend back home. But here, the ladies can't get enough of him! Lucky!

I wasn't sure who he meant was lucky, Tommy or the girls.

All Pup's letters ended with the same rant, which I thought was weird considering the dolphins and hearts.

You all think you're so civilized in Canada, with your big roads and Irving Oil jobs! But there's nothing civilized about living in a place where your piss freezes midstream! Back home, I can barely afford a snowmobile. Here, I live like a friggin' king for a few bucks a day! King Whynaught, ha! Got a nice ring to it, eh?

I tried to convince Mama that we, too, could be living like royals for just a few bucks a day. But it didn't go down well.

"Your daddy don't fuckin' know nothing about nothing! Who do you think's gonna pay for our flights? Who do you think's gonna put a roof over our heads and make sure you go to school and get your fuckin' vaccines? Eh? Speak up, Missy! God only knows what kinda trouble that hobo's into. I can barely put food on the table with the pennies he sends, never mind plane tickets. You're a fuckin' fool if you think he wants us over there cramping his style!"

I hated it when she talked about Pup like that. I rolled my eyes and slammed the door and waited by the phone, hoping he'd call so I could tell him everything. Hoping he'd prove Mama wrong, which he eventually did, always from a payphone, usually in the middle of the night, pissed as a mattress. "Oh, don't listen to that old bat," he'd say. "Your mama's just bitter. God only knows why when it was me who made all the sacrifices. Always having to work away from you guys so she could have her creature comforts. God, I miss you, Pet."

Mama always seemed uncomfortable, so I wasn't sure what creature comforts he was on about. The only time she ever looked comfortable was when she was drunk, watching her shows or sleeping. But it killed me to think of the things he missed out on over the years, birthdays and Christmas, so I didn't challenge him. Working day and night on those freezing ships so we wouldn't have to go without. And then, when he did come home, aside from me following him around like a stray dog, no one paid him any attention.

Randall always took Mama's side. "You're sixteen, for Christ's sake, fool! Open your friggin' eyes! He doesn't have to work away—there's enough construction work in this shithole town for any welder. And even if there wasn't, he sure as shit don't need to screw around in Cuba on his time off."

Pup said Randall only had time for him when he needed money, so he never sent him letters or invited him to visit. And Randall said Pup was a selfish prick, so he never gave him the time of day. Sometimes I blamed Randall that Pup never came to Saint John anymore. Sometimes I blamed Mama. But most of the time, I blamed myself.

About a month before my flight, Pup sent me a hundred American dollars and a list of things he wanted me to bring to Cuba.

A strong dog leash. I bought a pitbull puppy on the beach. I named him Bobo because he's so stupid. Ha! He's a good dog, but he keeps getting off his leash and killing the neighbour's chickens! Even got himself a goat once! I pay this young guy five bucks a week to walk him cause I'm just not strong enough to do it anymore. God forbid I lose control and he gets a hold of a kid or some little old lady! That's all I need. Thanks Pet.

Another dog! Mama always said if she'd had a tail maybe he'd have stuck around.

Lots of spices. As many as you can get. The food tastes like shit down here. The whole island is full of fruit and veg, but all they eat is rice 'n beans with nothing on 'em. I'm gonna show Veronica, the woman who owns the room I rent and cooks my food, a thing or two about cooking.

Nothing upset Pup more than a bad meal. One Easter, he went hunting with Big Red and snared a rabbit. Mama spent hours skinning it and stuffing it into a pie shell that she decorated with little bunny ears made out of the pastry. Pup took one bite, made a face like he was trying to poop, and spat it back on his plate. Mama locked herself in her room for the rest of the day. I wasn't sure whose side to take, so I ate the whole pie myself.

Some clothes for my new girlfriend. She's around your size. Size 8, I think she said. Something slutty, that's how the girls like to dress down here. It's not really my cup of tea, but, hey, who am I to judge?

My face went as red as my zits when I read that. It had been almost a year since he'd last seen me, and I felt sick wondering what he'd say when he saw that my ass and hips had grown again. For sure, me and his girlfriend weren't the same size. I was at least a size 12, closer to 14. That night I dreamt of Pup's girlfriend as a beautiful brown dog with a silky tail, running down the beach on all fours.

A top-of-the-line bike lock. I paid a guy fifty bucks to build me a bike. Only had it a week before it was stolen. I see the jerk who stole it riding around everywhere. He waves at me like he's the fucking president. I just got a new one, but God only knows how long it'll be before it gets stolen, too. I got no friggin' rights here, Pet. No friggin' rights at all!

I knew Pup would've bought the guy a bike if he'd just asked. Mama once made a list of all the money he'd spent on people other than us over the years and it came to thousands. "We could've paid off the mortgage years ago with this amount! We could've put in that fuckin' pool you've always wanted!" she said. "He's an irresponsible dumb-as-cum fucker, that man! *That's* what he is!"

Some BBQ tools. Made myself a portable BBQ. Gonna weld it to the back of my bike, so I can cook on the beach.

Before he started going to Cuba, he tried to open a mobile BBQ business in Saint John. He called it "Madonna Buns" and rode the rig from bar to bar, flipping patties. I'd been so proud of him. I even convinced myself he would settle down in Saint John for good. But he refused to get a permit and wouldn't accept his buddies' money, so it flopped something stupid.

And don't forget to buy some toys for the kids. Beautiful kids they got down here. Poor things don't have a pot to piss in, and I just hate running into them empty-handed.

I imagined his eyes getting all teary while he wrote about the kids. He was such a sentimental guy that sometimes I wondered if he was part woman. Until he did something stupid like punch Randall. Mama always said Pup liked little kids almost as much as he liked dogs. Randall said if we'd stayed in diapers, maybe he'd have stuck around.

I didn't tell Mama or Randall about the money from Pup. Mama would've for sure gone off about all the late bills and things needing fixing around the house. Just thinking about all the money he'd spent on my ticket, she said, was enough to keep her up at night. Instead, I skipped school one day and hitchhiked to the mall. A guy named Trevor, who smelled like Old Spice and looked like he could've been twenty-five or maybe thirty-five with a shaved head, picked me up in his pickup truck. When he leaned over from the driver's seat to open the passenger door, some candies fell out, but when I took a closer look, I noticed they were fruit-flavoured condoms. I also noticed he had a snake tattoo coiled around his fingers and wrist and forearm like prayer beads. For a second, I thought about refusing the ride, but it felt rude. Plus, the weather outside was blowing and thumping like a horny beast.

"Hop on in," he said. "Where ya going?"

"Cuba!"

"Ha! Well, I don't think I've got enough gas to get ya that far!"

The two of us laughed about that for a few minutes, which calmed my nerves about the fruity condoms. Then I told him all about my trip and how

I was going to the mall to buy stuff to take down to my father in Cuba. Trevor said he'd always wanted to go to a tropical island and that I sure was lucky to have a father like that.

"And he's lucky to have a daughter as helpful and as pretty as you, too," he added. "Hey, you think you can bring me back some cigars? I'll give you some cash and my phone number."

"Sure," I told him. I gave him my number, too, just in case I lost his. I was always losing things, and I really wanted to see him again.

I first went to the pet shop. The woman behind the counter had a cockatoo on her shoulder. She looked at me suspiciously when I gave her the American dollar bills, but when I told her about Cuba, Pup and Bobo the dog, she giggled and gave me free doggy treats. Like Trevor, she also said I was lucky to have a father like Pup.

I found the BBQ tools, bike lock, and spices at Kmart. The hard part was choosing the toys. I probably spent two hours loading and unloading my cart with things I thought the children might like. I decided on small stuff like marbles, Dinky cars, crayons, and Pokémon cards, things he could split up to make the feeling of giving go on a little longer. All that took the last of my money, even the money Trevor had given me for the cigars, which I figured Pup would cover once I was in Cuba.

I planned to leave the mall after buying the toys. I really did. I still had about four weeks left before my trip to come up with the money to buy clothes for Pup's girlfriend. I had even thought I could apologize to Big Red and ask if he had any more cleaning work to help me raise the cash. That was my plan when

I went looking for slutty clothes and ended up in the lingerie section of Sears. Just to look. But the next thing I knew, I was staring at my reflection in the changing room mirror, wearing nothing but a black thong and bra set, feeling as shy, dirty, and confused as I did after that doggy girl dream.

The urge to howl nearly killed me.

Randall said that not taking the tag off the lingerie before I walked out of the store wearing it under my clothes was a perfect example of me being a damn fool. Even the security guard who came rushing over to me when the alarm system went off said pretty much the same thing. "Young lady, only a damn fool steals something without removing the tags."

Mama did much worse than call me a fool, though. At the police station, the cops showed her the hot items, along with the other things I had legitimately bought with money, all lined up along the table together like the contents of a pervert's tool kit. When they told her that I'd said it was for my father, she began to cry as I'd never seen her cry before. Big, heaving sobs, body shaking. I thought she might be having a seizure. I kept saying, "It's okay, Mama," over and over again, hoping she'd snap out of it. But she kept crying until the police kicked us out.

"Ma'am," they said, "It's time for youse to head on home now. Things ain't as bad as they seem. A fine. Maybe a little probation, at most. But, until her case has been heard, she can forget about leaving the country."

I was devastated, of course. Not only was I not going to see Pup, but I'd wasted all that money. And Mama kept crying and crying. Every time she came out of her room and looked at me with her sad, puffy eyes, I felt like the worst human being on earth. I kept waking up in the middle of the night, forgetting for a second what happened, wondering if maybe I'd killed a puppy or a baby or someone's sick granny during one of my unreal moments and just didn't remember it.

Randall wouldn't let it go either. He followed me around, telling me I was the most selfish little moron ever. He said he wished I'd never been born. He also said he hoped Pup would get eaten alive by a Cuban shark. "The two of you are a match made in hell. Selfish to the core." Every time I tried to apologise, he held up his hand like he was gonna hit me. I thought he looked so much like Pup it was freaky. But I never told him that. He would've definitely knocked me out.

I was sure Pup would be angry, too, but when he finally called, he just laughed and said, between snorts, "What a waste!" Then his phone card died, and the call was cut off.

I wasn't sure if he meant that I, the stuff, or the plane ticket was a waste. I was desperate for him to call back so I could apologize. I had a plan to make it up to him if he'd consider sending me another ticket after the court hearing. I even started writing a letter in case he didn't call back.

Dear Pup, I am so sorry about what happened. But I have a brilliant idea to make it up to you. If I come to Cuba, you can stop paying people to do things for you. I'll do all your cooking and cleaning for free! The money you'll save will cover some of my ticket. What do you think? Good idea?

When the phone rang, I was finishing off the letter with my own drawings in the margins of a dog riding a bicycle with a cockatoo perched on his shoulder. I wanted it to be Pup so much that I was sure it would be him, but I didn't recognize the voice on the other end.

"Hello? Hello? Is anybody there? Missy?"

"Pup?" I asked, thinking maybe he was chewing on some pineapple or something, he sounded so unlike himself.

"No, it's Trevor," the voice said. "I picked you up hitchhiking a few weeks ago. You said you'd get me some cigars. Remember?"

Of course, I remembered. But when I opened my mouth to speak, nothing came out.

"Missy?" he said. "You there?"

"Oh, hey," I eventually said, trying my hardest to sound chill even though my hands were shaking so hard I almost dropped the phone. "Yeah, it's me. How's it going?"

"Good, thanks," he said. "How was your trip?"

"Well, actually. I didn't end up going."

I whispered that last part. Thinking he'd for sure hang up when he found out I didn't have any cigars for him, or worse, yell at me for spending all his cash. But I was wrong. We ended up talking for almost two hours. I was sure if he hadn't had to get ready for his night shift over at the refinery, we would have talked all night. I even told him the truth about what happened at the mall. He didn't call me a damn fool. Instead, he said, "The whole story's right sad." He'd been caught shoplifting once before, and knew how humiliating it was. "Fucking pigs."

I told Trevor how much I needed to hear that. For those two hours, I didn't have to worry about late bills or dangerous dogs or crying Mamas or Randall's fists. When Trevor asked if he could pick me up after his shift the following day and take me out for breakfast, I felt as though I'd just hooked myself a date to the prom, expensive hairdo, dress and shoes to match. I knew a breakfast sandwich and a double-double at Timmy's was no piña colada on the beach in Cuba, but it took the edge off waiting. At least until it didn't. Trevor made it clear as a right clear day that he couldn't wait to see me again. Cigars or no cigars.

8

Feet Guy

"Hi, Missy," said the voice on the other end of the line. It was a man. "Are your toenails painted white?"

At first, I heard, "Do you want your house painted white?" In the Maritimes, people are always calling around trying to score some work. "You need your wood chopped/snow shoveled/house painted?" Even though our house had been painted white back in the day, now it was the colour of dirty snow. As if God had ashed his big old God cigarette all over our house. It was a reasonable call to make.

"Umm, sorry, we can't afford it," I said, because we couldn't, and, "My mama's out," because she was. "Please call back later."

But he said it again.

"Are your toenails painted white, Missy?"

Not: Are you home alone? Not: I'm watching you, or what are you wearing? No heavy breathing or giggling in the background. Nothing like the predictable creepy prank calls that might leave you feeling freaked out, maybe mad. Calls that, if you're lucky, happen only once or twice in your lifetime, so they don't leave much of a mark. Nope, nothing like that. The calls were predictable. He called every Tuesday at five p.m. For months. He only wanted to talk about my feet. Politely. I called him Feet Guy. His calls marked me up like a bathroom stall in a girl's locker room.

I giggled that first time Feet Guy called, thinking it was Trevor, who'd ghosted me for a job in Fort McMurray several days after our breakfast date/make-out session in the Timmy's parking lot. Or some jerk from school just messing with me. How else would he know my name? I definitely didn't slam down the phone as I probably should have. Getting angry, unless it was towards Mama or Randall, just wasn't my style. So I said, "Sorry, gotta go, bye!" and set the phone down normally so I wouldn't offend him.

But Feet Guy kept calling. And I continued to answer.

We only had one phone in the house, which really pissed Randall and me off. We were always fighting over it. It was a phone for blind people that Mama had picked up at the flea market, with great big white and black numbers on it and a talking caller ID. The only phone jack was in the kitchen, so she bought one of those three-hundred-foot phone cords that was long enough to reach into other rooms. That's why, whenever Feet Guy called, I'd ask him to give me a minute to get settled. I'd take the phone into the bathroom, lie down on the floor, take off my pants and socks and prop my feet up against the toilet. Then I'd wrap the phone cord tightly around my bare legs, like they were hunks of strung-up meat Mama brought home for roasting on special occasions, and say, "Okay, I'm ready."

"Good. Are your toenails painted white?"

"No. That's weird," I might say. "My turn. What's your middle name?"

"Moby Dick," he'd joke. "My turn. Are your feet clean?"

"Of course!" I'd say, embarrassed. "Got any pets?"

"A cat. Cream 'em up for me."

"Cream your cat? Ha! What's his name?"

Feet Guy never got upset when I asked him questions. Or when I changed the topic if he got too pervy. Some things he gave up easily: brown eyes, brown hair, average height, average weight, Jon Bon Jovi, *Alien II*, Meat Lover's pizza, Boston cream. But when I asked about the important stuff, he said things like, "I'm sorry, Missy. It's complicated. Maybe one day."

Later on, I got bolder. When he asked if my toenails were painted white, I'd say, "Mayyybe." When he asked if my feet were clean, I'd say, "No. What are you going to do about it?" By then, I'd made Feet Guy into one of those strong, silent-type movie-star hunks, like Johnny Depp. But as soon as we hung up, I felt like I did the mornings after drinking a pint of vodka to myself and realizing, shit, that wasn't a dream, I really did go down on Dirk the Jerk again. Or the dreams I'd have about Kathleen Buzzell, this strawberry-blonde girl at school who dressed real preppy and was captain of every girls' sports team. In the dreams, kissing Kathleen felt so good, but when I woke up, I wished I was dead. What's wrong with me? I'm no lezzy! That's not normal! Same thing for the calls: I don't have a foot fetish! What the hell's wrong with me? This isn't normal! To get rid of the feelings, I'd eat a whole bag of cookies.

Looking back, it was Feet Guy's wake 'n' bake voice that I liked so much. So calm and smoky. That and the attention. But for him, it was always about the feet. Which was weird because my feet weren't anything to write home about. My feet were kinda like Grammy Whynaught's, even though we weren't blood related. Short, fat, rough and calloused, prone to corns. Sturdy and strong. Definitely not the feet you'd find in a shoe magazine or the ones Jemima inherited from her mama's side. When I visited Jemima when I was ten, she put her slim high-arched foot beside mine and said, "See? I got dancer's feet. That's why I'm a good dancer. And you got soccer feet to match your soccer calves and thighs. You should play soccer. Or go on a diet."

At ten, I didn't give a rat's ass if Jemima had long, skinny feet attached to long, skinny legs that would look good in heels. Heels that people like Grammy and me couldn't even squeeze into, never mind walk in. Her feet just looked like chicken feet to me, all bony-bumpy. Easily snapped. I didn't need 'em. I didn't want 'em. But by sixteen I knew that me and my soccer feet were nothing to get hot over. So why did Feet Guy choose me?

Mama said organized sports were too expensive, so I never played soccer. But I did, thanks to Kathleen Buzzell, play rugby. Kathleen had heard that the high school in Sussex, a little town about an hour from Saint John, had just started a team, so she wanted one too. She gathered a bunch of girls together in the cafeteria to sell us her plan. She stood on a chair, high above us all, waving her fists above her head like a warrior princess. Her golden curls made me think of seasoned curly fries.

"And it won't cost a thing!" she told us. "I know the rules, so I'll be the coach. And we don't need to buy cleats, because they're for sissies."

Being so close to Kathleen, especially after those dreams, made me nervous. The thought of having to wear shorts and show off my chubby thighs and calves made me nervous. I tried replacing the visions of Kathleen in shorts with visions of Freddy Krueger, but that made it worse because I started to worry that I was attracted to serial killers. That wasn't normal either.

At first, I wanted nothing to do with the plan. But Kathleen jumped off her chair and knelt before me like a prayer. She took my clammy hands with my nic-stained fingers in her powerful, warm ones and said, "Oh, please, Missy. Pretty please. Say yes. We need you. You look so strong!"

The wind, no lie, was knocked right out of me. The rest was rugby.

So there I was, the hooker on a team made up of flankers and props, all of us misfits. And we weren't that bad either. We kicked the Sussex girls' ass every time! Even Mama was impressed. Not only was it free, but she didn't have to drive me to any of the games or practices because they were all after school. She even got to brag to her friends when our team picture ended up in the local paper. *Saint John's First All-Girls Rugby Team!*

I got used to wearing my uniform in public, enjoyed plowing into people, and found all sorts of creative ways to avoid being alone with Kathleen. Until one day at practice I heard Kathleen tell the girls about this guy who kept calling asking about her feet.

"Seriously, cross my heart and hope to die, stick a needle in my eye. That's what he says," she said. "*Hi, Kathleen. Do you want your toenails painted white?*"

"Creepy-gross-puke-my-guts!"

"I know. He's called me, like, four times. I don't know how he got my number or knows my name. Like, who does shit like that?"

"What a freak!"

"I could tell he was getting off."

"Ewwwwwwwwwwwwww."

"My parents want to call the cops."

"He probably has sex with his mama."

"He probably has sex with animals."

"He probably has a micropenis."

"He probably doesn't even have a penis."

It was better than when Tara Cox's bloody undies were found soaking in the gym sink. Even better than when Joey McClintock got a boner during sex ed. They ate it all up. And Feet Guy became the talk of our team for weeks. The team crowded around Kathleen while she made fun of it all as if she were Jesus turned LL Bean magazine model handing out chunks of bread and the answers to the world's greatest mysteries.

"Hey, sexy feet!"

"Watch out, girls, I'm gonna take my socks off."

"How do you save a pedophile from drowning? Take your foot off his head. Ha!"

Kathleen christened us the "All Whites" after the New Zealand team but mostly in honour of Feet Guy. She even brought Wite-Out to one of the practices so we could paint our nails. Meanwhile, I held my breath and prayed to the Goddesses of Sexually Confused Teenage Girls that no one would find out that Feet Guy was calling me too. Or, worse, that I liked it. So I laughed along with them and painted my nails and said, "Yeah, those calls are the grossest."

But hearing them talk about Feet Guy felt like the night Dirk the Jerk pissed all over Madonna a few weeks before he and his buddies murdered her. We were in the woods behind the McDonald's doing what we always did. Once he'd blown his load, he turned to Madonna and rained golden showers all over her furry, blonde back. Dear Lord, had I ever wanted to protect that beast (the four-legged one). But I did nothing. I said nothing. I just stayed on my muddy knees, frozen, watching her droopy eyes look at me all, why-don't-you-kick-him-in-the-balls-and-tell-him-to-fuck-off-Mama-Missy? While I looked back at her all, I'm-so-sorry-I-can't-help-you-but-I-can't-even-help-myself-baby-girl.

Me and Madonna were the same to Dirk the Jerk.

That's how I understood that me and Kathleen were the same to Feet Guy.

I had a hard time sleeping as I waited for Feet Guy to make his next call. I didn't know how I was supposed to feel. I was mad as hell, but I was also flattered. How he knew our names, I'll never know. Out of all the girls in the world, he chose me and Kathleen. I was some jealous too. I wanted Feet Guy to be my dirty secret. When I did sleep, my dreams were of Feet Guy and Kathleen going at it in the shower, on the toilet, against the sink. Sometimes, I was Feet Guy. Other times I was Kathleen. Once I starred as yours truly, lying in the middle of the two while Freddy Krueger watched. It was all so scary and confusing.

Although he only called on Tuesdays, on the small chance he'd change things up, I hovered around the phone whenever I wasn't at school. Even Mama noticed my obsession. "Whoever it is you're waiting for to call ain't worth the jail time," she said. "Now, stop sulking around waiting around for scraps like a pathetic dog!"

Despite how much I thought about Feet Guy, on Tuesday I didn't skip school because we had a rugby game that afternoon, which was the only time

I managed to be distracted from my thoughts of him. I tackled. I elbowed. I growled. I grunted. I disappeared into the game for eighty minutes and even scored the winning goal. After that, I lay down on the field to catch my breath and looked up at the clouds. There was no Feet Guy at that moment. There were no bathroom dreams. No naked Freddy Krueger shoving his blistered tongue down my throat or Dirk the Jerk pissing on Madonna. I even forgot that Kathleen was close. It was grand. I should probably play more sports, I thought. It's good for my brain.

But my peace bubble burst when Kathleen came bounding towards me like a golden retriever and pounced right on top of me. I could feel her heart, wild with adrenaline from the wind and the game and maybe something else that I refused to think about. I could feel her panting breath. I could feel her breasts like water balloons pressing against mine. I wanted to kiss her as much as I wanted to knock her out. But there was no way in hell I would kiss a girl. I was no lezzy! Lezzy's didn't exist in Saint John! So I pushed her off me and started to run.

She chased after me.

"Missy! Missy!"

I kept running.

"Come back! We're going to Dairy Queen to celebrate!"

I kept running.

"Missy!"

I kept running until I couldn't hear her anymore. Through the soccer field, across the parking lot, down the street, along the highway. Until those soccer legs of mine brought me all the way to Poverty Hill. I kept running past Big Red's, where he waved at me because we'd made up. Past my big pine tree where the squirrels and the crows waved at me too. Up the gravel driveway, across the broken deck, through the living room and straight into the kitchen. I grabbed a bag of Oreos and sat down on the floor. And waited.

Thankfully, Randall wasn't home to hog the phone or give me shit about eating all the Oreos. It was just me and Mama, who was in the next room watching Ricki Lake interview some lady who'd lost five hundred and fifty pounds. I tried to rehearse what I wanted to say to Feet Guy, but I still didn't know. I could hear the TV through the wall as if Ricki Lake was sitting beside me. The lady explained how she hadn't left the house in five years. Like Grammy, the fire department had to cut a hole in the living room wall to get her out. It had taken six paramedics to get her into the ambulance. So far, she told Ricki, she'd had two gastric surgeries and was waiting to get a skin removal. She called it her "turkey-wattle skin," and I knew exactly what she meant. Grammy had also had the surgery, which failed. Mama was always saying if I didn't slow down with the cookies, I'd have to have the surgery, too.

"So, what do you feel was the turning point for you?" Ricki asked.

"Well, I couldn't walk anymore. I couldn't move," the lady explained. "I literally was stuck where I was at. I was dying."

I decided to leave the kitchen and join Mama in front of the TV. I'll run back as soon as he calls, I told myself. They showed before-and-after pictures of the lady, and I wanted to see them with my own eyes. I couldn't look away. Something about her face made me want to send her a present in the mail. Maybe a thank-you card or a bouquet of flowers. But what got me more than anything was when Ricki surprised the woman and the audience by bringing out her husband of ten years and their seven-month-old baby.

A husband?

Before the weight loss?

The man sat beside her and held her hand and kissed her cheek. He looked like a normal man; an average man. The kind of unremarkable man you see holding hands with an unremarkable woman, alongside their unremarkable children. The kind who made up 90 percent of the population and wouldn't stand a chance with the top-ten, supermodel type of woman, but also aren't forced, out of loneliness and horniness, to be with the bottom ten. Like a seven-hundred-pound woman. But there he was, telling the whole world: "It was love at first sight. I loved her just as much then as I do now. To me, she's the most beautiful woman in the world, inside and out, no matter how much she weighs."

The phone rang as the couple was in full smooch while Ricki Lake cuddled their baby. It startled me like a sucker punch to the head. I jumped out of my seat and waved my hands in the air like I was on a game show with only one minute to answer the question before the buzzer went off. As if I was saying, pick me, pick me, I know the answer! That's when it hit me: Two can play this game, Feet Guy.

I grabbed Mama's hand and sat down on the floor beside her recliner. I squeezed my eyes shut so tight they hurt. Although my feet tried gravitating back to the kitchen, I managed to keep them firmly tucked up under my bum. At that moment, I felt like the strongest girl on Earth. I'd summoned my inner Superwoman, that I didn't know existed until then—at least in regards to the male species. I was so proud of myself.

First ring.

"Screw you," I whispered.

Second ring.

"Screw you," I whispered, a little louder this time.

Third, fourth, fifth ring (in unison with the audience clapping).

"Screw you!" I yelled.

Mama snapped her head to look at me. "For Christ's sake, Missy! I can't fuckin' hear the show over your yapping! Whoever was calling has already screwed off! Now let go of me!"

And that's what happened. Until he called the following week. When my inner Superwoman was on vacation, I guess. I answered it. Again and again, he called; again and again, I answered. Until he didn't. Just like any other love story. The kind talked about on talk shows. The kind marked up on bathroom stalls. About girls like me all over the world.

9

Expat Part 1

I finally got to visit Pup in Cuba a few weeks after graduating high school. For eight days. I'd just turned eighteen. He'd been living there between jobs for years by then. He rented a bedsit in a village not far from Guantanamo. He told me not to worry about him getting locked up in Guantanamo because he wasn't brown or Muslim and didn't know how to shoot a gun very well. If anything, he'd get locked up for buying cheese off the black market or spending too much time with the local women. But I shouldn't worry about that either, he said, because it was more likely the cheese seller or the local women would get in trouble. Expats, he explained, got special treatment.

I didn't get why he needed cheese so badly. Or what the big deal was about spending time with local women. I didn't know what an expat was. I wondered if he was talking about his ex, Patty, which made no sense at all. I did worry about the jail part, though. Whenever he was home, Mama was forever bailing him out for something or other. It used to keep me up at night, expecting the worst. But at least in Canada, I could visit him. In Cuba, I didn't know what to expect.

Pup explained in a letter that he'd booked us a room at an all-inclusive resort. *You'll love it; it's like Disneyland,* he wrote. *There are free drinks twenty-four hours a day! Personally, I hate resorts. But it'll be more comfortable for you and less hassle for me. Immigration's on my ass for living off the resort property, even without having you in tow. But don't worry, we'll do day trips so you can see the "real Cuba."*

He sent money and a list of things I needed to bring for him in that same letter. It was similar to the list he'd sent the last time, when I tried but failed to visit him. *Toys for the kids, a CD player, disposable cameras, women's clothes, toiletries.*

He included a list of instructions, too. For dealing with customs at the airport. He wrote that part in uppercase letters. It read like a James Bond secret mission. Or a madman's diary.

DON'T TELL CUSTOMS ABOUT THE ELECTRONICS (but if they find them, just give them a camera so they'll let you through).

DON'T TELL THEM YOU HAVE A FATHER LIVING HERE (they'll for sure go through your suitcase).

DON'T PET THE GUARD DOGS.

I wasn't too worried about the customs agents or their dogs. I was more concerned about ruining my plans. I was so determined to go that I barely left the house in the weeks leading up to the flight. In case I found trouble again.

But, in the end, I had nothing to worry about. I made the flight. Neither an agent nor their dog gave me a second look. I was feeling pretty in the pink and white polka-dot halter dress I'd scored at a garage sale. I wore black kitten-heel sandals that were uncomfortable but made my legs look longer and slimmer. I painted my lips hot pink to match the dress. I teased and sprayed my hair into a bouffant. I'd read that Cuba was stuck in the '50s, so I resurrected my inner Betty Boop to look the part. When I walked out the door and into the airport parking lot, the air was so hot and wet it felt like I had my head in a dishwasher. It tasted like coconut cream pie. I wiped the sweat off my brow and put my hands over my eyes like a starlet looking for my lover. Cuba, finally.

That's when I spotted Pup with his back to me, leaning against the charter bus that took tourists to the resort. I hadn't seen him in a year, but I could tell by the way he swayed that he'd already had a few. He wore cargo shorts that came down to his shins because he was shorter than your average man and a T-shirt two sizes too big because he didn't care. He'd buzzed off his salt and pepper hair and wore sandals held together by duct tape. I walked toward him slowly. When he turned and saw me, he held out his arms like a mama eagle about to land in her nest.

"Aww, Pet," he sighed into my bouffant. All the hairspray in the world couldn't mask the smell of booze. "You finally made it."

"I did! I did!" I chirped.

"You ready to start your vacation?"

"Sure am!"

"Great!" he said, picking up my suitcase, heavy with gifts. "Let's bust this popsicle stand!"

When we arrived at the resort, I couldn't believe my eyes. Pup had been right. It did look like Disneyland. With its pillars and turrets and marble archway, the hotel was like something out of *Sleeping Beauty*. Instead of royal servants, hotel staff in stiff white collared shirts and navy-blue dress pants followed us around with fancy cocktails and snacks that looked like cat food. Instead of ball gowns, middle-aged ladies strolled around in flip-flops and bikinis looking like they'd just woken up. You could tell how long they'd been there by their tan shades. It made me think of Neapolitan ice cream: vanilla, strawberry, chocolate. The ones who'd avoided shade altogether or, like Pup, had long ago ditched their return ticket, were that rusty beef-jerky colour of all three flavours mixed together. Beef jerky in texture too.

"Close your mouth, or you'll swallow a tropical mosquito," said Pup.

"But, but," I stammered, "how can we afford this?" My tummy hurt as I had visions of Mama going door to door during snowstorms selling Avon. Her sore feet, her exhaustion. The way she sat in the dark or in front of the TV when she wasn't working, drunk, crying.

"Oh, don't let these folks fool ya. It's all for show. Back home, they can barely afford to heat their trailer," he told me. "Now, let's go enjoy ourselves. We deserve it."

So that's what we did.

In my first five days at the resort, I drowned my visions of Mama in piña coladas and experienced things I'd only read about in magazines. Day one: I swam with dolphins who looked perpetually happy. Day two: I got my first mani-pedi. Day three: it rained, so I ate great big mangoes in a great big bed watching movies on a great big TV. I spent day four on the beach and later received a massage from a George Clooney look-alike. "Coconut oil is *muy bueno* for cellulite," he told me. Day five, I went scuba diving and found a conch shell that whispered sea gossip if

I listened carefully enough. I couldn't wait to give it to Mama. Despite the night I had sex on the beach with a German tourist who pretended he didn't know me the next day, and the time I'd had to drag Pup off the dance floor because he'd passed out and pissed himself, I was having the time of my life.

On day six, Pup announced that it was finally time for me to see the "real Cuba." He wanted to show me his bedsit and introduce me to his landlady, Veronica, and her daughter, Teresa, who he was dating.

"It'll blow your mind," he told me.

"Your girlfriend?"

"No, silly. Teresa's pretty simple. The 'real Cuba' will blow your mind."

I didn't know how my mind could be more blown. By that time, I'd drunk enough rum to fill a jacuzzi. I'd almost fallen off a cliff trying to bachata in my platform sandals at four a.m. I'd dined with folks who looked like the mamas and the papas back home who played tennis all day and drove cars with built-in phones.

But it was true that I hadn't seen anything of the "real Cuba" yet. On our way to the resort from the airport, the bus windows were tinted, and I'd been too busy filling Pup in on what was happening back home.

Pup decided to rent a red convertible.

"You won't miss a thing in this baby," he slurred, patting the hood of the car. He'd been drinking all morning, and I was sure the rental guy would turn us away. I worried he might call over one of the guards with the big guns who hovered around the resort. I whispered to Pup that maybe we should spend the day watching movies; it looked like it might rain again.

"Are you trying to ruin my plans?" he growled. "Do you think anybody gives a shit if I've had a few drinks? Don't you remember what I told you? Expats get special treatment. And don't ask me to explain!" He threw his hands up like he'd been asked a complicated question he couldn't possibly know the answer to, and why the hell would he?

Again, I was confused about the term "expat." Pup hadn't spoken about his ex, Patty, in years. And she hadn't seemed all that important to him at the time. What on earth Patty had to do with getting in trouble or not was beyond me. The car rental man didn't know what to make of Pup's outburst either. We kept looking at each, hoping one of us knew what to do.

But Pup's mood lifted when a butterfly landed on his shoulder. The sun came out of hiding. The rental guy, after Pup gave him a disposable camera and a twenty-dollar bill, didn't bat an eyelash as he handed over the keys. And Pup, after packing up the trunk with a case of rum he'd bought for Teresa's father and a garbage bag full of the gifts I had brought down, was able to drive in a straight line. He popped an Elvis cassette he found in the glove compartment into the tape player and began to serenade me with "Are You Lonesome Tonight." It was entertaining enough to ease my nerves. I started to look forward to our adventure. As we drove away from the resort, I put my freshly pedicured feet up on the dashboard and said, "Vamos, Papa!"

As soon as we left the resort, I felt like we'd entered a new dimension. If the resort was a Disneyland brochure, the countryside was a National Geographic article. The resort a stuck-up poodle, the countryside a friendly mutt. Satin, cheesecloth. Chandeliers, burnt-down candles. All the cars looked like something out of *Grease*. All the houses were as proud and disheveled as a stood-up bride. Every few minutes, we passed gigantic billboards with bearded men on them looking terribly serious—lots of red stars and hammers and upside-down question marks. Just looking at them made me feel like I'd done something wrong.

I was about to tell Pup it was the most fascinating place ever when, all of a sudden, he took a sharp turn and almost hit a pig dozing in the middle of the road.

"Watch out!" I screamed as he slammed on the brakes.

"*Me* watch out? The fucker nearly killed us!" he yelled, shaking his fist at the pig, who'd already gone back to sleep. "I should run him over and roast him up just for being so ignorant!"

The car was stopped, but the engine was still running. I knew he was seriously considering killing the pig; he'd done something similar with a deer once. All he had to do was put the pedal to the metal and the beast would be a goner. I didn't want to criticize his creativity, but I didn't want to deal with a tantrum either. Or a dead pig.

I looked around, hoping for a distraction, a butterfly. When that didn't happen, I calmly said, "I don't know if that's a good idea. There's no room in the trunk. Plus, we can't get the car all bloody."

He looked at me and smiled. "Yeah, I guess you're right. He's pretty scrawny anyway. It's a good thing one of us has their head on their shoulders, eh?"

When we arrived at the village Pup parked outside a turquoise house that looked like something from an old Western movie. A group of people were hanging out on the rickety porch as if they'd been waiting all day, all week maybe. Pup barely opened his door when children swarmed him. There were big ones, little ones, and some that looked like adults. Even a small dog jumped into Pup's arms for a snuggle. A middle-aged woman, who I assumed was his girlfriend, Teresa, walked up with a tray of Coca-Colas.

"Veronica!" Pup said. "Missy, this is Veronica, my landlady. Teresa's mother."

Veronica said something in Spanish that sounded like, "Nice to meet you." She motioned to a girl around the same age as me and said something that sounded like, "This is Teresa, my daughter."

I looked at Teresa while Pup poured rum into his Coke. Teresa said something in Spanish that sounded like, "Hey."

Pup took Teresa's hand and kissed it. "Isn't she lovely, Missy?"

"Yes," I said, trying to compensate for my disgust with a big, stupid smile.

Her big eyes were the colour of caramel pudding. She wore a blue tube-top dress over her perfect size-eight body and a thick white headband in her shiny, long dark hair. Her neck and legs were long and slim like an elegant wolfhound. She was taller than Pup, even in her sneakers. She could have been a model. She could've been one of the popular girls that I went to school with, the pretty ones who always looked bored. Just looking at her, I knew Pup had done something wrong.

Suddenly, I had an overwhelming need to give Teresa something. Anything. Toothpaste, socks. I would have given her my sandals if I thought they'd fit her. I always did that when I thought someone didn't like me. When I was eight, I'd tried giving Madonna away to a girl who always excluded me from skipping rope at recess. I'd have given my virginity over and over again if I could have.

I turned to get the garbage bag of gifts from the car when Pup pulled me in another direction.

"Come and meet everyone, Pet."

"What about the gifts?"

"Oh, they can wait. I want to show you my room."

Pup took my hand and led me around the house. He introduced me to Rafael, his driver and Teresa's brother. To Belinda, Teresa's older sister, who washed his clothes. To Yonarkis, her aunt, who gave him foot massages. To Eduardo, her uncle, who worked at a resort and smuggled out cheese for him. To Carlos, a neighbour, who walked his pit bull, Bobo. To Bobo, that dog he'd bought from the guy on the beach who'd grow to be too strong for him to control. Bobo was always tethered to a post in the backyard so he wouldn't go after the neighbours' goats. Pup introduced me to Teresa's father, who bred canaries and drank rum in a rocking chair on the porch every evening. To Anna, Teresa's younger sister, who he paid to translate. According to Anna, Pup paid their family, who all lived in the same building, more than the average Cuban doctor's salary.

I wasn't sure what to make of Pup's dog walkers and masseuse. I tried not to remember how, a few weeks earlier, Mama's bank card got rejected while buying groceries. I tried not to remember how pathetic Pup had looked, passed out on the dance floor, covered in piss, while everyone laughed at him, drinking the tenth round of mojitos that he'd bought. I wasn't sure if he'd become the Godfather or the village idiot.

I followed him to the top floor of the building to see his bedroom. Teresa and her sister, Anna, joined us.

The room was small but tidy. In it was a bed, a kettle, a desk. On the wall, he'd tacked a picture of Jemima and Bobby on their wedding day and another of me and Randall with Santa Claus when we were little. I remembered sending him that photo along with a letter saying that we'd try not to have too much fun without him. The window in the room was open and I could hear Bobo whimpering. I felt like crying, too.

"What do you think, Pet?" Pup asked as he sat down on the bed and pulled Teresa down on his lap. He wore the same cargo shorts and T-shirt he'd been wearing all week. Some of the duct tape holding his sandals together had come off, exposing long, yellow toenails.

"It's great!" I squeaked, tapping my feet awkwardly to the bachata music coming from downstairs. I started rummaging through my purse to offer Teresa my lipstick. But then I saw her look at Anna, roll her eyes and say something in Spanish that sounded like, "This is boring. Please think of something to speed this up."

That's when Anna asked if I wanted to see her room. It was next to Pup's. She shared it with Teresa and their other sister, Belinda. Anna said she had a new poster she wanted to show me. The timing was perfect. I wanted to get away from Pup and Teresa. I was sure they didn't want me around, and I'd give Teresa the entire contents of my purse if I didn't have a distraction. I was sure Teresa thought I was annoying, and I knew that when I tried to give pretty girls my things, they found me even more annoying.

Anna didn't seem to find me annoying at all. She reminded me of Kathleen from high school, except I didn't want to kiss her, which was a huge relief. She was athletic-looking like Kathleen, spoke quickly, and knew many things like Kathleen, too. Anna was in law school and loved Celine Dion. Her side of the bedroom wall was covered in posters of the Canadian superstar. Her newest poster was of Celine with black leather pants and big hair. In the background, there was a picture of the Titanic and the caption, *My Heart Will Go On*.

Anna was excited to talk about Celine Dion. "Have you seen her perform? Do you like her? Don't you think she's the best singer in the world?"

I did like Celine Dion but had been pretending for a long time that I didn't. All the cool kids back home were into the Grateful Dead and Phish. Celine Dion just wasn't cool. Pup said every time he heard Celine Dion sing, it made him fart.

I was about to tell Anna about my complicated relationship with Celine. About everything, really. About my untreated brain damage. The unspeakable event with Rudy. How I was scared the German tourist might have knocked me up. How I worried Pup might be dying because he never ate anymore, only drank, and kept shitting himself. I worried Eduardo might get locked up for smuggling cheese to Pup. I worried Teresa might get locked up in Guantanamo for spending time with Pup. Part of me even wished Pup would get locked up in Guantanamo. But if he did, Teresa's family wouldn't get paid the same as a doctor's salary anymore.

But just as I was about to share it all, we heard Pup moaning and groaning in the room next door.

"Can you put some Celine on?" I fidgeted on the bed while Anna pulled out her cassette collection. The moaning and groaning got louder.

"Which song should I—"

"Any song. Please. Just hurry."

Anna chose "I Drove All Night."

We couldn't hear the moaning and groaning anymore.

We couldn't hear the bachata music.

We couldn't hear Bobo whimpering.

Still, I felt like crying.

Before getting in the car to return to the resort, Pup and I handed out the presents. Toys for the kids. The toiletries to Anna. The strong dog leash to Carlos. The electronics and rum to Teresa's father, who never got up from his rocking chair. The clothes to Teresa, who barely waited for us to get into the car before leaving the house and going somewhere, anywhere we weren't.

As Anna and I were exchanging addresses, I caught a reflection of myself in the window. My skin was strawberry pink. My hair was frizzy from the humidity. My hands and feet were swollen like pizza dough. I thought I resembled Pup's ex, Patty. Just looking at myself, I knew I'd been part of something terribly wrong.

10
Expat Part 2

Me and Pup were having lunch at the resort's beach bar with two of his buddies when he said he had to piss like a racehorse. "Grab another round on your way back, man, will ya," English Paul called out. "And poulet frit," French Paul hollered. "J'ai la langue à terre!"

Pup winked and said he'd be back in a jiffy. He knew I didn't want to be left alone with his buddies, and I knew he'd never make it to the hotel beach baños without pissing himself. English Paul, a retired cop from Ottawa, never stopped complaining about the heat. And the Quebecois trucker smelled like cheese-curd farts. Pup went to piss in the sea. I watched as he hobbled across the hot sand, slightly bent over, hands over his crotch, thighs squeezed together as if he were about to lay an egg in the world's largest toilet. He'd given his swim trunks to a beggar on the beach, so he was wearing my purple boy-short bikini bottoms. We'd had a good morning so far. I was looking forward to finishing up our lunch and spending the rest of the day together. Pup had promised snorkeling after his afternoon siesta.

Fifteen minutes later, still no Pup. I put my hand over my eyes to block out the glare of the sun and looked up and down the beach. No Pup.

I looked towards the water then the bar. No Pup.

I worried he might be dead. All the likely scenarios flashed through my mind. He'd been swallowed by an undertow, too drunk to swim his way out. Caught in a bloom of venomous jellyfish, tentacles stuck in every orifice of his body.

I kicked off my flip-flops and was about to sprint the four metres across the sand to take on whatever sea creature had got hold of him when all of a sudden French Paul burst into laughter.

"Regard!" He pointed a stubby finger towards the ocean. "Pup's been caught by a sirène!"

English Paul spat a mouthful of mojito all over my shoulder. "Bwahaha! A fucking mermaid! Jesus Christ. A man can't even take a piss in Cuba without someone trying to trap him!"

I was still in fight mode, frantically trying to remember the details of the First Aid course I'd taken in high school. Was it two breaths every thirty compressions, or thirty breaths every two compressions? A vague recollection of Dirk the Jerk violently humping the CPR dummy exactly the way he humped me flashed through my mind.

But then I saw the mermaid. Waist-deep in the water, she wore a silver mesh bathing suit with a cut-out over her tummy and something sparkly in her belly button. Long, wavy hair fanned down around her shoulders like black seaweed. And in her arms, cradled like a baby, with his head tilted back, smiling at the sky gods, was Pup.

I looked out at the mouthwash-coloured ocean. What was more uncomfortable? The Pauls' talking shit about Pup as they sucked back the third pitcher of beer he'd bought them? Or Pup, gripping a bottle of rum that had magically appeared, waving at me to join him and his catch of the day? I noticed a pair of serious guards with scary dogs on leashes carrying shotguns walking up and down the beach between the bar and the surf. I started to panic that the mermaid would get in trouble for being with Pup, just like Pup was always complaining about. But then I remembered that we'd hung out with a ton of locals so far, and not once did anyone get in trouble. Nada. I guess I misunderstood, is what I told myself. I'm such a worry-wart. Of course, I want to join them. They look like they are having so much fun. Otherwise, I'll be stuck with the Pauls all day. Or worse, spend the day alone.

I sucked in my tummy and walked towards the water, covering my butt with my hands. The Pauls laughed as I walked by them and I was sure it had something to do with me. The slight wind made the palm trees wave their feathery branches in all directions, as if they didn't know if they were coming or going. As if they couldn't make up their minds about the shenanigans happening all around them.

Once the water was deep enough to avoid risking a neck fracture, I slipped on my goggles and dove in. I half-expected to see a shimmery green tail under the water. But there were only Pup's short, hairy legs in my purple boy shorts wrapped around a pair of long, slim brown ones. His captor had a silver anklet around her human left ankle and a silver toe ring on her human right foot.

"Missy!" Pup chuckled when I surfaced. "Glad you could join us, Pet. This is Serena. Serena, this is my daughter, Missy."

Serena smiled, showing human crooked teeth. She squinted human seafoam green eyes, two shades lighter than turquoise, one shade darker than peppermint. She pushed some human hair from her human forehead. She brushed some seaweed off her human pockmarked chin. She took my hand in her two human hands as if we'd known each other forever, as if we were the best human girlfriends in the world, and said, "Hola, Missy."

The three of us played in the water for a good hour. We finished off the bottle of rum and played monkey in the middle with my goggles. Serena won the handstand contest, but I won the race out to the buoy and back. We poked fun at Pup, and we laughed so hard I nearly swallowed a seahorse. I was glad I had accepted Pup's advice and the rum to loosen up. Serena was just one year older than me, and fun and exciting.

Unlike Teresa, Serena seemed genuinely interested in him. She kept diving under the water and bringing him presents. A pretty shell, a heart-shaped stone, a necklace of braided seaweed, someone's soggy pink hair scrunchy that he wrapped around his wrist gratefully. It reminded me of the weirdo gifts I used to send him when I was little. Like that blown-glass fish I bought for a quarter at the flea market that broke in the mail. And the Tupperware full of Christmas dinner leftovers that arrived rotten. It's the thought that counts, right? Pup meeting Serena was a lucky hookup for us all, I was sure of it.

When we got out of the water, Serena invited us to a party that evening at her friend's place. She said there would be music and a pig roast and dancing all night long. In the meantime, she wanted to go home and change. And Pup wanted a nap back at the hotel. We made plans to meet up again in a few hours.

"In the parking lot in the back of the hotel. Where it's more discreet. I'll be in a red Fiat," Serena told us after she kissed us both goodbye on the cheek.

"Sure thing, doll. Whatever you think's best."

"Sí. It's best."

"Roger that. Now, adiós, amigos. I gotta catch me some zzzs," he said, yawning.

As Serena walked away, the late-afternoon sun lit up her silver bathing suit like a sparkler, and I was convinced that my new friend really was a mermaid. She must have traded one hot tail for those fabulous legs of hers. I didn't question what else Serena might have sacrificed to be so lovely.

Back at the hotel room, I was too wound up to nap. Every time I closed my eyes, I saw the silvery silhouette of Serena. Every time Pup's snoring skipped a beat, I jumped out of my sunburnt skin. To pass the time and squash the little voice in my head that said Serena might ditch us, I sat out on our balcony and ate three mangoes, a loaf of bread, and a super-sized avocado, while smoking half a pack of cigarettes. Afterwards, I washed and styled my hair. I slipped on a black kaftan, my platform sandals and a layer of burgundy lipstick. Then I walked around the hotel and bought a phone card to make a two-minute and thirty-two-second call to Mama.

Randall answered.

"Jesus Christ, Missy, I still can't believe you went to Cuba. You know you can't keep your shit together around Pup. He's a friggin' sponge and you're the goddamn ocean."

"It's fine. I'm having a great time. We spent the day on the beach and now we're going to a pig roast with this girl we met. Serena's so cool."

"I'm sure she is," he said sarcastically. "How's Pup?"

"Good, I guess. His spirits are high, but he's drinking a lot and sometimes shits himself. He kinda smells like a homeless guy, to be honest. I'm really worried about him."

"Fuck, Missy. He *is* a homeless guy. He's a fucking parasite. Don't you—"

I was glad my phone card ran out mid-conversation. "Screw him," I said out loud and hung up. Who was Randall to judge my relationship with Pup when he was still asking him for money left, right and centre anyway? He was as bad as the Pauls and Pup's exes and Mama for taking, taking, taking and giving nothing, nothing, nothing in return.

I went back to the beach to pick a bouquet of wildflowers and put them in an empty rum bottle on Pup's bedside table. Their perfume covered up some of his smell, but my movements woke him up.

"Get off me! Get off me! Get off me!" He jumped out of bed and waved his arms as if he were on fire.

I backed up to a corner and kept my voice calm while Pup threw the bedsheets on the floor. He knocked over the bouquet, spilling the water and flowers on himself.

"It's just me," I whispered. "You're fine. You were dreaming."

"Jesus fucking Christ, Missy! Don't do that to me! I thought you were a spider. And what the fuck's with the flowers?"

"Sorry. I—"

"What fucking time is it? Did we miss the party? I bet we missed the party!"

"Not yet. That's why I tried to wake you."

"Oh, right. Perfect. Thanks, Pet. What would I do without you?" His expression melted from angry pit bull to adoring puppy. "Mind going down to the lobby and ordering me a beer while I get dressed? I'll meet you in ten."

Half an hour later, Pup joined me in the lobby bar. He wore a big smile, his signature cargo shorts, and his sandals with a fresh layer of duct tape. His powder-blue T-shirt brought out his blue eyes. He carried my bouquet in one hand and a case of rum in the other. Cleaned up, I thought he looked like a cross between Frank Sinatra and Papa Smurf.

"Hey, Pet!"

"Hey, Pet. Hey, Pet. Hey, Pet," squawked the green parrot behind the bar.

"Not you, bird. I'm talking to my daughter." Pup waved a scolding finger at the cheeky bird before turning his attention back to me. "Hope you don't mind if I give these flowers to Serena? I bought a case of rum at the canteen to bring, too. Can't arrive empty-handed to a party now, can we?"

"Party! Party! Party!" said the parrot.

"Shit, man, your bird's a menace," Pup said to the bartender as he handed him an extra-large tip.

"Menace! Menace! Menace!" the parrot called and swooped off the bar and began flapping around my head. "Menace! Menace! Menace!"

Pup downed his drink. "Come on, Pet, let's get out of here."

"Get out! Get out! Get out!"

I was relieved to spot the red Fiat at the far end of the hotel parking lot—but a man was in the driver's seat and Sarena was nowhere to be seen. I was about to tell Pup that we'd been ditched as I'd predicted, that we should turn back, maybe check out the karaoke party by the pool instead. But then a hand popped out of the car's back window and I heard a woman's voice.

"Hola! Quick! Get in!"

The back door opened. Serena was crunched down in the footwell with her legs folded into a perfect golden pretzel. I didn't recognize her at first. She wore a blonde cornrow wig and white-rimmed sunglasses. She was laughing nervously like she was playing hide-and-seek. As if we were invited to share her hiding spot if we would just hurry up, get in, and never speak a word of it to the other players.

Pup put the rum in the trunk and squeezed in the back beside Serena while I sat shotgun. I was so excited that my tummy felt like it was full of salsa dancers. I turned to say something playful to Serena, like how I wished I'd worn a disguise too, maybe a gentleman's fedora and mustache, but Serena put her finger to her glossy lips and whispered, "Shhh. No talk to me. Act like I'm not here. Act like you going for a drive to sightsee. Act like Jorge is your tour guide."

I took my role in this game very seriously. I sat up straight and didn't look back. Didn't nod; didn't laugh. I pretended I was a bored teenager going for a drive with my boring father, and that there was no incognito mermaid between his legs. I pretended not to notice how handsome Jorge, the driver, was. I pretended to know what Serena was hiding from. I felt like the world's first chubby Bond girl.

Jorge turned off the main street onto a dirt road bordered by tobacco fields. It was dark and he drove slowly. Eventually we came upon a dozen or so thatch-roofed houses and a whole lot of banana trees. Some houses were painted baby pink and butterscotch yellow, with lace curtains and pretty terracotta tile roofs. Others looked like run-down garages, the ones back home littered with old motors, patched together with mismatched metal sheeting like steampunk quilts. A gutted pig hung from the rafters of one house like a fleshy windchime. Another had Virgin Mary candles on each of its front steps and a Mickey Mouse poster tacked to the front door. The flickering light of the candles made Mickey look like he was dancing.

We got out of the car and followed the bachata music to behind one of the huts. There, forty or so folks—big and small, young and old, human and beast—were dancing around a fire. A roasting pig was impaled from butthole to throat. Its tongue hung out the side of its mouth like a limp penis.

"Hola, muchachos!" Pup hollered over the music as he lifted the case of rum above his head like a trophy. "Now, *this* is my kind of fiesta!"

The crowd greeted us with a cheer, and within seconds we were served fruity drinks and paper plates piled high with rice and beans. Pup, Serena and Jorge sat down at a picnic table by the fire, while a group of children ran circles around me. One little girl brought me a chick to hold, and another gave me a handful of shiny pebbles. I felt like the popular girl. I lifted each child by their armpits and spun them around and around and around.

It was like the field parties I went to back home, except instead of being spit on or taunted by chants of "Piggy," there were lineups of people waiting their turn to dance with me. Instead of bumming cigarette butts and beer bottoms once my supply ran out, I was offered drink after drink and enough roast pork to make a vegetarian turn in his grave. I finally understood why Pup had given everything up for the Caribbean dream, and I stumbled drunkenly through the crowd to tell him as much. I found him sucking face with Serena under a banana tree beside a bitch nursing her pups. I smiled at the dog and went to pet her behind the ears, but she lifted her lip in a snarl.

"Pup!" I said, backing up. "I get it now! I want to stay here forever, too. What do you think? I don't need to go back to Canada; I graduated! I can get a job at the hotel or something!"

Pup suctioned his lips off Serena's, reached into his pocket, and pulled out a wad of American dollar bills. He waved them at me as if he were swatting a fly.

"Sure, Pet. Sure. Let's talk about it tomorrow. Now, take this and go have a fling of your own. It'll do ya a world of good."

I was upset that Pup shooed me away like that, but the money he gave me—more money than I'd ever held in my life, more money than Mama made in a week—was thrilling. I felt so grown up. I felt powerful. I felt like I'd been given the keys to a new car or a house. A new life even. I didn't know what I'd do with it in the middle of a field, but the possibilities seemed endless. Something was bound to turn up.

Not a minute later, I dropped one of the twenty dollar bills. When I bent down to pick it up, I saw a shadow in the dirt. It was Jorge. He crouched down to meet me and whispered with a sexy lisp, "Mithy."

The rest of the night was a blur of fire and mud and Jorge.

Jorge's hands on my hips.

Jorge feeding me papaya from his salty fingers.

Jorge writing my name in the dirt and tracing a heart around it.

Jorge driving us back to the hotel, where I paid the concierge seventy-five dollars for him to stay over.

Jorge taking a shower and using the fancy doll-sized bottles of shampoo to lather his chin-length, curly black hair.

Jorge asleep on his tummy, one arm dangling over the bed, the other cupping his cheek. I was as eager for him to wake up as I was for him to stay like that forever.

That's how Pup found us. He stumbled in around noon despite the DO NOT DISTURB sign on the door. The bags under his eyes looked like water-filled blisters. His powder-blue shirt was stained with black beans and pork grease. The duct tape had come unwound from his sandal again, revealing his long dirty toenails, and his hands were shaking like they always did when he needed a drink. He looked older and weaker than his fifty-two years.

Pup didn't seem to notice that I was naked under the white sheet. Or care that I was with Jorge. "Hey, Pet. You up for some brunch?"

All the disappointment I had felt the previous night when he'd ignored me was replaced with the need to run him a bubble bath. To clip his toenails. I wanted to butter him some toast and squeeze him fresh orange juice.

But I wanted Jorge more.

"Jesus, Pup," I whispered, pointing to Jorge. "Can't you see I'm busy? Can't you go for brunch with Serena or the Pauls?"

Pup shook his head. "The Pauls left this morning. And Serena's not available. She got picked up last night."

"Picked up?" I said louder than I meant to. Jorge was stirring.

"Yeah. Cops showed up at the hotel and took her away. Locked her up, I suppose. It's too bad. Nice girl, that Serena."

I felt sick. "For what?"

Pup paused for a moment as if I'd just asked about tomorrow's weather forecast. "Not being careful enough, I reckon."

"Holy shit. Does that mean they're gonna come for Jorge?"

"Doubt it. Jorge's a dude. Plus, from what the maid told me, Serena had been warned to stay away from this hotel before. Seems she's a regular with the tourists, which, I'll have you know, is illegal in Cuba. Just my luck to get mixed up in something like that."

"You're in trouble too?"

"Nope."

"Why not?"

"Fuck, Missy! Quit it with the interrogation. I told you before, don't ask me to explain how things work around here! No one tells me diddly-shit. I'm just gringo! An ex-pat! A hungry ex-pat. Now, how about that brunch?"

Jorge sat up. He lit a cigarette and smiled peacefully at Pup.

"Oh, hey, Jorge," Pup said as if he'd only just noticed him. "How 'bout you? You up for some brunch?"

I was thrilled Jorge wanted brunch. The three of us sat at the bar and laughed every time the parrot repeated something we said. We had omelettes, fresh mango on sticks, and mimosas. By the second round of mimosas, I concocted a plan to break Serena out of jail. By the third round, I replaced my escape plan with a list of presents I planned to give to Jorge to bring to Serena to make her comfortable. Toiletries, magazines, maybe some of that cheese Pup liked so much. By the fourth round, Jorge asked if I wanted to go on a road trip for the last two days of my trip.

At that point, I couldn't remember Serena's face; all I could remember were her fabulous legs.

By the time I realized what they'd cost her, my road trip with Jorge was over and I was on the way back home to Canada. The money Pup gave me plus the extra two-hundred for the roadtrip was long gone, too. As for the parrot, he'd seen it all before. He couldn't tell one hotel guest from the other, and that was fine by him. Pet. Party. Menace. More. More. More. It was all the same.

11
Te Quiero

When I got back, Mama asked me about my plans. September was just around the corner, and everyone I graduated from high school with was either getting a job, going to college, or moving out West for the trees, drugs, and ski hills. I was doing none of the above. Not even getting pregnant, the last option. I didn't have any plans at all. I don't know how I missed the future-plans part leading up to graduation. I hadn't even had a conversation with Mama about my future. I guess we'd both been hoping I'd stay with Pup in Cuba.

The closest I had to a plan was the idea of moving to Montreal with Jorge. At least, I think that's what we'd planned. No matter how many times I'd told Jorge that I lived nowhere near Montreal, he wouldn't stop mentioning it.

In bed, after too many rum and cokes and sloppy sex, he said, "Te quiero, Montreal."

On the last day of our road trip, I took him on a shopping spree. Just after leaving the shop where I'd bought him a surfboard and a wetsuit, we stopped at a street vendor. With the pocket money I'd given him, he bought me a bag of roasted peanuts. As he offered it to me, he got down on one knee, like he was proposing, and said, "Por favor, llévame a Montreal."

The last thing he said after he dropped Pup and me off at the airport was, "¡Nos vemos en Montreal!"

By the time I got back home, my neck covered in fresh hickeys, I was fantasizing about nesting with him in one of those colourful apartments you see on Montreal postcards. Ours would be turquoise with yellow trim, with a steep, spiral staircase that I couldn't for the life of me figure out how thousands of people went up and down without breaking their necks every winter. Those fantasies were the only thing that got me out of bed in the morning.

When I told Mama her response was swift. "Well, ya better hurry up and get yourself a fuckin' job! Montreal and Cuban lovers are expensive. Just ask your fuckin' father!"

I got a job quickly enough, not even a week after I got back, at the Tim Hortons in downtown Market Square, making donuts, working the till, mopping the floors. Whenever someone I knew came in, I made sure to sweep my hair off my neck so they could see the hickeys, kept fresh with a thin layer of burgundy eyeshadow. I'd drop the fact that my job was just a means to an end.

"I'm moving to Montreal with my boyfriend soon," I'd say.

"Yeah?"

"He's meeting me once I've saved up enough money." I pulled out the photo of us I kept in my purse. The one Pup took with my disposable camera. A quarter of the photo was Pup's thumb. The other three-quarters were Jorge—tall and gorgeous, wearing the fluorescent green wetsuit bathing suit I'd bought him. If you looked closely, you could see his arm was around a short, plump human's pink sunburnt shoulder.

"That's me."

"Yeah?"

"Yeah." Then I'd point to my shoulder, which was still a little pink and peeling. "Cool, eh?"

When things were quiet at work, I wrote letters.

Dearest Jorge, I miss you so much. I think of you all the time. I'm saving up for your plane ticket. When do you want to come? I can meet you in Montreal. You can take French classes while I work. Let me know so I can start looking into an apartment.

Te quiero, Missy.

My beloved Jorge, I hope everything's okay. Pup always told me that the Cuban post sucks, so maybe you're not getting my letters. I wish I could call you. I can't wait to live with you in Montreal. Should we get a pet? What do you like better, cats or dogs? Birds or bunnies? Are you allergic to anything? I can't believe I don't know these things about you. We've got so much to learn about each other! I prefer dogs, but it's hard to have a dog in the city. Maybe just a little tiny dog. Like a chihuahua. Te quiero, Missy.

My love, why haven't you written? What about Montreal? I don't know what to do. Please write. Te quiero, Missy.

Dear Jorge, I worry you're dead. Like, maybe you've been run over or murdered or got stung by a bee and had a deadly reaction. Just the other day, this guy at work was telling me about an old lady who was out mowing her lawn and got stung by a bee and died. She had no idea she was allergic to bees. No one found her for hours. The mower was still on. Crazy sad, eh? Te quiero, Missy.

In my tenth letter, I included a Spanish-English dictionary.

In my fifteenth letter, I sent him fifty dollars from my small savings to move to Montreal.

By the time I wrote my twentieth letter, I'd stopped trying to keep my hickeys alive. I rarely spoke about Jorge anymore. My skin had faded from strawberry to toffee to vanilla again. If someone asked when I was moving to Montreal, I'd say, "Oh, there's been a slight delay. But, hopefully, soon."

When I looked at the photo of Jorge and Pup's thumb, I realized it could have been any old tourist's shoulder. Mama figured it out too: "Looks like you need a Plan B."

12

The Montague Suites

Plan B was to rent a room at the Montague Suites, a rundown Victorian mansion-turned-boarding house on Orange Street, one of the poorest, most dirtbaggiest streets in the South End of Saint John. It wasn't Montreal or Cuba, but it was far enough away from Poverty Hill that it felt like a step forward.

The rooms at the Montague Suites had each been painted with a different theme. There was the Flower Suite, the Naval Suite, the Rainforest Suite, the Black and White Suite. Mama thought herself quite the comedian when she came up with: *There's nothing sweet about the Montague Suites!* But there was a lot of truth to it. Despite the fancy name, the rooms were so rundown and filthy, it might as well have been a squat house. The murals looked as though they'd been painted by either a child, a drunk or a blind person. A blind, drunk child. Although my room was advertised as furnished, it only came with a stained, lumpy mattress on the floor, a greasy hot plate that only worked at max heat, a mini-fridge that smelled like sour milk, and a window that didn't close properly or have curtains. On every floor there was a communal bathroom with a rusty claw-foot bathtub. The bathroom door on my floor didn't close properly either, so I peed with one leg outstretched to keep it shut.

I rented the Rainforest room on the first floor for $235 per month. The first-floor rooms were fifteen dollars cheaper than the other floors because homeless people were always sneaking in to sleep in the vestibule. We were supposed to call the cops when that happened, but I never did. I gave them food and spare change and sometimes, especially when it was cold, invited them to sleep on the floor of my room. They never caused any trouble. I was grateful for the company. Otherwise, I was stuck with the useless rainforest crew. One wall was painted with a toucan riding an elephant with a particularly large trunk. Another had a gorilla holding a sceptre that looked more like a baby rattle or, depending on my mood, a dildo. The other animals were covered in graffiti. *Jay wuz here. Suck my dick. I loved a boy who didn't appreciate me, and it fucked me up. Have a nice day.* The ceiling was painted to look like a sky, and I was always picking white and blue paint chips out of my hair. One time I told my landlady, "The sky is falling."

"The sky's not falling!" she said. "That's just a crock of alarmist propaganda from a bunch of left-wing wackos!"

At least half a dozen cats lived in the Montague Suites, sleeping and pissing wherever they wanted. I never did much like cats. I didn't understand them; I didn't trust them. When I was eleven, I'd been curious about reincarnation. "If you could come back as anything, anyone, who would it be?" I'd asked Mama.

"A house cat," she said, which blew my mind and put everything into perspective all at once.

Still, like the squatters, having the cats around made me feel less lonely. When I used the bathroom in the middle of the night, there was often a fat ginger cat in the bathtub, licking droplets off the tap. I named him Big Red because the real Big Red had always been lying on his couch, watching TV, sucking on a beer, just like the fat ginger cat did with the faucet.

I called the fluffy white cat Little Mama. Little Mama was always lounging next to the door, cleaning her luxurious fur coat, not budging an inch when I tried to get by. When I did laundry in the basement, Little Mama would be dozing on the washing machine, blocking me from putting my clothes in. You could always tell where Little Mama had been because she left little tufts of white fluff that smelled like a makeup drawer. Like my own mama, Little Mama had a way of looking at me that made me feel like I was a nuisance, like I was the one keeping her from getting the beauty rest she needed. The Mamas acted like they carried the world's woes on their pretty shoulders, and I knew from experience that there was nothing I could do to make them feel differently.

The skittish black cat with a missing eye I named after my classmate, Magda. With her long, dark ponytail and sweet smile, human Magda got knocked up in high school and never told anyone until the police found the dead baby in a trash container. Afterwards, she couldn't step into the cafeteria without someone throwing food at her. She stopped keeping her hair in a ponytail and let it dangle in her face, like window blinds for her eyes. At the drop of a pencil, she'd jump out of her seat and run out of class crying. After she got beat up so bad that one of her eyes became permanently lazy, she dropped out of school for good. No one ever bothered her boyfriend, who swore up and down the baby wasn't his. Mama had said, "Once damaged, always damaged." But I wasn't so sure. I secretly believed that if enough of the silky white cat kinds of people took in the Magdas of the world, they might be fixable. But still, I avoided the Magdas at all costs. As if their brokenness was contagious and I was at a particularly high risk of catching it.

It took me a while to name the muscular, handsome silver tabby. He would sit outside my window staring at me with his amber eyes, deadpan, then up and leave five minutes later. Even in the bitter cold, I would leave my window open for him, but he never set a paw inside. I left tins of sardines, but he never took the bait. What did he want from me, if not warmth or sardines? Sometimes I wasn't even sure I'd seen him at all. I'd take my eye off him to pick something up off the floor or change the radio station, and he'd vanish like a shooting star.

The tabby's showing up unannounced and then leaving again reminded me of Pup. But the tabby wasn't loud or emotional and didn't demand anything of me. He was agile. So I didn't name him after Pup.

In other ways, the tabby reminded me of Dirk the Jerk. The way he used to sneak through my window in the middle of the night. He often arrived in a taxi and had the driver, his uncle, wait for an hour. Sometimes he paid his uncle; sometimes, I did. But at school, he acted like we were strangers. Like he hadn't farted during our sixty-niner the night before.

But the tabby was able to hold eye contact and kept a respectful distance. So I didn't name him after Dirk the Jerk.

Sometimes he even reminded me of Jorge. The strong, silent type. But I was still reconciling myself to the fact that I'd never see him again and trying not to think about him. Plus, Jorge's eyes were much, much darker than the tabby's. So I didn't call him Jorge.

In the end, I decided the tabby didn't remind me enough of anyone I knew. He was his own cat. I looked forward to the way he stared at me without lust or need, and made me feel that maybe I could be a cat person after all. I gave him a noble name, a peaceful name. Godfrey. I'd never encountered another Godfrey and doubted I ever would.

Things went well between Godfrey and me for a few months. But one night, in the deepest darkest hour, as I was dreaming of Jorge choking to death on a roasted peanut after proposing to me, I was woken by a terrible thud. The sky was finally falling, I thought. I braced myself, sure the ceiling was about to come crashing down—gyprock, the fan, the upstairs toilet, everything. I'd once seen the collapse of a Korean shopping mall's ceiling on TV. It started with a few cracks and ended with five hundred and two casualties, with thousands more trapped inside for days.

When I didn't hear a second thud, I wondered if a robber had snuck into the apartment. That happened a lot at the Montague Suites, too. Maybe someone was standing by my bed, trying to decide whether to leave or kill me in case I'd caught an identifiable glimpse of him. I felt kinda bad for whoever it was. I had nothing to steal. He must be so desperate, I thought. I would have let him in if he'd have just knocked. I didn't know what I'd say to him, so I stayed as still as possible so as not to spook him, recalling a conversation I'd had with Mama while I was moving in.

"I should ask Big Red to come and put some bars on them windows," she said. But she'd forgotten about it, and so had I, and now they were wide open.

A minute or so later, when I was pretty sure there was no other human present, I thought that Godfrey had finally decided to come inside. At long last, I've gained his trust; he's ready to become *my* cat. We were going to move to the next level. I felt almost giddy as I lifted the covers slowly off my head and reached over to turn on my bedside lamp.

It wasn't ceiling debris.

It wasn't a robber.

And it wasn't Godfrey. At least not inside the apartment.

Lying on the floor, at arm's length from the window, was a half-dead squirrel. It was missing a quarter of its face, and one of its legs dangled lifelessly by a few bloody strands of muscle. When it tried to stand up, its eyes popped out like it was trying to poop, and it fell back down in exhaustion. A shriek like a shriek from the tiniest woman in the world came from its mouth. Outside, staring, as poker-faced as always, was Godfrey.

I remembered hearing that carnage was a cat's way of giving a gift to its human, so I wanted to appear grateful. I hoped my voice would cover the tiny shrieks of the squirrel.

"Thanks, Godfrey," I said. "This is very thoughtful of you."

The shrieks were getting louder. I kept talking.

"You gonna at least come inside?"

Diarrhea squirted out of the mangled squirrel's ass.

"If you're gonna eat it, you'll have to come inside. I'm sure not bringing it to you!"

The squirrel was lying on its back; its paw was moving back and forth as if it were begging me to come closer, to do something.

"Come on, Godfrey, you gotta at least finish it off."

He didn't even blink.

I started to get angry.

"Please!" I yelled at him.

And angrier. "What the fuck am I supposed to do with it?"

I was sure he was laughing at me in his silent, cat way.

The squirrel shrieked louder.

"It's not right!"

I could have sworn Godfrey smirked. "Fuck you, too, Godfrey!"

I grabbed a Sobey's bag and scooped up the squirrel. I tied the bag shut and beat it against the window frame as hard as possible. "I hate you!"

I beat it and beat it and beat it until the bag split open. "You coward!"

Now there were squirrel guts all over the window. Squirrel guts all over the wall with the elephant with his stupid trunk. Squirrel guts all over the gorilla with his ridiculous dildo. Squirrel guts all over me, on my face, in my hair.

"Don't you ever come back! Do you hear me? Never!" I screamed.

But Godfrey was long gone by then.

The smell of blood made me queasy, but the only cleaning supply I had in my room was a tiny bottle of dish soap. I didn't even have a bucket. And I was too tired to clean; it was four a.m. Instead, I took my pillow and blanket under my arm and made my way to the communal bathroom.

I picked up Big Red from the tub and threw him out the door. Then I made a little bed for myself in the bathtub and went to sleep.

I dreamt that I was sleeping on that gutbucket Big Red's dirty couch while he took nude polaroids of himself. I kept willing myself to wake up so I could get away, but it wasn't until he'd stacked hundreds, maybe thousands of Polaroids, still warm from the camera, onto my legs like pancakes that I finally woke up. Magda was curled up on my legs, peacefully catnapping. Her lazy eye was undetectable; her suffering impalpable.

I had a terrible crick in my neck. My bladder was ready to burst. The squirrel guts had crusted around my chin and were as itchy as a new mosquito bite. But I didn't dare move an inch. Not even a twitch. Magda was warm and soft, and feeling her purr against my skin was soothing in a way that was unfamiliar. I was pretty sure the feeling was mutual. I was pretty sure that if we could stay in that position, exactly in that position, I would feel a little less alone, and Magda could be an unbothered housecat. And if that was the one thing we could do for each other, I would make sure we did it well.

I really needed to make some friends.

13
Naked Lady

It was shortly after the dead squirrel that I started to see a lady on the staircase that led to the second floor of the Montague Suites. Naked as a jailbird, she was. With long, straggly, platinum-blonde hair. She was skinny, skinny, skinny. That veiny, muscular, I've-been-running-my-whole-life (but not as a sport) kind of skinny. And tall. The sort of tall woman with small tits and broad shoulders that no matter how feminine she presented, people treated her like a man. Her skin was covered in scabs. Like she'd spent the night in a swamp. She was so pale, she glowed.

At first, Naked Lady scared me shitless. I was in my nightie, half asleep, having just peed, and she appeared out of nowhere. I was sure she was a ghost. It was three a.m. She stood on the stairs with her head down and her arms at her sides, hair covering her face. I dashed to my room so quickly that even if she'd been bald, I likely wouldn't have made out her features. I unplugged the mini-fridge and pushed it against the door. If she really was a ghost, a mini-fridge wasn't going to stop her, but still, it helped me get back to sleep.

Over the next few days, I decided that Naked Lady was either an *unreal* or one of those half-awake, half-asleep hallucinations I was prone to when I was little. I once woke up to get a glass of water and saw Mama kissing a zombie. Another time, during a camping trip, I saw a giant raccoon the size of a bear, with big flashy disco-ball eyes. In a Cockney accent, the raccoon said to me, "Ello, Missy!"

Mama hadn't been concerned enough about my *unreals* to take me to the doctor, but she was worried enough that I'd do something dangerous in my sleep that she eventually made an appointment. "It's called Complex Nocturnal Visual Hallucinations," the doctor told us. "Totally normal for a kid her age. Nothing to worry about. She'll grow out of it." Which, unlike my *unreals*, I eventually did.

Whatever it was, I told myself, it was all in my head. I'd recently watched an Oprah episode about not letting irrational fears interfere with quality of life and that was exactly what I planned to do. I was an adult now. I wasn't in danger. A creepy, naked lady was certainly no reason to start peeing in a potty in my room. Chill out, Missy, you're safe.

But then I saw her a second time.

In the middle of the night. Half-asleep, half-awake, I left the communal bathroom to go back to my room and there she was. On the staircase. Same nakedness, same pose, same scraggly hair, same swampy scabs. But this time, she was holding Godfrey.

Godfrey! Of all the cats! In all my attempts to connect with him, the closest we'd ever come was when he gave me the gift of that mangled squirrel. I'd assumed he was on the far end of the reserved-cat spectrum.

Apparently not.

"Godfrey?" I said. "Is that you?"

Godfrey, being Godfrey, looked at me like, "Who I am is of no concern to you, and who you are is of no concern to me."

So I spoke to Naked Lady.

"Hey," I said. "I'm Missy."

But she didn't look at me. She didn't move. "Okay, well, goodnight to you both," I said.

I didn't bother blocking my door with the mini-fridge this time. She didn't scare me that much anymore. Like Godfrey, it was clear that I was of no concern to Naked Lady. Real or not. Ghost or not. I was, indeed, safe.

During this period, I was volunteering at the SPCA. One, because of the animals. Two, because, dear God, was I lonely. So lonely. Like, walk into my apartment and be grateful to be greeted by a house-fly lonely. Like, leave the radio on 24/7 because, if I didn't, I'd start talking to the walls, or, worse, reach out to Dirk the Jerk kind of lonely. Even though I was only a seventeen-minute drive from Poverty Hill, moving to downtown Saint John was like moving to Paris minus the fancy cheese and elegance. I was failing miserably at making friends, and not for lack of trying. When I wasn't working, I walked the streets, hoping to run into someone I knew. I'd go to bars by myself. I ordered a drink for anyone who made eye contact with me. Sometimes that led to an invitation to their table or a one-night stand, but mostly it didn't go beyond a "Thanks, man, have a good one." Other times, I'd buy a couple bottles of vodka and a carton of smokes and go to King's Square to hang with the drunks and the squirrels. That usually worked out well enough, but I couldn't do it too often because it was so expensive. At home,

I treated myself to some R&R: a litre of red wine and a big bag of Ringolos.

My volunteer shift at the SPCA was every Wednesday evening. I loved it. I cleaned the cages, walked the dogs, and kept an eye out for hamsters that weren't suitable for adoption. Eventually I noticed a trend and developed a screening tool that they still use at the Saint John SPCA today: If a hamster pisses on you, it's more likely to bite its baby's head off. If it bites its baby's head off, it's more likely to bite you. Sandy, the volunteer supervisor, said, "Missy, if you keep up like this, you might land a job here one day. You're a natural."

It was at the SPCA that I finally made a friend. Nadine was a year younger than me. She was in her last year at RCS, the fancy boarding school just outside of town, and needed volunteer hours to graduate. She didn't even like animals very much. "But they're, like, *way* better than geezers and sickos," she said. She rolled her eyes a lot. I never saw her without a French manicure and a messy, naturally blonde ponytail. She always wore forest green jogging pants and a hoodie with her school's logo on them. Every fifteen minutes, she applied her Body Shop kiwi lip gloss, which she carried in a Guess purse. Her parents were diplomats, so she saw them only a few times a year. She was a pathological liar in the way I've noticed that people who have too much money and not enough love can be.

"I fucked this guy on an airplane once," she told me on the first day when we were out walking the dogs. "He was on his way to meet up with his fiancée in Australia. He told me that he really loved her but that it scared the shit out of him knowing that she would be the only person he'd ever be able to have sex with for the rest of his life. He was crying and everything. So I told him I had a rare, life-threatening disease and that being part of the mile-high club was on my bucket list. Maybe we should help each other out, I said to him. He thought it was a great idea. So when the lights went down, I just climbed on top of him."

Another time, while we were comforting a cat birthing her kittens, she said, "I spray-painted *Jesus was a homo* on the chapel door at school today."

She liked to pee with the bathroom stall door wide open. "I pierced my labia with a safety pin and an ice cube," she once told me. "Wanna see?"

She loved it when I told her stories of my own too. She'd get excited and ask lots of questions and then try to one-up me. And then I'd try to one-up her. Some of my stories were real, some weren't. But it didn't matter. It was just a game.

For example, when I told her about Pup's teenage girlfriends, she said, "Uggh, I hear ya. My dad owns a brothel."

"Crazy!" I said. "Did he ever try to pimp you out? My dad tried to pimp me out once."

"Whoa, that's hardcore! No, his lawyer told him pimping me out would be too risky. But he lets me dance at one of his strip clubs sometimes," she said.

When I told her about Feet Guy, she said, "Gross. I once dated this guy who couldn't get it up unless we watched video clips of bees or wasps. Just before he came, he'd scream, *'Sting me, sting me, baby!'*"

"I once dated a guy who liked me to suck on his nose."

"That's fucked up," she said.

"Totally."

One day while cleaning the turtle aquarium I told Nadine about Naked Lady. She was leaning against the sink, applying lip gloss.

"Hmm," she said. "She either *is* a ghost, or she's on crack. The scabs are a telltale sign. Maybe she's the ghost of a dead crack addict. Either way, you must keep trying to connect with her."

"Yeah?"

"Absolutely. You're lucky. I'd give anything to see a ghost junkie in the middle of the night. In my dorm, the creepiest thing you'll see is the cage the house mother puts us in if she catches us masturbating."

"How does she get away with that?" I asked.

"Oh, that's nothing. You should see what the headmaster does if he catches us kissing."

I didn't know if Naked Lady had an apartment in the Montague Suites. If she was an *unreal* or a ghost, she wouldn't need one, right? But I was bored and I wanted a story for Nadine, so I started with the assumption that Naked Lady was a real human with an apartment. And what better way to connect with a human, especially a Maritime human, than by giving them something from Tim Hortons?

Over the next six days, I brought home a family pack of Timbits each night from work and knocked on one of the apartment doors. There were four units on each of the four floors.

An old man answered the first door. He was wearing striped pajamas and was holding a banana.

"Sorry to bother you, sir," I said. "I'm Missy, your downstairs neighbour. I'm looking for a really tall lady with long blonde hair. Does she live here?"

"No," he said.

"Ok, thanks anyway, and sorry for the bother."

I gave him the Timbits. He took them and shut the door quickly.

At the second apartment a girl about nine years old opened the door. She held a baby on her hip. In the background, I could hear more babies crying. She had the tired eyes of a fifty-year-old.

"Hi," I said. "I'm Missy, your downstairs neighbour. Does a tall lady with long, blonde hair live here?"

"No."

She took the Timbits before quickly shutting the door.

Same thing with the third, fourth and fifth apartments. Knock-knock. Sorry for the bother, here are some Timbits for your time.

Finally, after my sixth failed apartment attempt, I saw her again. Same place on the staircase. Same pose. Wearing nothing but her scabby birthday suit.

"Oh, hey! I've been looking for you. I wanted to give you some Timbits," I said cheerfully. "I don't have any left. But stay right here, K? I'll be right back. I've got a Tim Hortons mug you can have."

But when I returned less than a minute later, she was gone.

I told Nadine that Naked Lady was most definitely, most undeniably, a ghost.

"For sure. There's no doubt about it. Like, everyone I asked in my building had no clue who I was talking about."

"Spooky. I wonder what she wants from you then?"

"Well, nothing from Tim Hortons."

"Maybe we should call an exorcist," she said. "My cousin, Cheryl, was exorcised, you know? Like, one day, she was this gentle, normal kid, and the next, she killed her neighbour's kitten. Choked it with her skipping rope. When her parents caught her trying to drown her little brother in the pool, they called in an exorcist. They made it into a huge event. Catered and everything. Invited all the family and a few famous people, like George Michael and the mayor. The exorcist put my cousin in a straitjacket and poured holy water all over her."

Nadine left me hanging while she applied lip gloss.

"And? What happened next?"

"Well, all of a sudden, a horrible smell came from my cousin. It was worse than rotten eggs. Like, *so, so* disgusting. She started weeping and wailing, and so did her parents. The next thing I knew, everyone was weeping and wailing, even George Michael. It was super intense."

"But, did it work? Did she go back to being a normal kid?"

"Hard to say. They sent her away to boarding school in England, and we haven't heard from her since."

"Wow. A bunch of guys burried my dog alive when I was fourteen. She died, too. My Mama said evil spirits were involved, but I think the guys were just assholes," I said. "But Naked Lady's not bothering anyone, so I don't think an exorcist is necessary. I think she's just sad."

I was having more and more R&R evenings. It made me feel rotten the next day, but it was the closest I came to having fun on my own, and it calmed me down. I'd put on a movie and pause it every twenty minutes or so to contemplate ideas that came to me. They always felt crazy deep at the time but ridiculous when I sobered up. *Pet Sematary* was one of my favourites. I watched it over and over again. What a story. Like, what would you do if someone you loved more than anyone else on earth died and you knew you could bring them back to life? The only condition: they'd return as an evil, murderous zombie. If I could have brought Madonna back to life, even as a murderous zombie dog, I would have. I could handle it. I'd love her even if she tried to kill me. Mama said I had an infinite supply of compassion for predators and bullies.

Nadine's story about her cousin and watching *Pet Sematery* got me thinking that Naked Lady had probably once been a normal woman with a normal life too. And then somehow, somewhere, she ran into some bad luck and was banished to a life of purgatory, roaming the Montague Suites in the middle of the night covered in scabs. What happened to Naked Lady? What did she really need? A million bucks says Nadine's cousin didn't turn evil overnight.

I hadn't seen Naked Lady in a while, but I knew she had to be in the building somewhere, so I kept looking for her. I left a few notes around the Suites: on the staircase railing, the front door, and the bathroom door.

Dear lady with the long blonde hair (calling her Naked Lady felt judgemental), *if you ever want to go out for drinks, just knock on apartment 2. My treat! Missy.*

Dear lady with the long blonde hair, if you need to borrow sugar or milk or clothes, knock on apartment 2. I'm usually around after five. Except for Wednesdays when I'm at the SPCA. Missy.

Dear lady with the long blonde hair, I noticed you're friends with Godfrey. I can get cheap cat food from the SPCA. Just knock on my door. Missy.

I didn't hear back from Naked Lady. At least I tried. At least if she was real, she knew I wasn't scared of her, which was strangely very important to me.

Then, one night a week later, around the same time I usually saw her as I was leaving the bathroom, I heard rustling from the front door of the building. I thought Naked Lady had maybe changed up her location. Or that one of the cats or squatters was caught between the heavy doors of the vestibule.

I peeked through the door's window.

Something large and dark; much too large to be a cat and much too dark to be Naked Lady.

It was a man wearing a fur coat. Bunched up in the corner, reading a book.

I opened the door.

"Hey," I said. "You okay?"

"Yes, I'm perfectly fine," he replied, looking up from his book. "Just came in to warm up for a bit. It's freezing out there."

"November's the worst," I said.

He stood up and put his book in this black leather backpack. He was almost as tall as Big Red. With dark hair, dark beard, dark eyes, dark-rimmed glasses. I guesstimated his age to be twenty-nine-and-a-half.

"You don't have anywhere to go?"

He cocked his head and winked at me. He was also very handsome.

"Nowhere but here for the moment."

"Oh," I said. "I'm sorry to hear that."

"No need. It's actually a social experiment."

"Huh?"

"I'm experimenting with what it's like to be homeless," he explained. "How to survive, how people react to me, how people end up homeless, stuff like that. I'm writing a book about it for my doctoral thesis."

"You're gonna be a doctor?"

"In a manner of speaking, yes. A social behaviour doctor."

"Wow. That's like my friend Nadine," I said. "I mean, she's not a doctor or anything, but she loves pretending to be someone she isn't. She's super rich, but she likes to sneak away from her boarding school and pretend she's a squeegee kid. She says the look in people's eyes when they think she's poor and lost makes her feel more alive than when she cuts herself. She says it's almost orgasmic. It's hard to know if anything Nadine says is true or not, but I guess that's kind of like a social experiment, too, right?"

He blew into his cupped hands, looked at me from under his steamed-up glasses and said "Brrrrr."

"Ya wanna come in for a cup of coffee?"

"I'd love that, thanks. I'm Nathaniel. And who might you be?"

"Missy," I said. "Welcome to the Montague Suites, Nathaniel."

I didn't want Nathaniel to leave. Ever. Which was a wonderful thing because, from the moment he stepped inside my apartment, he never did leave. He never wanted to go outside. Not even for a walk around the block. Not even when I offered to take him out for dinner. I don't even recall him leaving the room to use the communal bathroom in the hallway.

Starting that first night when we stayed up drinking coffee while he read me excerpts from his book, we fell into an instant partnership. I stopped noticing the houseflies. He got a dry roof over his head and a place to plug in his word processor to finish up his very important book. I had someone to talk to; he got unlimited coffee, Timbits, Tia Maria, hash, back rubs, sponge baths, free meals and rent. I got a live-in boyfriend; he got a sounding board for his torment. Usually about his inability to finish his book, but sometimes about *her.*

Like this:

Sob, sob, sob. "Oh, Missy. I'm so close, but so, so blocked. The words, it's like they're trapped inside this mind that is my prison and nothing, nothing can get them out. Now I know how Van Gogh felt. And Ernest Hemingway. And Tennessee Williams. I should throw myself and all these pages off the Reversing Falls Bridge."

I didn't know who those people he was comparing himself to were, but I'd cheer him on from the floor while massaging his feet. He had scabs between his toes that neither one of us mentioned. I told myself they were flea bites from the cats. "I believe in you, Nathaniel. You can do this! You're so brilliant! You're even smarter than those guys!"

"Brilliance has nothing to do with it! I'm doomed! I'm possessed! I can't take it anymore! Don't you understand?"

"Sure, I do. When I—"

"Of course you can't! How could you possibly understand a torment like this?"

"Try me."

"No! No! I've already asked too much. I can't contaminate you. I need you to stay pure and simple. You're my angel and sanctuary. If I hadn't found you, this book would be dead. If I hadn't found you, I'd be dead. I was running out of fire until you came along to stoke me up."

"I'm here for you, Nathaniel," I'd say. "I'm not going anywhere."

He'd take my face into his big hands, kiss me with his long, thick tongue and say, "Thank you. Thank you." We'd try to make love, but he couldn't get it up. He blamed the unlimited supply of Tia Maria and hash. He'd say, "Why are you so fucking kind to me, Missy? What the fuck is wrong with you?" Then he would apologize for snapping, and hold me all night in his big arms, while I told myself: at least he didn't mention *her.*

Because mentioning *her* went like this:

Sob, sob, sob. "She wanted to kill my book. She wanted to kill me. That she-devil wanted to suck the fire out of me until I was nothing but a fucking useless piece of coal."

"Who, Nathaniel? Who's a she-devil?"

He'd never answer. Instead, he'd make me wear the blonde wig he kept in his backpack and position me facing the wall. "You stupid, fucking bitch," he'd snarl. "Who do you think you are?" We'd try to make love, but he couldn't get it up. He blamed it on my legs being too short and my tits being too big, unlike *her* long legs and small tits. He'd say, "Why are you so fucking kind to me, Missy? What the fuck is wrong with you?" Then he'd apologize for snapping, and hold me all night in his big arms, while I told myself: at least *I'm* in his arms and not *her.*

Once I asked if he'd ever seen a tall, naked, blonde lady in the building. I hadn't seen her since he'd moved in.

"No," he barked. "But if I do, I'll punch her lights out."

I never mentioned Naked Lady again.

While I was at work, all I could think of was Nathaniel. Even though he never left the apartment, I was so anxious he'd be gone by the time I got home that my nerves were on constant edge. When I wasn't with him, I felt like I was watching a horror movie that I'd never seen before. Of course, something terribly scary was about to happen; it was just a matter of when.

I stopped drinking coffee. I chain-smoked on my breaks. I kept getting everyone's order wrong and miscounting the till. Over and over again: will he still be there? What will I do if he's gone? What if he's an *unreal*? What if he gets up and leaves without a second's notice, like Pup does? What if today is the day? My heart was in a constant state of thump, thump, boom, boom, wham-bam, get-me-out of-here-so-I-can-get-back-to-my-man.

I was so jumpy and tongue-tied that even when I was with him, all that came out of my mouth was mumbling gibberish.

"Please be quiet!" he'd snap. "I'm trying to think!"

Eventually, even in silence, I couldn't keep my cool. I kept spilling his Tia Maria. I rolled his spliffs too tight or too loose. I burnt his French toast and forgot to put the plug in for his bubble bath.

His snaps got louder. "Stop being so clumsy/wasteful!"

More proof. More fears. More mess. More snapping. More proof.

The pattern seemed so simple. Such an easy fix. Like those claw machines at the fair. Come on, Missy. Position the mechanical claw directly over the stuffed toy that's sticking out the most. Aim. Click. Grab. Easy peasy. Except it never sticks. Never.

I hadn't told Nadine about Nathaniel. I was worried she'd judge me and I also didn't want them to meet. She was so much prettier than me. But when she confronted me about how wound up I was, I finally let the cat out of the bag. I told her everything: his book, his brain, his toe scabs, his fur coat, his long, thick tongue, his difficulty getting it up. I told her about my overwhelming and ever-present fear of him disappearing and how I wondered if he might be hiding something. Or that maybe I had finally lost it, and he was just a figment of my brain-damaged imagination. It was a relief to get it all out. But for all our fantastical one-upping exchanges, when it came to Nathaniel, Nadine was a stark realist. She wasn't reassuring at all. And, just as I'd expected, she judged me.

"Of course, he's hiding something, Missy," she said. "I mean, the University of New Brunswick Saint John doesn't even have a doctoral program. It doesn't even have a sociology department."

"How is living in your apartment experiencing homelessness?"

"Like, you don't think it's weird that he doesn't want to go outside? And he hasn't offered to pay for anything? No rent? No food? Nothing? What a deadbeat! What the fuck, Missy? You can do better than that! Lose the loser!"

"If you can't kick him out, you really gotta get your shit together. You absolutely can't let him see how much you care. Here, hold this."

She passed me a puppy.

"Whenever you start to spin, pretend you're holding her and imagine you're her mother and you have to stay calm to protect her with your life. It works for me. Except I imagine that I'm the puppy. But I'm not sure that would work for you."

She offered to sneak over on the weekend. "Just to suss him out, you know? I have really good instincts about these things," she said. "And if he's really as hot as you say he is, it doesn't really matter if he's hiding something. I mean, we all have our secrets, right? And maybe we can have a threesome. That'll solve his boner problem! Haha!"

The puppy-holding worked to calm me down. But the thought of her meeting Nathaniel made me feel worse. I didn't think she was joking about the threesome at all. I didn't trust that naturally blonde vixen wouldn't try to hook up with him without me any more than I trusted her to clean the hamster cages. Thank God I hadn't told her the details about the blonde wig. Or my address.

Around five weeks into Nathaniel living with me and two weeks into my feeling so shaky, I started seeing Naked Lady again. Every. Single. Night.

On Friday: Same time, same place on the staircase. Same pose. Same hair over her face. Same scabs. But now she was wearing a bra. A pale pink bra with dainty eyelet straps. I smiled and waved and said hello. She didn't respond. I went back to my room, slid into bed with Nathaniel, who put his big arms around me, and fell back to sleep.

Saturday: Same pink bra. This time she had matching pink panties and no scabs. Her skin was normal. I smiled and waved and said hello again. She didn't respond again. I went back to my room, slid into bed with Nathaniel who put his big arms around me, and fell back asleep.

Sunday: She added ballet slippers and sheer stockings to her outfit, and her hair was tied back in a bun. I could see her face. It wasn't beautiful, but it wasn't ugly. She'd put on a little weight. Her tits had gone from an A- to a B-cup. As usual, I smiled and waved and said hello. As usual, she didn't respond, but she did hold eye contact. We stood there for a few seconds looking at each other. I went back to my room, slid into bed with Nathaniel who put his big arms around me, and fell back asleep.

Monday: She wore a dress. It wasn't a beautiful dress, but it wasn't ugly. A dress that you might see on a bank teller or a teacher, long-sleeved and navy blue. When I smiled and waved and said hello, she waved back! I went back to my room, slid into bed with Nathaniel who put his big arms around me, and fell asleep.

Tuesday: She smiled. A sly, sneaky, mischievous smile. Like she knew a joke, and the joke was on me. I didn't say hello this time, but smiled back in a what's-so-funny-please-let-me-in-on-the-joke kind of way. Then she said, "Hey, Missy. You got any of that cat food left?"

On Wednesday, I told Nadine about it while I was cuddling puppies. As well as what happened afterwards.

"Cat food?" said Nadine. "Did you say cat food?"

"Yup."

"Why the hell would she ask for cat food?"

"We have a lot of cats in the building. I'd offered to give her some. Cat food is expensive."

"Fine. But then what happened?"

"I went back to my room to see if I had any cat food, even though I knew I was all out. I wanted to get away from her. She looked like she hated me. Like she was about to hurt me."

"She *is* an evil ghost! I knew it!"

"No, I don't think so. She reminded me of this mean girl in high school who pretended to be my friend so she could get me to come to a party where all the other mean girls were waiting to beat me up."

"Ooof. That happened to me once, too. Except it was my mother. She pretended she was taking me shopping, but three doctors were waiting for me when we got to the shop. They took me to the back room, held me down and shot me up with Seroquel."

"That's horrible!"

"Whatever. Seroquel is pretty awesome. Except for the weight gain. Anyway, get on with the story, will ya?"

"I went back to my room. But when I got into bed with Nathaniel, he was... he was..."

Nadine handed me another puppy. "He was?"

"Gone." I burst into tears.

"Gone?" Nadine said. "I don't understand? Did he leave out the window?"

"He wouldn't have fit. He's a really, really, really big guy, Nadine. Practically a giant."

"He didn't sneak by while you were in the hall with Naked Lady?"

"There's no way I would've missed that."

"What about Naked Lady?"

"She was gone too!"

"Did you look for him?"

"Who?"

"Nathaniel, dumbass!"

"Of course! That's how I got this," I said, lifting my sleeve to show her the two-inch cut on my forearm.

A few drops of blood were oozing through the gauze. "When I couldn't find him, I ran out into the street and accidentally locked myself out of the building. I was only wearing my nightie. It was two a.m. It was, like, minus a million. I thought I was going to freeze to death. I ran around to the back of the building to get in through my window. Fortunately, I live on the first floor. I couldn't get the window open, so I ripped off the bottom of my nightie with my teeth, wrapped it around my hand, and punched the glass. That's how I got back in."

"Shit. That's harsh. Why didn't you ring other apartments until someone buzzed you in?"

"I didn't want to bother anyone so late."

I paused for a minute, hesitating whether to tell her the next part. The worst part. I chose to whisper it. "You know what else? When I was outside, freezing my ass off, covered in blood, I saw the silhouettes of two tall people in an apartment on the top floor. I'm sure it was my imagination, but for a second, I thought it was Nathaniel and Naked Lady. Weird, eh?"

"Ya think?" Nadine said. "Well, duh. Of course, it was them."

I started crying again. I dropped the puppies, and they went running off in four different directions.

Nadine's face softened. "Oh, hun, I'm so sorry. I've been there, I really have," she said. "Deception's a bitch. Remember that guy on the airplane I told you about? The one going to meet his fiancée in Australia? Well, I didn't tell you that we kept in contact. And I later found out that there was no fiancée at all. He was actually a surf instructor, and his modus operandi was to tell ladies he needed one more fuck before he could settle down for good. Can you believe it?"

That winter ended on an icy but uneventful note. I went to work. I watched movies. I drank too much, ate too much. I visited Mama and Randall on Poverty Hill on Mondays and Nadine at her boarding school on Sundays. I increased my volunteer hours to three evenings a week and developed a fondness for two female rats that a biology student had rescued from his lab, but that kept him up all night, so he couldn't keep them. They were such sweet, playful little creatures. And smart! I was worried no one would adopt them because they were rats and their tails were as disgusting as rats' tails usually are. I considered adopting them if no one else did, even though I knew the cats would probably kill them. But then one day, a punk girl came in. "I'd like to adopt a rat. Ya got any rats?"

Punk Girl took both rats. Every once in a while, she sent an email addressed to me at the SPCA with pictures of her and the rats doing fun, normal things. Punk Girl and the rats at the mall. Punk Girl and the rats chillin' at home playing video games. Punk Girl and the rats in a mosh pit at the Green Day concert in Fredericton. She wrote: *I love these little furballs so much. Coming home to them every day makes me happier than you can imagine. They're exactly what was missing in my life. Thanks so much, Missy!*

Punk Girl's story made me feel happy. And hopeful that I'd one day have someone to come home to. Ideally with only two legs, but I'd take four.

I never saw Nathaniel again. But I did see Naked Lady in the middle of the night every once in a while. Sometimes naked, sometimes clothed. Sometimes scabby, sometimes not. Sometimes a scrawny A-cup; sometimes a perky B. We just ignored each other.

14
Ninja Baby

A week after Nathaniel disappeared, Pup showed up unannounced at the Montague Suites wearing shorts, sandals and his beef-jerky tan. It was three days before Christmas, and he'd been MIA in Cuba for six months. Instead of a suitcase, he carried a red camping cooler full of Cuban lobsters, two quart-sized bottles of rum, and wild orchids. We put the orchids in a Mason jar. They were magenta with lots of fat heart-shaped buds. We put our heads and arms through black garbage bags and feasted on lobster. They were itty-bitty in comparison to Canadian ones, and so delicious. Then we settled down on the little blue loveseat I'd recently dragged off the street with the help of one of the squatters, and got drunk on the rum as he told me how he accidentally knocked up a Cuban teenager named Yolanda. Now the baby was eight months old. That's why he'd come to Saint John. He'd wanted to tell me face-to-face. That and go shopping.

His story went that he had invited Yolanda as part of a surprise party for Randall who, despite saying he'd never go, visited him in Cuba the year before. Pup set up the party in the backyard of Veronica's rooming house. "Even though God only knows how much I hate organizing things," he said. "Rum, cigars, a pig roast. Pretty girls. I invited all my buddies. I even hired a DJ. You know me! I went all out for Randall! The whole kit and caboodle! Only the best for my son!"

He said he handpicked Yolanda because she was petite and short like Randall, and Pup knew how much Randall hated being around women taller and larger than him. He was sure the two of them would hit it off. He said it would've done Randall a world of good to have a vacation fling. What more could a young man ask for?

"But you know how your brother can get when he's in a mood. Right high and mighty," he growled. "She'd come all that way all dolled up, and he ignored her. It was *so* embarrassing." He paused for effect. "But, what can I say, she was more into older guys. Like me. One thing led to another, and, well, the rest is history. We all make mistakes, right?"

I'd already heard an entirely different version from Randall, minus the baby. It was a story Randall liked to tell when he needed proof that he and Pup were nothing alike. According to Randall, Yolanda was all over *him*, not Pup. He'd said to Pup, *thanks, but no, thanks. I don't do prostitutes. I got morals and a girlfriend back home.* So Pup fucked her instead. It was *so* embarrassing.

I waited for Pup to finish and poured myself another rum. "Yeah, we all make mistakes. You guys in a relationship now? And what about Teresa? Aren't you still living in the same boarding house as her?"

"Teresa? As long as I pay her family for my room and board, Teresa doesn't give a shit who I'm with," he said. "As for Yolanda, well, she wouldn't have been my first choice for the mother of my child. Different interests, language problems, ya know?" He stopped to sniffle. "But here I thought I had nothing to live for anymore, and then surprise! Juan-Howard came into my life."

"One what?" Between the crying and the rum, I had a hard time understanding.

"Juan-Howard," he said.

I leaned in closer.

"One hour?"

"Juan-Howard!"

"I'm sorry, but I don't—"

"Juan-Howard! Juan-Howard!" he cried. " J-U-A-N hyphen H-O-W-A-R-D."

"*Juan-Howard?* Seriously?"

"I wanted to name him Howard, after my father, but Yolanda wanted to call him Juan, after her father. So we compromised on Juan-Howard."

"Got it. That's sweet. You might want to work on your accent though."

"Oh, he's sweet, alright," he gushed. "He's sweeter than ripe mangoes. He's sweeter than a kitten. He's the sweetest thing in the whole world. Juan-Howard's the best thing that ever happened to me, and he won't want for nothin' his whole life. It's my fourth and last chance to be a good father, and I ain't gonna fuck it up this time. And that's a promise. I have a plan."

By this point, Pup had wrapped himself up in my grey, itchy army surplus blanket. All I could see were his face and his hands that he used to hold his rum and roll smoke after smoke. There was loose tobacco all over the couch, all over the blanket, all over the floor, and stuck to his cheek from when he'd wiped away his tears. Godfrey had shown up at the window a little earlier, and miraculously, Pup had managed to lure him in, and now he was curled up under the blanket on his lap, purring. It sounded like Pup's crotch was vibrating, which made me laugh. But Pup and his plan were serious. Especially the parts about The Marias.

I thought I'd misheard again. "The Marias?"

"Yes, Missy, The Marias!" he snapped. "Now stop interrupting and just listen, will ya?"

The Marias, Pup continued, were Yolanda's relatives. Her sisters, her aunties, her cousins, her mother, her grandmother. All of 'em living together in one rundown, dirt-floor shack. There were so many, and all with versions of the same name, that Pup didn't know who was who. Maria. Maritza. Marissa. Marisol. Marta. He was sure they did it just to confuse him. He was sure they didn't like him, and the feeling, he said, was mutual. Every time he tried to visit Juan-Howard, one of the Marias was holding him, feeding him, changing his diaper, or taking him for a walk. They were like Juan-Howard's personal bodyguards, he said, protecting him for everyone, even from his own father!

"It's like I'm not even important!" He yelled so loud that Godfrey jumped and made a beeline for the window. "It's like all they care about is whether I give them enough money to feed all fucking fifteen of their mouths! I'm like, *hola, remember me? Yo soy Juan-Howard's padre.* But, they're like, *we don't give a merde. Dinero, por favor.* Sometimes I wonder if they think I'm not his father at all! It's a total nightmare!"

I wondered about that too. Especially after he showed me the picture of Juan-Howard that he carried in a Ziploc bag in his back pocket. Pup had dark hair with blue eyes; Juan-Howard was blonde with brown eyes. Pup's natural complexion was as pallid as a foggy day; Juan-Howard's was dark Coppertone.

But I wasn't sure if it mattered, and I couldn't find the right words to ask. So I waited for him to finish, opened the window to let Godfrey out, and yawned. "Wow, that does sound like a nightmare. So, what are ya gonna do?"

"Well, Pet. Moving in with them just ain't an option. There's no room for me, and even if there were, I sure can't fucking handle being under The Marias' feet all day. That would be the death of me. Plus, they don't have a shower, they don't have a fridge, they don't even have a kettle. If I want a cup of tea, I have to boil a big pot over a friggin' fire like a goddamn witch! And they wonder why I drink so much rum! Fuck 'em!" he said. "I tried convincing Yolanda to move into the rooming house with me. But of course, she won't consider moving anywhere without The Marias."

"So," he said, breaking into a sneaky Cheshire Cat grin, "I plan to build a house. Three houses, one on top of the other. Yolanda and the baby upstairs, The Marias on the second floor, and I can have my own space on the ground floor. While it's being built, I'll continue living at the boarding house."

Oh, his house was going to be so big that all The Marias would have their own bedrooms! It was going to be so strong that it would laugh in the face of those powerful tropical storms! It was going to have so many mod cons that Cubans all over the country would be talking about it! Even Castro would be jealous! Yolanda and the baby could come and go as they please, but his floor was off limits to The Marias. He had solved the problem of The Marias.

"Most importantly, no matter what happens to me, Juan-Howard will always have a roof over his head. When he's older, he can live in it, sell it, rent it out to tourists. It will be as much his nest egg as my legacy," he said. "And, of course, you and Randall can come and visit whenever you want. Wouldn't you like that? Even your Mama can come if she wants. A nice vacation is exactly what that old bird needs!"

I had a flashback of the time I'd visited him in Cuba. The STI I got from the German tourist, all that money I spent on Jorge. I still felt sick when I thought about Serena, the mermaid who'd gotten locked up for spending the night with Pup at the hotel. No, I didn't think I wanted to go back to Cuba. And Randall sure as shit wouldn't. As for Mama, she needed money to fix the big leak in her basement. There was so much mould down there she could start her own penicillin business.

But that's the last conversation I wanted to have. I was done talking. It was two a.m. I'd worked a double that day at Tim Hortons. My head was spinning from the rum and his story. I got up from the couch and wobbled over to my mattress on the floor. "Sorry, but if I don't go lie down now, I think I'm gonna puke."

I didn't want to go shopping the next morning. I was exhausted and my brain hurt. It was finally the weekend and I wanted to sleep in. But Pup was pumped. As if he hadn't just travelled halfway across the world and polished off a quart of rum the night before. I woke up when he sat down on the end of my mattress. "Wakey-wakey, Pet! Up and at 'em! We got things to do, places to go. You can't lie around all day like a half-baked barnacle!"

He promised me lunch at the food court. He promised we would visit Randall and Mama afterwards. He couldn't wait to see them, he said. It had been *way* too long.

"But, first and foremost," he said, yanking the blanket off me, "I need to buy supplies because I can't buy shit in Cuba. Nada. No tools. No materials. People keep telling me they'll get stuff for me, but once I give them the dinero, they vanish into thin air."

He pounded his fist into the sofa's armrest. "They're all thieves, Missy! The whole island is made up of thieves, believe me. Why I keep going back is a fucking mystery to me! I got no choice but to take matters into my own hands if I want this house built before Juan-Howard says his first word. And if there's one thing Canada is good for, it's shopping!"

That's how I found myself hungover at McAllister Mall at ten in the morning, the taste of rum and lobster still in my mouth despite having brushed my teeth twice. Walking up and down the aisles with Pup, who was wearing a pair of my red long johns under his cargo shorts, a pair of his old welding socks ridden with burn holes with his sandals, two of my sweaters over his Hawaiian shirt and a multi-colored tea-cozy crocheted by Mama on his head.

By eleven his shopping cart was full: a pickaxe, a garden hose, plastic sheeting, silicone sealant for the solar-powered shower. Circuit breakers, a hacksaw and a voltmeter for the electrics. A rubber ducky and an inflatable paddling pool for Juan-Howard. He bought a bike that he gave to a random teenage boy so he could stuff everything in the box. He'd heard from a buddy of a buddy that you didn't have to pay an extra luggage fee for sports gear. The bike box was so stuffed that items kept popping out of the sides, so he wrapped it up in a triple-layer of duct tape. It looked like the torso of a silver pregnant donkey.

"Jesus Christ!" he yelled over the Christmas music blaring from the mall's sound system as he peeled off one of the sweaters. "They're trying to boil me alive in there! What do they think I am, a fucking lobster? Goddamn, North Americans are as bad with blasting the heat in the winter as they are with the air-conditioning in the summer. Like, make up your fucking minds, will ya! That's why layers are the only way to go. I could walk around in my bathing suit in this place even though it's friggin' December. No wonder the Cubans are ahead of us by, like, a trillion in saving the environment. You don't see them wasting precious energy like it grows on trees. You don't see them driving around in big-ass trucks spending money on stupid-ass plastic junk, drinking soda out of jumbo plastic cups, do ya? No, of course not! You Canadians pride yourselves in being these tree hugging environmentalists, but all you do is waste, waste, waste."

"You done?" I asked.

"Oh, yeah, sorry, Pet. I fucking hate this place."

"I meant with your shopping?"

"Yeah, pretty much. I just want to pop into the travel agent to look into flights. I'd like to get back to Cuba before New Year's. Meet you in the food court in a half an hour, okay? Here." He handed me a fifty-dollar bill. "Order a family-size platter of fried clams at Deluxe. The whole ones, with the big bellies."

I called Randall from a payphone while Pup went to the travel agent and told him about the house. I told him we were coming over after the shopping spree. I told him all about our new baby brother, Juan-Howard.

Randall burst into laughter.

"No way, man! There's absolutely no way that baby is his. He was too loaded that night to ever get it up," he said. "And she's a fucking prostitute! I'm sure Pup was one of dozens she slept with that month!"

"I don't know. Maybe it really *is* his baby? Maybe he really is gonna do it right this time?"

"And maybe pigs really do fly. What's wrong with you, Missy? Yolanda's just using him. She's taking him for a ride, and I hope she rides him right to his grave 'cause he deserves a dose of his own medicine."

"Umm, isn't *he* the one who took *her* for a ride?"

"Yeah, him and every other ex-pat down there."

"Well, then it's a good thing one of them is stepping up, no?"

"I wouldn't waste your time worrying about her. I'm sure she's got a hand in all of their pockets. She's probably got a boyfriend on the side who's laughing his head off at the luck of it all. Like, the amount of money Pup throws around..."

I held the phone away from my ear as he continued. I found myself thinking about Serena again. I'd been with Jorge when she was arrested, so I hadn't witnessed it. But I imagined two policemen escorting her out of the hotel in handcuffs. I imagined a group of tourists standing by gawking. And that green parrot swooping by and squawking. *Arrest her! Arrest her!* Pup had put his arm around me when I suggested we bail her out. "I know it's sad, Pet. Serena's such a nice girl, and it's a right shame what happened to her. But there's nothing we can do. I've got as much power in Cuba as that damn parrot."

I waited for Randall to finish. "Yeah, whatever. I gotta go, see you later," I said.

I ordered the clams and waited for Pup at a table in the food court. "Jingle Bell Rock" played over the loudspeaker. A mother with so many boys that she didn't know what to do sat down beside me. One of the boys rolled around under the table, his snow pants covered in ketchup. Two other boys pushed fries up their noises and barked like walruses. The toddler dumped soda all over himself on purpose. The mother kept screaming, "Just wait 'til your father hears about this!" But none of them gave a hoot, as if they knew their father wouldn't give a hoot either.

It wasn't until Pup showed up that the boys quieted down. At first, they weren't sure what to make of the man with the tea-cozy on his head pushing the shopping cart with the strange duct tape-wrapped box in it. Maybe they thought he was a homeless clown? They looked to their mother, but she looked back and forth between Pup and me as if she was trying to make up her mind whether to flee or not. I smiled and nodded at her reassuringly. Pup offered to buy them all donuts. He offered the mother some of his clams. Then he smiled at them with his captivating smile and winked at them with his sparkly blue eyes and chuckled his contagious chuckle and said, "Listen up, boys, and I'll tell you a story. Once upon a time, there was a—"

"Ninja!"

"Poop!"

"No," said Pup, "a baby."

"Ninja baby!"

"Okay. Once upon a time, there was a ninja baby," Pup said. "And he was the cutest, strongest, smartest ninja baby in the whole world. As soon as he was born, he could already walk and talk. At three weeks old, he could climb walls with just his bare hands. At five weeks old, he could pick up a goat and throw it across the room. But Ninja Baby was a kind baby and he would never throw a goat. No. Ninja Baby used all his strength to do good deeds, like carry old ladies up and down the stairs and push stalled cars out of the road. People all over the country wanted to visit Ninja Baby because he was a miracle, and they were sure he was destined for great things. But one day, his wicked witch aunties started to worry that someone would kidnap him. They got so scared that they decided to lock him away in their home and refuse to let anyone see him. They wouldn't even let his own father see him! Can you imagine that?"

"That makes no sense!"

"You're full of poop!"

"Well, maybe there was a good reason for his aunties to—" began the boy's mother.

"Bullshit!" Pup interrupted. "The wicked aunties were crazy! And jealous of Ninja Baby's love for his father. But you *are* right that it doesn't make sense! Nothing makes sense in the land where Ninja Baby lives! And don't try to figure it out; you never will. Believe me, I've tried! But here comes the twist," he continued. "They even went so far as to put a spell on the little guy so that he would be too sleepy to try and escape. And the only way that the spell could be broken was if someone brought the wicked aunties a cup of Christmas snow from Saint John delivered on—wait for it—no other than Christmas Eve."

"That's tomorrow!"

"Exactly!" cried Pup. "But there's no need to worry, boys. You see, the wicked aunties were sure that no one in their hot, tropical village where nothing makes sense would ever be able to get their hands on Christmas snow. Especially not snow from Saint John. It was too far away! Plus, who had ever heard of Saint John? But what they *didn't* know was that Ninja Baby's father just happened to have connections in Saint John. So, even though there were only a few days left before Christmas Eve when they announced the antidote to the spell, he travelled as fast as he could, across land, sky, sea and outer space, all the way to Saint John to get a cup of Christmas snow, only to turn right back around again to make it on time. The end."

"No way. I don't believe you."

"You're definitely full of poop."

"Oh, it's true, alright. And you know how I know? Because *I* am Ninja Baby's father. What do you think is in this box? It's full of Christmas presents for him. The only thing I'm missing before I leave tonight is a cup of snow. So I wondered if I could have one of your cups after you've finished your soda? And then, of course, I'll have to bid y'all goodbye because my plane leaves in a few hours."

"Really?" I piped in.

"You said you were staying for Christmas."

He looked at me as if he'd forgotten I was there. "Yeah, Pet," he said, shaking his head apologetically. "They had a half-price sale on last-minute flights that I just couldn't pass up. Sorry 'bout that."

The lady at the airline reception desk refused to have anything to do with Pup's bike-box plan. "Sir, that exception only applies to things such as tennis rackets and gold clubs. You have to pay based on the weight of the box." He screamed and complained. He jumped up and down. He waved his fists in the air threatening to call a lawyer that he didn't have. But it was a firm *absolutely not, sir,* until he finally gave in and dumped the box's contents on the departure area's floor.

He made three piles.

The rubber sheathing, circuit breakers, and hack-saw were in the medium pile that went in the cheap suitcase he had begrudgingly bought at the luggage shop. He checked that in as he muttered about double standards for athletes.

The voltmeter, garden hose, and rubber ducky got stuffed into the plastic bag the lady gave him to use as a carry-on. The rubber ducky almost didn't make it, but he couldn't come back empty-handed for Juan-Howard.

And the leftover pile, the biggest pile, was for me. I was to hold on to it for his next visit. But the pickaxe I could give to Randall.

"Now he'll have no excuse not to fix your mama's basement," he chuckled. "If that brother of yours spent even half as much time helping your mother out as he spends on playing that godawful stuff he calls music, it would be one less thing for me to have to worry about."

"Wait'll she hears that you're building someone else a house," I muttered under my breath.

Pup heard me. He was shocked. He put down his plastic bag, put his hands on his hips. "And what is that supposed to mean, young lady?"

"I dunno. Nothing, really. Forget about it."

"Come on, Missy. Speak your mind for once, why doncha?"

"I guess I just mean Mama's been struggling a lot lately. She's working extra jobs just to make ends meet. I try to help her out a bit here and there, but I'm certainly not bringing in big bucks from Tim Hortons—"

"And you think I'm bringing in the big bucks? You think I should be the one bailing your Mama outta debt after all these years?" His face went red and he began to pace. "I got my own debts to worry about. I got a new baby that depends on me for everything, thank you very much. You and Randall are all grown up. I already did my duty with you two. Your mother and I have been split for—"

"That's not what I'm saying."

"Well, what *are* you saying?" he snapped. "Why don't you tell me what you *really* think, Missy? Instead of pussyfooting around all the time. You're about as hard to read as a fucking Chinese menu!"

"Sometimes I just wonder if Yolanda even *wants* a house. Like, why *do* The Marias want you away from Juan-Howard? Is it because of what happened with Serena?"

"Serena? Who the fuck is Serena?"

"Serena, Serena. The one they locked up because she was with you," I said. "The mermaid."

"Jesus Christ, Missy! Are you still thinking about her? You're so dramatic. What happened to Serena was her own damn fault. She should've been more careful. The situation with The Marias is a whole other kettle of fish. Weren't you listening to what I told the boys? The Marias are wicked. The more difficult they make it for me, the more dinero they think they'll get. No one's going to jail because of this. No, siree! Because *I*"—he pointed a finger to his chest—"*I* am Juan-Howard's legal father. And there's nothing in this whole fucking world that's gonna keep me away from him. Not Yolanda. Not you. Not The Marias. Not the police. Not even father fucking Christmas! You understand me?"

I nodded but I had a hard time figuring out what was right and wrong about it all. All I knew is that I hoped The Marias and Yolanda were more robust than the most stable house in the world. And I hoped Mama would manage to get a good rest over Christmas. And that Serena was free. And that Randall would stop being so angry. And that Godfrey would come back again because, when I thought about it, he was actually such a sweet cat. Maybe I was a cat person after all. A cat was an easy thing to hope for.

I didn't tell Pup any of that. I knew he'd translate it into me not caring about him. I waited for him to calm down. "Yeah, I get it," I said, smiling as blandly as I could. "Sorry 'bout that."

•

The next day was Christmas Eve. I slept in until eleven, then put the lobster shells in the garbage bags. I took a long bubble bath and shaved my legs carefully. I hung out with Magda the lazy-eyed cat in the hallway for a bit. I crammed the bag of Pup's overflow in my closet that barely had enough room for my own stuff. Then I packed up the pickaxe, orchids, and the second bottle of rum in the red camper cooler Pup had left behind and went to visit Randall and Mama. On my way, using the money I'd pocketed from the clams, I bought a roast chicken, a tub of potato salad, some eggnog and a pack of smokes.

I told Randall and Mama that the pickaxe, orchids, and food were gifts from Pup and apologized on his behalf for not coming to see them. He was *so* sad to have missed them, I told them. He tried his best, he really did. But he couldn't pass up the cheap ticket.

"Good riddance," Mama said.

"Good riddance," Randall echoed.

The three of us sat around the table and feasted on chicken and potatoes, drank rum and eggnog, and reminisced about Christmases past. Mama used the orchids as the centrepiece. Several of its buds had since bloomed, and their heads hung heavy as if they felt ashamed. But that only made them more beautiful.

15

The Beagle and The Head, A Love Story

The following summer, I fell in love with The Head. Not just any old head. Not the kind of head that could disappear into a crowd or be mistaken for another head. No. I fell in love with *The* Head. The most wonderful, most charming, most gorgeous, noble head in the whole wide world.

The Head had dark, wavy hair that hung just below his heart-shaped ears. A Romanesque nose unblemished by blackheads, not even one. His lips were a perfect 1:1 top to bottom ratio. When excited or lit up by the sun, his eyes were the colour of fancy pickles put out in little crystal bowls for special occasions. Moss when happy; a hint of mint when sad. Crocodile when angry. The Head, I told anyone who would listen, was like a famous sculpture, the kind scholars devote their entire lives to understanding. The kind people save money to travel across the world to witness in real life. The Head, I believed, was perfect.

Of course, The Head wasn't *only* a head. He was a human being. A young man otherwise named Scott Miles who once upon a time was one of the best skateboarders in the country. But when he broke his neck in a half-pipe accident, he pivoted his energy into designing a logo: a severed zombie head riding a skateboard. Written in Permanent Marker font across the zombie's forehead: **HEAD**. Then he spent the insurance money from the accident marketing **HEAD** skateboards and T-shirts and stickers. Then skate shops up and down the Atlantic coast bought **HEAD** merchandise and sold it for a pretty penny. And then, soon enough, no skater, no groupie, no gangsta wannabe style fashionista did not own at least one item of **HEAD** merchandise. By the one-year anniversary of his accident, Scott Miles had renounced his name, his whole identity, in favour of his Head empire.

The Head was a local superstar.

Not being a skater or a groupie or a wannabe style fashionista, I had never heard of The Head or his merchandise. Not until Nadine invited me to a fundraiser party at McKibbin's Pub one evening. I don't remember what the fundraiser was for. Mikes for Bikes? Save the Whales?

"Look!" Nadine shouted over the crowd. "There's The Head!"

"The what?"

"The Head!"

"The who?"

"The Head, Missy. The guy hosting the party. The one in the wheelchair. I can't believe you don't know him. Like, *everyone* knows The Head."

He was wearing a navy-blue hoodie and a flat-brimmed **HEAD** cap perched slightly to starboard. His neck was long, sinewy and white, like a swan's. By the way the others leaned in to hear him speak, I could tell that he was a very important person who only said very important things.

There were two empty spaces next to The Head. Nadine sat down to his left, and I sat to his right. This turned out to be a stroke of luck because the right side of his upper body had more mobility than his left.

He turned to face me. Those moss-green eyes.

He cocked his chin, that hallmark move of many a great professional. Exceptional confidence. Total preparedness.

He smiled and said something that might have been "Yo," or "Can you please move out of my way? You're blocking my view," but to me sounded exactly like, "I've been waiting my whole life to meet you."

Then he lifted his right hand, bent at the wrist like a broken talon, and held it out for a fist bump.

It was love, I told anyone who would listen, at first fist bump.

The Head and I spent the rest of the evening together. I soaked him up like the sun. Everything he said sounded like poetry. Now that I was familiar with the logo, I saw it everywhere. The men's bathroom had a sticker on the door with the zombie wearing a top hat. For the women's, the zombie wore a tiara. There were **HEAD** coasters, **HEAD** napkins. Behind the bar were photographs of a six-foot-four Scott Miles riding the world's biggest skateboard ramp around a section of the Great Wall of China; Scott Miles rocketing down Mount Washington at 130 km/h; Scott Miles holding a gold trophy, flanked by two girls in hotpants and bikini tops.

It didn't take long for me to realize that **HEAD** was a cult and The Head was its leader. Sitting beside him made me feel so important. Everyone who entered the bar came to greet him, and me by association. All he had to do was nod, and the bartender brought him a whiskey. Gentleman that he was, he made sure the bartender brought me one, too. The Head drank in tiny sips from a silver straw that he carried in his **HEAD** fanny pack. Trying not to down mine, I found myself fantasizing about kneeling before his wheelchair and kissing his hand. Like a royal servant would for her king on his throne.

"What does it taste like, Missy?" he asked.

"Whiskey."

"Alright, let me try again. What does it *feel* like? Does it feel like the embers of a summer bonfire, like the engine of a race car, like the memory of a forbidden lover?"

"All of the above," I sighed, even though whiskey was my least favorite booze. "All of the above."

The Head, I could tell, was a romantic. A modern-day Maritime Renaissance man. I'd never met anyone like him. He knew as much about hip hop as he did about jazz. As much about skateboarding as chess. And best of all, most refreshing, most surprising of all, was that he wanted to know everything about me.

Tell me about *you*, Missy.

What interests *you*, Missy?

He became concerned when I told him about my *unreals*. Charmed that I had a thing for climbing trees; interested that I volunteered at the SPCA. He didn't believe me when I said I knew all the homeless folks in town until I pulled out a little notebook from my purse with a list of their names, where to find them, and how they liked their coffee. I take after my father that way, I told him.

At first, he was reluctant to play my game of matching people to their totem dog.

"Look," I said, "the bouncer is a bull mastiff!"

"Childish! Absurd!" he said, which came as no surprise to me. The Head, I'd observed, was a no-nonsense individual. Not someone prone to dippy, frivolous games. Imagine a judge or a palliative nurse. But I could tell by his eyes that turned from moss to pickle that he was having a blast. He looked as if the lights had just turned on after an epic power outage. Like, man, I'd forgotten how much better and easier things are with electricity. How did one ever live without it?

"And Nadine, with her wavy blonde hair and big brown eyes, is a golden retriever!"

He was trying his hardest to remain composed.

"And the barman," I continued. "That beard! For sure, a wire-haired dachshund. And your little buddy over there, a whippet."

He couldn't contain himself any longer. He burst into laughter. Whiskey shot out of his nose. He lost his grip on his glass, which fell on the floor and smashed.

"My bad!" I yelled loudly to all the heads turned in our direction. I knelt to clean up the mess and slipped a **HEAD** napkin into his right hand so he could wipe the whiskey-drenched snot off his face. From the floor, I looked up at him with lowered eyes and pouty lips, wishing I could do something even naughtier to make it up to him. "Oops," I mouthed, as I grabbed hold of his armrest to hoist myself back on my feet.

I sat down again, lit a cigarette, and blew smoke rings towards the ceiling. The way they dissipated into the light made me think of jellyfish pulsating through the ocean. I casually rested my arm on the same armrest, shook my head loose of the jellyfish, and said, "Sorry about that. Maybe dogs aren't your thing."

He went serious. "That's my body."

"Huh?"

"My wheelchair," he said. "It's my body. No one other than my caregivers and my family touch it."

I jerked my arm away. My eyes burning with whiskey-sharp shame, I stood up. "I'm so sorry. I'm such an idiot. I'll go."

"No, not an idiot," he said. "I haven't laughed like that since the accident. Sit back down, little beagle."

He struggled to take my hand and place it back on his chair. It took several tries. I could have helped him, but I sensed he wanted to do it himself. He put more effort into me in that one minute than all the men I'd ever been with combined.

"But," I said, "beagles run away. They howl too much. They're prone to getting fat."

"Not if they're trained properly." He winked at me.

The party was still in full swing, but The Head's lift was scheduled for nine p.m. and he had to leave. If he missed his lift, he'd miss Vince, his caregiver who came to prepare him for bed every night. If he missed Vince, he'd have to sleep in his wheelchair. And if he slept in his wheelchair, he'd be exhausted the next day. "There are rules," he said as we waited outside. "The rules of my current predicament sadly force me to cut the evening short. But how does coffee tomorrow sound? I make a mean cappuccino."

I was devastated he had to leave. Convinced tomorrow wouldn't happen because it never did. I'd been dumped more times than an outhouse. But just as I was trying to think of a way to prolong the evening, luck jumped in my corner again. Or was it fate? Or was it just because everybody knows everybody in a small town like Saint John? Whatever the reason, the Head's adapted taxi-van driver, Mr. Gould, was one of Pup's drinking buddies. A jolly fellow who didn't think twice about asking if I would be joining The Head on his ride home. And when, to my great surprise, The Head agreed, Mr. Gould asked if we'd like him to take the scenic route. He parked the van at the Fort Howe lookout, then got out and went for a stroll, leaving the radio on as "Purple Rain" started playing. Was our attraction so palpable that even Mr. Gould felt compelled to speed things along?

"Kiss me, Beagle."

I obeyed.

We kissed for the four-minute, seven-second duration of the song.

We kissed as Mr. Gould got back in the van.

We kissed when we got back to his apartment.

The only time we paused was when The Head called Vince and gave him the night off.

All night we kissed. The Head in his wheelchair, me on his lap.

"Do you feel it?" I asked him.

"The lips make up one million out of seven trillion nerves in the body."

"But do you *feel* it?"

"I feel something I thought I'd never feel again. Something I didn't *want* to feel again."

He fluttered his long eyelashes against my cheek and ran his Romanesque nose along my jaw. He nibbled my chin, my neck, my ear. My whole body tingled as if it was coming off of Novocaine.

It was the most erotic moment of my life.

Like any good love story, The Head and I melted into a honeymoon phase. The only time he left my side was when Vince came for his morning and evening routines. He cancelled his therapy. He skipped his physio. He took time off work, something he told me he hadn't done even when he'd had a nasty UTI. Not even when his grandfather died.

"No, I'm not being reckless," he told his mother over the phone while I circled my tongue around his succulent earlobe. "Business is thriving. I need to focus on other, more neglected needs." When he got off the phone, he smiled sexily and said, "Down, Beagle." I got down on all fours, arched my back, and wiggled my hips and ass just the way he'd asked me to.

The only time I left his side was to go to work at Tim Hortons, pick up extra clothes at the Montague Suites, and get to my Wednesday evening volunteer shift at the SPCA. Since meeting The Head, I ditched the two other shifts.

Nadine, of course, was full of questions.

"What about his cock? Does it work?"

"There are little blue pills for that," I said as we were cleaning out the guinea pig cages. "But ejaculation can cause heart attacks and that's not a risk we're willing to take."

"But can he get you off?"

"Oh, let me count the ways.

"But don't you miss it?"

"Miss what?"

"A good cock, ya dummy!"

I sighed deeply. "On the contrary, Nadine. Cock has never been further from my mind."

"You're the most delusional person I've ever met, you know that?"

"Why? What has cock ever done for me anyway? I don't even know what a *good* cock is. I wouldn't know a good cock if one jumped up and slapped me in the face. And even if I did, I wouldn't trade one for The Head for a million bucks."

When we weren't kissing, we'd sometimes go to Rockwood Park to visit the petting farm. I'd hold baby bunnies against his cheek, and lure the ponies close enough so The Head could touch their muzzles and feel their hot breath on his face. One day, we witnessed ducklings poke their way out of their eggshells. The Head, who had told me he wasn't an animal person, said it was a transcendent experience. The last time we were there, a rowdy goat jumped up on The Head's lap and punctured his urine bag. He was furious. "If I could, I'd fucking strangle you with my bare hands!" he yelled at the beast. But then I grabbed a sprinkler and spun it around us, goat included, to make it look like we'd had a water fight. After the shock wore off and he had confirmation that his wheelchair wasn't damaged, The Head laughed and laughed. "Where did you come from, darling Beagle?" he asked. "Where on Earth did you come from?"

Other times, we went to the City Market. He'd close his eyes, and I'd hold a sprig of basil or a bag of dulse under his nose. I'd bend down at eye level so he could slip a cherry, a chocolate-covered coffee bean, or a piece of saltwater toffee into my mouth. Once, the lavender vendor offered us free soap, which The Head graciously accepted, but out of her earshot, he snapped. "I'm not a fucking charity case!"

To which I replied, "Certainly not! You're the famous Head! Do you think she'd make Prince Charles pay for his soap? No way!" The Head rolled his eyes. "What am I going to do with you, precious Beagle?"

One time, I suggested we go to the racetrack when it wasn't in use. I hitched a ride on the back of his wheelchair, wrapped my arms around his shoulders, kissed his swan neck, and yelled, "Faster! Faster!" I felt like the heroine in *Top Gun*. He took it to max speed around and around the track until the battery died. While we waited an hour for his adapted van taxi to pick us up, I could tell he was annoyed. I kept apologizing.

"It's okay, my feisty Beagle," he eventually said. "You're still learning. I should have known better. But now you know."

Mostly, though, we stayed inside, kissing to "Purple Rain" on repeat. As of nine p.m. (once Vince had completed his nighttime routine): in his hospital bed. As of eight-thirty a.m. (the second Vince left after the morning routine): circling each other all over his apartment like randy dogs, memorizing each other's scars and smells. I'd undress and guide his right hand over my body, between my legs, in my mouth, while he recited poetry.

"My feelings for you aren't optional anymore, Beagle," he said while I danced for him.

"I'm terrified that you will see that I am not what you saw," he said as I straddled his wheelchair.

"You, my hungry Beagle, are thirst, and thirst is all I know," he said one night as I sat on his face..

I wasn't always sure what he was talking about, but it always made me cum.

After lovemaking, we'd often nap. Me in his bed; him parked up beside me in his chair. If he fell asleep first, I'd watch him. He was such a peaceful sleeper that sometimes I thought he'd died. Panicking, I'd hover my hand over his face. Close enough to make sure he was still alive, far enough not to wake him. Mama, who thought herself a medical expert after a two-month cleaning gig at a nursing home, had planted the sudden-death seed in my head.

"For someone like him, a common cold is a death sentence," she said. "A fuckin' fever could take him out like a sniper! If it weren't for modern medicine, he'd be long dead. He'll be lucky to make it to thirty, if you ask me. But maybe that'd be a blessing. For both of yas. I mean, what kind of fuckin' life is that for him? What kind of future is that for you? It just ain't worth it. But knowing you, my bet's on him croaking before you come to your senses and leave."

"There's only one valid reason to dump someone, Mama. And that's if the love is gone. And my love isn't going anywhere."

"That's fuckin' ridiculous, Missy! What if you found out he was a pedo? Or a murderer? You'd stay with him anyway?"

"But he's not."

"Sure. But what I mean is, what if he's an asshole. Who hurts ya. And I don't just mean throwin' you around."

"You're one to talk. Like, no offense, Mama, but Pup isn't always, how can I put this, the best husband to you."

"Exactly. Look how far love got me in life. Take it from me. Love is just gravy on a fuckin' turkey dinner. If the turkey's off, you're both stuck on the shitter all day, if not dead. One of ya's gotta throw the rotten bird away. Don't be like me, throw the fuckin' bird away."

Mama was confused. Me and The Head were nothing like her and Pup. She was just jealous because my relationship was a perfectly healthy turkey dinner, trimmings and all. I wouldn't have traded one minute of it for a guaranteed lifetime with someone else. Even if she was right about the expiry date.

What scared me more than death was remembering being with other men in other beds. Mean men, bad men. Men that always left. Men like Dirk the Jerk and Nathaniel. Or the bartender who'd woken me up after sex, screaming, "Get out! Get out of my house! This was a mistake!" It was four a.m. and raining. I was sure the bartender guy was into me, too, but he changed his mind as fast as he fell asleep after getting laid. What's stopping The Head from waking up and doing the same?

But that panic went away after I woke once to *him* watching *me*. He looked as if he'd seen a ghost.

"You okay, darling?" I asked him.

"I'm afraid I've fallen in love with you, my Beagle."

I had the best sleep of my life from that moment onwards. With the L-word sealed, there was no reason for him to bail. No one was throwing away no bird.

A few days after The Head proclaimed his love, our trials and tribulations, as he called them, started. It was a rainy Saturday, and we'd asked Vince to come and get him ready earlier than usual so we could have a movie night in bed. Pizza boxes open, we lay side by side in his bed in our pajamas watching *Dirty Dancing*. After *Pet Sematary* and *Nightmare on Elm Street*, it was my favourite movie. I'd seen it a hundred times and could recite every line. At one point, I stood on the edge of his bed and reenacted the part where Johnny teaches Baby to dance by balancing on a log. But I tripped over one of the side railings and crashed to the floor. I wasn't hurt and neither was he. He wouldn't have felt it anyway. No biggie, I thought. I'll make lemonade out of lemons and do like Baby does for Johnny. I'll curl my index finger and playfully summon him from the floor. He loves me on all fours. I'll add some extra wiggles.

"Come here, loverboy," I sang seductively, as I crawled towards his bed.

But The Head loved nothing about it. He wasn't having it. He burst into tears. Big, heaving, painful, minty tears.

"For fuck's sake, Missy!" he sobbed. "Do you want to break *your* neck, too?"

I was shocked. I'd never seen him so upset. And it was the first time he'd called me Missy since we met. He lay on his back and cried at the ceiling, tears streaming down his face and soaking the collar of his blue flannel pajamas.

I slipped back into bed and pulled him towards me, but he resisted. I kept apologizing, asking if he was okay, but he refused to look at me. Refused to talk to me. Finally, after I begged him to at least tell me what he wanted me to do—should I stay? should I go? should I call for help?—he turned to face me.

His eyes, now so crocodile angry, scared me. Those 1:1 lips, so pursed, they scared me, too. But what scared me most of all was being kicked out.

"Go sleep in the guest room," he snapped. "Now! And don't come out until I tell you to. I can't look at you right now!"

All night through the wall that separated the guest room from his bedroom, I heard him wail like a sick child. A trapped animal. A spirit stuck in purgatory. It was hell. But I didn't dare leave the room. I clung to the fact that he hadn't told me to go home, and I couldn't risk him changing his mind. I could take any punishment as long as it wasn't expulsion.

The next morning, I listened as The Head and Vince started their morning routine. I'd managed to relieve my bladder by peeing into a mug and dumping it out the window, but only The Head could relieve my spinning brain and aching heart. Waiting, I heard the hum of the sling transferring him from bed to commode, then from commode to wheelchair. His wheelchair hummed as he moved from bedroom to bathroom, then bathroom to kitchen. The kettle whistled as he prepared his first cup of Earl Grey, then bread popped from the toaster. I could picture The Head buttering it with his utensil-holder wrist strap, then, after switching to his page-turner wrist strap, reading the newspaper. First the sports section, then politics, then arts. What felt like three hours later but was likely closer to one, I finally heard Vince leave. The Head made his way to the guest room, the motor humming louder the closer he got. Then it went silent in front of the door for a good five minutes before he entered.

"My Beagle."

Relief washed over me like a bucket full of Calamine lotion, and I jumped into his arms so fast I almost knocked us both over.

"I'm sorry, I'm sorry, I'm sorry," I said, between kisses. His face was a bit colder and paler than usual, but I figured it was from lack of sleep and my warm body.

"I know you are, my Beagle," he replied. "And I am too."

"Do you still love me?"

"I do. Desperately."

"Do you still want me?"

"More than anything. But—"

I cupped his face and shut him up with kisses. I kissed his forehead. I kissed his chin. I kissed his cheeks, now rosy and flushed. I'd been right: my kisses were the best medicine.

"But," he continued when he finally managed to wrangle his right hand between our faces. "I need you to be more careful. I need you to see me for who I am. I need you," he paused to make sure I was listening, the way he paused when he was about to say something profound, "to stop mistaking me for your own pleasure. Can you understand that, Beagle?"

I nodded while I lifted his shirt and kissed his chest.

"Do you? Do you *really* understand?"

"Oh, yes. Totally," I moaned while undressing. Desperation made me a horny bitch. I would have said yes to just about anything so he would keep me. That is what I longed for above all else. For him to keep me. Like a pet.

I tried to be more careful, but from that day on, my blunders, which he had once found endearing, or at least tolerable, made The Head even angrier.

When I left my towel on the floor and he couldn't get into the bathroom to brush his hair with his adapted hair brush, he made me set the egg timer and sent me to the guest room for an hour. Later that evening I noticed chunks of hair in the brush and cleaned it. But the chunks kept reappearing.

When I broke the George Foreman grill, the only cooking tool he could use on his own, he set the egg timer for two hours. Shortly after the grill came back from the repair shop, he lost his grip while cooking a steak and burned his hand. When Vince asked about it, The Head blamed the repairman and threatened to sue. No one mentioned the elephant in the room: his right hand, his good hand, had become too shaky.

When I suggested we have a baby, he screamed. "What the fuck is wrong with you? I can't even look after myself! I can't even look after a goldfish! Do you even see my wheelchair?" I was sent to the guest room without dinner. He didn't even set the egg timer because he was already in bed by the time I could come out. While Vince got him prepared, I overheard him say, "You've been losing weight, sir, is your health okay?"

The Head snapped, "Your observations are not part of your fucking job description."

When we had a dinner party, and he caught me showing Nadine how to use his voice-controlled keyboard, he looked at me as if I'd just exposed his poo bag. "You *don't* understand, do you?" he growled through gritted teeth. After the party, I took myself to the guest room for the rest of the weekend.

His mother dropped by that Sunday and I listened to them through the door.

"Scott, I know it's not my place to meddle, but your stock prices are dropping and you're looking haggard. I can't help but wonder if it has to do with that scruffy girl you dragged home. You've been spending an awful lot of time with her."

"You're correct, Mother," he replied. "It's not your place to meddle. In fact, I'd like you to stop coming over unannounced. More tea?"

With each banishment, I'd whimper from behind the door, counting the seconds to our final goodbye, thinking, for sure, this is the final act. There's no way he'll keep me after this. Especially without his mother's support. But, no. He became more committed. More devoted. He said our relationship was like a business project in the make-or-break stages. He even had me write up a *(Not) To Do* list to help our cause:

no smoking inside, no adjusting the thermostat, no discussing my personal hygiene with your friends, no raiding the fridge in the middle of the night and leaving the dishes unwashed, no leaving things on the floor, and more. He said the list would bring us structure, which would bring us peace. He didn't want to choose between love and peace because he couldn't fathom the idea of losing either. It was the greatest length anyone had ever gone for me.

For my twenty-second birthday, he bought me a diamond-studded choker with *Beagle* engraved on it. It came with a double-sided sterling silver leash. He ordered me to strip and tie one end of the leash to his commode and the other end to his wheelchair. As he backed up until the tug of the choker bordered on life-threatening, he cried out, "I am pitiful in my love for you," and I came and came and came.

Weeks went by. Months. Four and a half, to be exact. I spent so much time in the guest room that I thought of it as my own. I'd never been happier. I'd never felt calmer. I would take myself there just to self-soothe, something The Head insisted I master. I learned to spend time alone, and I enjoyed my own company for the first time in my life. The Head introduced me to so many new activities, music, and books that I rarely got bored. Jazz appreciation, knitting, crossword puzzles. He even bought me a *Teach Yourself Italian* kit. It was like finishing school. The ones for rich girls to learn how to be a proper lady. I'd always fantasized about going to finishing school. Or was it obedience school?

I could have lived like that forever. When neither of us was working, which he was doing less and less of, and I wasn't in my room, we played chess, watched documentaries, and dined on fancy foods I'd never tried before, like camembert and sweetbreads with creamy truffle sauce. His palette was so highbrow.

We barely went out anymore either. Partly because it was winter, and it was impossible for him to manoeuvre his wheelchair in the snow. But also to avoid mishaps. *Remember the rowdy goat?* he'd ask whenever I whined to go out. *Remember the racetrack? Remember how you get when we run into friends of mine, especially of the female nature?* It was true. Whenever that happened, I was certain they were asking themselves and each other, "What in the hell is The Head doing with someone like Missy Whynaught? He could have any woman he wanted. What a mismatch!" Then I'd get insecure and clingy, and if there was anything he disliked about me almost as much as my messiness it was that. "That's not a good look on you, Beagle. Not a good look at all." That was number twenty-one on the *(Not) To Do* list: *no doubting my feelings for you.*

So we stayed inside, in our little bubble of love.

Then, one glorious spring day close to our five-month anniversary, after a week of good behaviour, The Head asked me to officially move in. Your room, he said, you can decorate it however you like. Make it your sanctuary. Make it as special as you are. Keep it as messy as you want. He promised to take a whole day off work and book a taxi to take me shopping at McCallister Mall. I could choose the paint, the curtains, the carpeting, little accessories like picture frames and my own alarm clock.

I was ecstatic. It was one step closer to the engagement ring I was pining for. And starting a family—

he'll be ready one day, I'd told myself, and I could bear the brunt of the work, no problem!

But in the midst of it all, I sensed a deep despair in his voice. His eyes were mintier than ever, like he might burst into tears again. He kept scrunching up his perfect face as if he were in pain or had just learned some terrible news. And it was paler than usual, with big dark circles under his eyes. It didn't make sense. Why wasn't he as on top of the world as I was? I didn't want to consider it, but I couldn't help it: could he, God forbid, be coming down with something? I didn't dare ask, though. He hated being reminded of his fragile immune system as much as I hated thinking about it. I'd worked my ass off to bury those awful death seeds Mama had planted. I had my own explanations whenever I noticed something off. Hair loss? *Premature balding, of course.* Shaky hand? *Stress certainly does take its toll.* Sure, it was taking longer and longer each time to warm up his skin after one of my banishments, but it was just another example of how addicted he was to my kisses.

That's it, I concluded. Mystery solved. He's in kiss withdrawal. Possibly constipated. Definitely exhausted. That certainly explains the bags under his eyes. After all, we'd cancelled Vince again the night before so we could stay up later, which meant he slept all night in his chair again. Not to mention the obvious: he was just as overwhelmed by the depth of our love as I was. He just expressed it differently than me. The Head loved intensely and painfully, like that sexy Heathcliff guy from *Wuthering Heights*, which we'd read in high school. Which made me his Catherine, minus the trust fund, natural dark locks, and beauty. He couldn't live with me; he couldn't live without me. For better or for worse; in sickness and in health. Like Catherine and Heathcliff, he was stuck with me forever, even in the afterworld. Why else would he ask me to move in with him permanently if it weren't forever love? I had better, much more important things to do than trigger an unwanted conversation about his bowel movements. Why ruin the romantic moment? Focus on the positive, Missy. Like decorating your forever home. Like warming up that long face of his with a million kisses. He'll soon perk up.

Leading up to the move, I pored through decor magazines. I was leaning towards Mediterranean with a hint of Gothic. Turquoise and umber and various shades of red. Velvets and lace and scented candles. It was the opposite of The Head's style, which was grey and white and stark and utilitarian. Red was The Head's least favourite colour, but when I told him about my plans, he just sighed. "Whatever makes you happy, precious Beagle. It's not like I go into that room very often anyway."

When the special day finally arrived, we almost had to cancel because he'd thrown up that morning. But, after his second cup of Earl Grey and an Adderall, The Head, who abhorred last-minute schedule change, said he had recovered enough to stick to Plan A. I wore a tight grey **HEAD** T-shirt under my denim jumpsuit. The Head wore black baggy jeans and a black hoodie over his cap, his face barely visible. It was hard to tell if he was hiding his face because he looked sickly or he was going incognito. He'd once explained that the evolution of the hoodie dated back to the Middle Ages, when monks needed to hide their identities. It was the same for graffiti artists, he said, and protesters and gangsters and working-class boxers. It's a counterculture statement, he said. Everything we wear is representative of who we are. The Head was so smart! But the point is, looking back on that fateful day, I remember only three things. What we wore. That Sinéad O'Connor's "Nothing Compares to You" was on the mall's loudspeaker. And the red paint.

It was just a plastic gallon of paint with a red dot sitting on top of the 50 percent sales bin at Sears. A lonesome gallon of paint someone, once upon a time, had thought would be perfect but then returned. Hadn't it been the right fit? Could they not bear the thought of living with that colour day in and day out for the rest of their lives? Maybe they'd just bought too much? Whatever the case, I hung it on the back of The Head's wheelchair. It was heavy. When he spun to see what I had done, it slipped off his chair, fell to the ground, and popped open.

Splash! Red paint flew everywhere. All over the aisle. All over me. Over the nearby shoppers. Parts of The Head's wheelchair. All over The Head, except for his face, saved by his cap and hoodie. The place looked like the aftermath of a bloody massacre. I tried to speak, but my mouth was filled with paint. I tried to see, but red paint got in my eyes and stung them shut. Finally, I took off my shirt to wipe the paint off my eyes but what I saw made me wish I was blind.

Not just because of the mess. Or the horror of the other shoppers. It wasn't even the shock of the paint potentially seeping into the mechanics of The Head's expensive electric wheelchair. The hundreds of dollars' worth of repairs hadn't entered my thoughts yet.

No, it was much, much worse.

The Head was barely recognizable. It was as if I was looking at him for the very first time. What

I saw was terrifying. It took everything I had to keep a neutral expression. His once model-worthy chiselled face was so shrunken he could have been wearing a Skeletor mask. His gorgeous green eyes, now flashing danger red, threatened to pop out of their sockets. With barely any cheeks left, his Romanesque nose looked grossly out of proportion, like a wicked witch's. His hood was down and his cap had fallen, exposing an almost bare scalp now covered in infected, pus-filled boils. His previously blemish-free skin was so membrane-thin and translucent that red and purple veins were visibly pumping hard to keep what was left of him alive. His long swan neck quivered from the weight of his head, as if it was ready to snap all over again.

His body, that body that I had worshipped, even with clothes on, looked starved and almost lifeless, like an old geezer who'd given up food to speed up the inevitable. I suddenly knew I could break him with just one little shove. Kill him, even. He bore a striking resemblance to his zombie **HEAD** logo. The metamorphosis from Scott Miles to The Head was finally complete.

I tried to get close to him, but he spun around and around in a frenzy. "Love is a dog from hell! Love is a dog from hell!" he kept yelling.

A crowd had gathered around the chaos and continued to multiply like wasps at a picnic. Still, the Head, whose reputation and self-discipline were his prize possessions, didn't stop spinning and screaming in rage.

Shirtless, I ran in circles after him. "Please stop, my love!"

"Love is a dog from hell! Love is a dog from hell!"

"I love you! I'm sorry!"

"Love is a dog from hell!"

He went faster and faster.

"I don't know what to do! Tell me what to do!"

Someone grabbed me and I turned around to see a little girl. She had blonde pigtails and couldn't have been more than seven. "I think he wants you to leave him alone, lady," she said, taking my hand. "I think he's scared of you."

That's when it hit me.

True love really is a dog from hell. And that dog was me.

I left the crime-scene with my head hung low. Trailing bloody footprints down aisle number nine.

Unfortunately, my strength only lasted seventy-two hours. But it was enough time for him to change his phone number, move back home with his mother temporarily, and get a restraining order. The only contact we had after that was a quick phone call early one morning.

"I called to say a proper goodbye, Missy."

"I hate it when you call me Missy. I'm your Beagle. I'm your love. I didn't mean to hurt you. That's the last thing I ever wanted. Please believe me. Please forgive me. Let me prove to you that I can do better. I didn't try hard enough before. I took you for granted, I know that now. And I'll never ever do that again. I'll go to therapy. I'll quit smoking, I'll—"

"Stop. This is already extremely hard for me. My love for you hasn't fully dissipated yet."

"But if you still love me, why would you let me go? That doesn't make sense. We are the luckiest people in the world to have found this kind of love. We'd be fools to throw it away. Our love is stronger than our issues. Love is all we need."

"Goodbye, Missy. And don't try to contact me again. I wish you all the best."

Click.

This heartbreak was nothing like any pain I'd ever experienced. Much, much worse than I imagined salmonella from a rotten turkey would feel like. More like being force-fed a cake covered in thick layers of blood-red icing made out of ingredients from the most toxic person in the world: me. I was both the force feeder and the feedee. If only I'd given him more space. If only I kissed better, smelled better, looked better. Flushed the toilet more; brushed my teeth more. Spoke less; farted less. If only I weren't so dangerous. What if I'd killed the guy? Maybe I should turn myself in for attempted manslaughter?

I couldn't take the torture of being me anymore. I couldn't even look at myself in the mirror. Mornings were the worst. The second I woke up, it felt like a runaway train was seconds away from crashing through the Rainforest-themed bedroom wall. My body and brain were in a perpetual state of bracing for the most brutal, fatal blast. The fact that it never happened was the most torturous part of all. Death felt like the only solution to my misery. Where was my equivalent of when I put that mangled squirrel in a plastic bag and beat it to death against the wall?

Death didn't scare me; it never had. Putting more on Mama's plate did, though. I didn't want to cramp Pup's style, either. We were in high-season plane ticket prices. To soften the blow, I tried to provoke an accident. I started crossing the street without looking. I intentionally left my hot plate on. It was winter, so I kept the windows open and slept in my bathing suit, praying I'd freeze in my sleep. I tried to starve, too, but apparently red wine and coffee are enough to keep you alive.

When that didn't work, I turned to Nadine. But instead of giving me her pills, she fuelled the real reason I hadn't followed through on the dare: a tiny glimmer of hope that The Head would realize he couldn't live without me. That I was his Catherine, after all.

"Oh, Missy. You're not toxic, you're fun and colourful and the kindest person I know! You're definitely not a murderer. That's too delusional for even *me* to wrap my head around. Seriously, if you turn yourself in for attempted manslaughter, they'll lock you up in the loony bin. But, hey, if you *did* almost kill him, at least you can say you saved someone's life, right? I once saved this old lady from getting run over by a steamroller. She turned out to be a bitch, so I should have just left her to become part of the pavement. Anyway, you *can't* kill yourself. Who would screen the hamsters for adoption? You couldn't pay to touch those disgusting creatures. And then I wouldn't get my credits to graduate. But, yeah, maybe you're right. There *is* a possibility he'll come back. I think I read in *Marie-Claire* that there's a thirty-percent chance the dumper has regrets. Tell me his exact words again? *My love for you hasn't fully dissipated yet*. Hmm. Sure, let's analyze that again."

Mama, on the other hand, wouldn't hear another word about it.

"For fuck's sake, Missy! Enough already! You got dumped. He's not coming back. Live with it. You're fuckin' lucky you got out when you did. You'll bounce back. Pinky says he won't."

Mama and her sidekick psychic, Pinky, were right. Eleven months later, The Head died. Pure bad luck came back to finish him off. His adapted van got sideswiped. Nothing to do with his health; nothing to do with me. In fact, word on the street was that he'd been living his best life since our breakup. He'd just gotten a **HEAD** tattoo on his shoulder, adopted a Bouvier support dog who'd done wonders for his independence, and was dating a rising-star corporate lawyer. Apparently, she was *so much more his type than that Missy Whynaught.*

No one bothered to let me know, of course. I found out about it at the SPCA. The TV was on in the background, and the funeral was televised. I'd been cleaning a particularly obstinate Pekingese's ears. As I listened, my hands began to shake so hard I had to shove the little dog back in its cage, cotton ball still in its ear. I wished I could fit in the cage with him.

I stood there and read the captions scrolling by on the screen: *Quadriplegic business mogul, The Head, dead at twenty-six. The Head: Gone too soon, but his legacy will never stop rollin'.* Outside the funeral parlour, streams of people were pushing their way past security for a glimpse of what the reporter called "Saint John's biggest event of the year." Inside, a DJ launched a new song in honour of The Head. An opera singer sang "Requiem for The Head." A politician used more words than necessary to say, "The Head rocked, and we're going to name a skatepark after him."

Near the end of the funeral, an artist unveiled a bronze bust of The Head. The crowd was so big that it was hard for the reporter to get a good shot. Everyone was pushing to be as close to the bust as possible, knowing it was the closest they'd ever get to the real thing. I knew exactly how they felt. I would've given anything for just one hour of straddling him in his wheelchair, kissing to "Purple Rain." To hear him whisper one last time, "I love you, my Beagle." But he didn't want me anymore while he was alive. Death would be no different. In the afterlife, he'd be forced to get another restraining order out against me.

The Head was gone and so was that tiny glimmer of hope of reunification that had been keeping me alive. I was a fool to think I was his Catherine. The heartbreak pain was back in full force. But I no longer felt I deserved to die. I didn't even deserve to be at the funeral. Watching his loved ones mourn felt like another assault against him. Why should I be the one to be put out of my misery? I never wanted to hurt him or anyone else again. My only job now was to make sure no one else ate the toxic parts of whatever food group I was. Maybe I could even find a way to tolerate it myself. But how? I knew dogs were safe enough. They're so much more forgiving and have much stronger stomachs. Thinking of dogs, I remembered that Pekingese I'd been grooming. I turned off the TV, took him out of the cage, and cradled him in my arms. He was a squirmy little guy, so I held him tight. Then I cried so much into his fur that he needed to be blow-dried afterwards. He hated it, the poor thing.

16

Lillian's Pad

Lillian was next in the long line at Tim Hortons. I tried to predict what she would order. It was a game I played at work to keep from obsessing over whatever I was obsessing about that day, thoughts about The Head included. Medium black for the curt businesswoman with the tight buns. Three sugars for the soft-spoken metalhead. A dozen donuts, no nuts, for the mama with rat's nest hair and breast milk leaking through her tomato sauce-stained *That's it, I'm moving to Florida* T-shirt. I got it right about 50 percent of the time.

Lillian was a tough one. She looked my age but was dressed like a middle-aged 50s housewife, along with a string of pearls with matching clip-on earrings, and carried a white patent clutch against her chest like one, too. She had the posture of a soldier in full regalia—from taping her shoulders blades together so she wouldn't slouch, I later learned. Even without makeup, she looked like a cherub, all creamy and round with auburn curls and naturally red cupid's-bow lips. I was guessing a bran muffin and mint tea until this guy butted in front of her. I didn't catch what he said, something about being really busy and needing a double-double *now*. I didn't catch exactly what she said in response either, but it was something about not giving a shit if his wife was giving birth to triplets in the parking lot, he had to wait like everyone else. She threatened to hit him with her clutch if he didn't move to the back of the line.

"Wow! You've sure got some balls! I could never do anything like that! Let me guess, hot chocolate with whipped cream," I said when she took a confident step to the counter.

"Balls have nothing to do with it," she said. "Balls are one of the major problems with this world. We really should stop giving them so much credit. If I had a penny for all of the problems caused by balls, I'd be a rich woman. Do you know how unhygienic they are? It should be mandatory for all men to shave their balls."

"Yeah, totally," I said.

"And yes to the hot chocolate, but no whipped cream. Whipped cream is made from animal products."

"Oh yeah?"

"You couldn't pay me to put that in my body. And I'll have a jelly donut too, please." She looked me up and down. "You're wearing too much foundation. And it's the wrong skin tone. Go two shades lighter next time. But you seem nice. I'm looking for a roommate. You should move in with me. I'll leave my address. Come by any time after five. Don't bring any furniture that you can't fit in your bedroom. I have particular tastes."

And that's how we became roommates.

After my shift, I went back to my Rainforest room at the Montague Suites, packed up my stuff, and walked the ten blocks uptown to Lillian's. I didn't inform my landlady. I didn't say goodbye to the cats or leave a note for Naked Lady. I didn't bring furniture because I didn't have any. I didn't even empty the mini-fridge.

Lillian's pad was an extension of herself. It had a fireplace with a mantel crowded with a milk-glass knick-knack collection, and a cold room for pickling and dungeon play. She had tole-painted affirmations onto driftwood and hung them up above pieces of furniture that she'd refurbished herself. ***Play hard, Work harder*** over a sage-green wingback chair. ***The Best Revenge is Massive Success*** above her mustard-yellow chrome kitchen set.

She had a mean Siamese cat named Roosevelt who wore a gold collar and ate gourmet cat food from a milk-glass saucer. She introduced Roosevelt to me as a good boy prone to biting anyone who tried to pet him except her. He was absolutely never to be let outside. She believed people who let their cats run wild should be fined and banned from ever owning pets again. If I agreed to these conditions, she said, I could rent her craft room and sleep on the wicker daybed under **LIFE IS BETTER WITH CATS**.

I knew life wasn't necessarily better with cats, but it did feel better with Lillian. She never ceased to amaze me. There was never a dull moment. Hanging out with her was like spinning the wheel on *Wheel of Fortune*. You win some, you lose some, and there was no telling when, why or how. When she was a vegetarian, meat-eaters were to blame for the Earth's demise. When she was a meat-eater, lettuce was three times worse for gas emissions than cattle. She studied political science at UNB-SJ and was a card-holding Conservative but worked as a dominatrix on the weekends and was extremely vocal about legalizing sex work. Her disdain for balls was palpable, but even through her sex work, she couldn't get enough of them. When you called her out on her contradictions, she'd look at you with the confidence of a man and say, "Your point?" In that way, she was like Pup. But way smarter.

Most people didn't get her sense of humour, but she had me in stitches regularly. Once, after her daily seven p.m. lavender salts soak, she came out of the steamy bathroom wrapped in her towel. "Hey, Missy. What do you think of Rosie?"

"Who's Rosie?"

She dropped her towel, bent over, and spread her rosy butt cheeks. "This is Rosie! Come and give her a big smooch!"

Another time, one of her clients stayed and joined us for tea and a joint after his session. For some reason, the man, who was in his fifties and quite dapper, was fixated on the milk-glass poodle on the counter. Was it the dope? Was it that only thirty minutes before he'd been spanked by the woman who was now serving tea from a primrose china set? Hard to say. But his eyes, even when he spoke to her, even when he was answering a direct question, never left the poodle.

"Why are you talking to the poodle?" she finally asked.

"I'm not."

"You're doing it now."

"No, I'm not."

"You're still doing it. Please stop looking at my poodle while I'm talking to you. It's rude."

"I'm not."

Lillian picked up the poodle and held it against her cheek. "Now you can talk to the poodle," she said, deadpan.

I guess you had to be there.

There were downsides to living with Lillian. She was always on my case about something or another: "Missy, stop slouching. Missy, stop mumbling. Missy, clean the bathtub after you use it. We don't live in a barn." Sure, it annoyed me sometimes. But, mostly, I loved how much she fussed over me. I was like one of her pet projects. In a way, our relationship was similar to the one I'd had with The Head. But because I wasn't in love with her, it was easier not to screw it all up. And the stakes were so much lower. It was actually Lillian who helped me get out of my heartbreaking grief over him.

"Does your grief bring you joy?" she said. "Does it help pay the bills? No? Then snap out of it! And throw away all that nonsense that you made him sick. You're just not that powerful. Move on. Go get laid; it'll do you the world of good."

It was also Lillian who encouraged me to go to college: "Missy, you need a career. I encourage you to try something in the helping professions. It's high time you stop helping people for free. You need to cash in on that." She would bring home pamphlets: nursing, social work, teachers' college. Eventually, I applied to be a vet tech. When I was accepted, she said, "Well, that wasn't exactly what I hoped. But it sure beats pouring coffee. I'm proud of you."

A client had just paid her two hundred bucks to pretend she was his mother for the night. He even wore adult diapers. With the money, she took me to Billy's Seafood, a fancy restaurant, to celebrate. We dined on oysters and the most expensive white wine they had. "See, Missy? *This* is the only thing balls are good for!"

It took me a while to figure out why Lillian made such an effort. What was in it for her? Then I noticed she barely had friends, and the few acquaintances she did have were either scared of her or could only tolerate her in small doses. In spite of her stack of self-help books in alphabetical order—*How to Start a Conversation, The Science of Making Friends, The Social Skills Guidebook*—no one except her parents or clients ever came around. I told her she didn't need to keep doing stuff like making little cards with pressed flowers glued to the front to thank me for being her friend, but she did it anyway, and I knew I'd have been sad if she'd stopped.

On Halloween, we went to a sex shop and bought matching fishnet stockings, bodysuits, feather boas, and heels. I was a blue Water Goddess, she was a red Fire Goddess. We painted our faces to match and went to a karaoke bar down the street. We danced, we drank, we danced some more. We sang "You're the One That I Want" (I was Sandy, she was Danny). As a dog person, by the end of the night, I'd befriended half the bar. Lillian's a cat so no one knew how to approach her; still, she had the pick of the litter to drag home. She made the lucky guy shower before coming to bed and kicked him out before sunrise. The next morning, she was teary-eyed over breakfast. The red sparkles still on her cheeks made her look more cherubic than ever.

"Missy," she said. "That was the best night of my life. Swear you'll never let anything come between us."

"Sure."

"No, not like that," she said. Her eyes got all froggy, like I had touched the silverware without washing my hands first. "I need you to say it as if you *mean* it. Like you *really* mean it."

"Okay, okay," I said. "I double-dog-honky-hog-rinky-dinky-pinky-swear ya."

Of course I meant it. I wasn't going anywhere.

If there was one thing that could come between Lillian and me, it was Pup. Smart women unnerved him. Women with good posture and fierce eye contact frightened him. He hadn't gone past grade nine. When I was a kid, me and Pup ran into my favourite English teacher downtown once, the large one with the big ideas. All she said was something like, "Oh, you must be the illustrious Mr. Whynaught! Does Missy get her wonderful imagination from you? No? Well, it is my sincerest hope that you grace us with your presence more frequently! There exists no substitute in this world for the guiding presence of one's father."

I swear he shrank three inches right on the spot. Afterwards, I told him I thought my teacher was a bitch. I said she was so cocky with her fancy words and fake smile. I said she was always sticking her fat nose into everyone's business and what she should really do is lose some weight. When he got his inches back, he said, "Yeah, she seems as useless as a nun's cunt."

I knew Pup would have a similar reaction to Lillian's particular ways and intense stare, so when he called to tell me he'd be coming soon, I tried to prepare him. "Difficult?" he said. "Oh, you know me, I can handle anyone." "High maintenance?" he said. "Well, all I need is somewhere to put my head down for the night and a couple of sandwiches, and I'll be no bother at all. She won't even know I'm there!"

As for Lillian, all the preparation in the world couldn't change the fact that she'd decided before she even met Pup that she didn't like him. *Her* father had worked himself to the bone as an elevator repairman to send her to university. *Her* father had stayed in a loveless marriage because that's what a good family man does. *Her* father gave up his dream of sailing around the world because it was irresponsible, and wasn't that the most selfless thing ever?

When I told her that Pup was a lost soul, she said, "Lost soul, my rosy asshole! He sounds like a stray dog. He sounds like a baby. And you know how I feel about stray dogs and babies."

Lillian made Pup leave his muddy sandals outside. She made him smoke on the balcony. She made him wash his dishes immediately after he finished with them. Listening to her interact with him gave me tummy cramps, like the ones I got at the SPCA when I had to put the dogs back in their cages after a nice long walk, knowing they'd be put down the next day. But she bossed him around with a smile, and he smiled back, so what could I say? She baked him a blueberry pie; he bought her a bouquet of tiger lilies. She cut his hair; he gave her an expensive bottle of brandy. They got stoned and watched *This Hour Has 22 Minutes* together.

"Don't you think Americans should just keep their mouths shut, like *all* the time? Like, *all* of them?" she asked, after they agreed that Canadian comedy was superior to American.

"Right on, sweetheart," he said. "Never met a Yank that could make me laugh. They shouldn't be allowed to make comedies. If you ask me, they shouldn't even be allowed to interact with the rest of the world."

"Absolutely. I hate Americans," she said. "But, don't call me sweetheart, Pup. Ever. There's nothing sweet about me."

"You can say that again!"

They laughed and laughed.

Toward the end of his visit, Pup asked if he could use our address to avoid losing his NB residency and therefore his pension. Pup was drinking his morning Guinness on her pumpkin plaid Pottery Barn sofa under *I am enough (Just as I am)*. He was going on about how unfair it was that he couldn't enjoy his hard-earned cash in the country of his choice.

Lillian stared him down. "Well, if you want to have your cake and be able to eat it too, you better give me a slice."

"What's that?" Roosevelt was fast asleep on Pup's lap, purring like a luxury car.

"It's called tax fraud," she said. "Why would I take that risk without getting something in return?"

"Don't listen to her," I quickly chimed in, nearly choking on my coffee. "She's just messing with ya."

"No, I am not!" she said. "Fifty bucks a month for my address, take it or leave it. I'll put it towards my trip to Vegas."

Pup gently shifted Roosevelt off his lap and stood up. I was sure he would walk out, and I was ready to walk out with him. Instead, he took the money he carried around in his zip-lock baggie out of his pocket, and handed Lillian a wad of cash. "Here's four hundred until I come back next time," he said.

"Stop! Both of you!" I yelled. "I'll pay it!"

Pup looked at me and winked. "It's nothing, Pet. No one favours me in life, and don't I know it. Lil's got a point."

"And, I hope you pay that Cuban teenager of yours for all of her 'favours'," Lillian said, making finger quotes.

"He's building her a house. A big one! Right, Pup?" I said.

"I'm trying, Pet. I'm sure tryin'. But you know I can't get shit done in Cuba. Eighteen months in, and I'm already out ten grand! And all that's done is the foundation and the walls! Bleeding me right fucking dry they are and laughing at me as they do it. Sometimes I just wanna punch them behind their cocks! Crooks, I tell ya, the whole island is made up of crooks!"

"Maybe you should bring a gun with you next time," Lillian said.

"Ha! Good idea, Lils! Let's drink to that!"

Pup and Lillian got along peachy-keen. It was me who pouted around the apartment like a scolded schoolgirl. Lillian finally cornered me and ordered me to speak my mind. "I can't believe you asked Pup to pay you," I told her. "Since when are you going to Vegas? You said you hated Americans. Like, stick to your story for once."

"I've always wanted to go to Vegas, Missy. Las Vegans, I'll have you know, are very different from other Americans. A totally different species. Plus, Pup doesn't mind me keeping him in line. It's you who minds. Limits are good for him. He likes them. It makes him feel useful."

To make it up to me, however, she offered to throw a dinner party on his behalf. Pup thought that was a great idea, so I softened up. I invited some of my vet tech friends, and Lillian invited some of the political science students she'd been trying to befriend. She served roast beef and Yorkshire pudding, Irish coffees, a chocolate fountain and melon balls. She gave everyone a melon-ball scooper as a party favour. I contributed a party pack of Timbits that Lillian arranged on a crystal cupcake tower.

Pup hit it off with the vet techs like a tick on a deer, but the poli-sci folks were a whole other animal. He showed them pictures of his beloved Juan-Howard, but they wanted to discuss Castro. He showed them the plans for the house he was building, but they called out colonialism. I tried to steer the conversation toward something more neutral, like hurricanes, but when they brought up sex tourism, Pup got as uncomfortable as a rooster in a pond and upped and left for the bar down the street. I told him I'd join him later, but I ended up having sex—against the bathroom sink, under OLD WAYS DON'T OPEN NEW DOORS —with a guy named Josh who had snowdrifts of dandruff piling up on his shoulders and used words like *pragmatic sanctions*. And then I passed out.

The next morning, I wanted to make it up to Pup by taking us to a fry-up breakfast, but he and his things were gone.

"This is all your fault," I snapped at Lillian, who was slicing red peppers for pickling. She was wearing a homemade avocado face mask and a pink shower cap.

"What are you talking about? He could use a few pointers on his arrival and departure manners, but otherwise, I found him delightful," she said. "Really, Missy, you don't give him enough credit. You make him out to be incapable of anything. But in fact, he's quite remarkable. And handsome! We should all take a page out of his book and live life on our own terms. Oh, and please don't forget to douche today. That Josh is a nasty piece of work, I doubt he's bathed in months. I do wonder about your standards sometimes. But I'm happy you've started spreading your legs again. Looks like your mind is finally getting off The Head."

With that, she lifted her left butt cheek off her chair and yelled, "Booty bomb!"

Over the next year, Pup's letters got weirder and weirder. As always, they were written on something random, like a menu or a disco flyer, and had Canadian stamps. I imagined him running into someone at a beach bar or a restaurant and being, like, "Hey, buddy, you Canadian? I'll buy you drinks if you send this to my daughter when you get back home. Can't trust the Cuban post. Fucking Commie spies!" Then he'd find the closest thing to paper, borrow someone's pen and write whatever came to mind in whatever state he was in. He knew my address by heart.

Hi Pet. I had a dream that Madonna was thirsty and hungry. So I gave her milk and leftover fat from your Mama's slow-cooked ribs. 'Member how she used to shove her whole face in the pan, and her fur would get all slicked back like Elvis? Ha! She loved it! God, I miss that dog. She was such a good girl. Tell Randall and Queen Lillian I said hola. Not sure if I'll get the chance again. So maybe tell them toodle-lee-doo. And a toodle-lee-doo to you too! Don't forget to pay my union dues.

Hi Pet. Did you pay my taxes? Fuck the pigs and their taxes! I am the Egg Man, I am the Walrus. Don't you think the Joker's after you? What a song! John Lennon was a fucking genius! If that ugly Chrétien-fucker had half the brains Lennon did, we'd be living our best lives. If capitalism doesn't kill ya, communism sure the shit will. Believe me, I know what's really going on behind closed doors. They're all heartless mother fuckers who only look out for themselves. Love you.

Hi Pet. Everyone in Cuba's after me. The Marias want me dead. They think I don't understand, but I do. And now they've taken Juan-Howard from me. But do you think they can stop me? No way! I'm like a pig's snout, and you can't wear that out! Look into getting me one of those baby bike seats, will ya? I'm gonna ride me and JH right off this island if it's the last fucking thing I do. I miss you so much.

Meanwhile, Lillian also got weirder and weirder. She took a philosophy class and became obsessed with Simone Weil. After Martha Stewart, Simone Weil was her new idol. She went from being on my case about slouching to being on my case to give up my material goods. She boxed up all the milk-glass knick-knacks except the poodle and put them in storage. She gave her pearls to a homeless guy. She gave up sugar and masturbation for a month. She made another tole-painting—***Look at Food Without Eating It***—and hung it above the stove. She said refusing to eat for pleasure was also a good way to lose some weight, despite repeatedly telling me that wanting to lose weight was just another example of my low self-esteem fueled by internalized gender-based discrimination. Or something like that. She informed me that in addition to devoting herself to feeding the poor, Simone Weil starved herself to death. She told me that with the same tone of admiration she used for Martha Stewart's cake decorating techniques. I questioned her about giving the homeless guy her fake pearls instead of food.

"Well, he can sell them," she said. "Learning to be industrious is also a gift. I refuse to indulge his idleness."

Amongst Lillian's lifestyle changes was telling her parents, who she was otherwise very close with, particularly her father, that they might not hear from her for a while because she needed to detach herself from loved ones. She was convinced that's what I needed to do with Pup. She said if we don't weep, we won't need to be comforted. And if we're not comforted, we won't become attached. And if we're not attached to something or someone, they can't hurt us. "Let Pup go, Missy," she said. "Just let him go." It all sounded like a Jon Bon Jovi song to me. When, in turn, I suggested she give up Roosevelt, she rolled her eyes. "It only applies to humans, Missy."

Lillian giving up her attachments to humans was as easy as the rich voting for tax cuts. For me, it would have been easier to learn Mandarin. Pup and his letters kept me up at night. Especially when they abruptly stopped. I kept dreaming that he was dead, but not really dead. I mean, I'd hear from someone that he'd died, but then he'd sneak up on me and say he was just pretending. Ha, ha! Then he'd die again and reappear again. Like Jesus, but less holy. In one of the dreams, he drowned trying to swim out of Cuba. We had a big, fancy funeral, similar to The Head's, where everyone tried to one-up each other about the great times they'd had with Pup and how much they'd miss him. But then I saw him on a TV show in Florida. I knew it was him even though he had a mustache and had dyed his hair blonde, but I couldn't for the life of me figure out how to reach him. I'd wake from these dreams and wonder all day long if he was dead or not.

These feelings, of course, weren't anything new. But they were more frequent and heightened. Like the difference between hearing on the radio that a thunderstorm is about to happen versus breathing in that boggy pre-storm air. Sometimes I thought that if anything could bring me peace, it would be knowing he'd finally croaked, which also made me think I was a monster. I guess that's why, when he showed up a few months after his last letter, I was as disappointed as I was relieved. He arrived one afternoon with groceries and a guy named Bert he'd met at the bar across the street from the bus station. They'd been drinking and were both in a right state. Lillian was gone for the day at some meditation workshop that she needed like a hole in the head.

"I hope you're hungry, Pet!" Pup slurred as he and Bert pushed their way past me into Lillian's pad, as unceremoniously as if he'd just seen me the day before. "We stopped off at the Super Store on our way over. Got the makings of a feast fit for a king! All the food I can't fucking get my hands on in Cuba is right here in these bags!"

Now, if this was a choose-your-own-adventure story, it might read something like this:

If you want me to convince Pup and Bert that the three of us should have our feast at the park next door because it's a beautiful sunny day, go to page 4.

If you want Roosevelt to unleash his inner guard cat and bite Pup's and Bert's ankles, so they run away and never come back and I get to continue my day as I please, go to page 11.

If you want me to summon the courage to ask Pup and Bert to kindly not come back until they've sobered up, go to page 26.

But this is not a choose-your-own-adventure story. Unlike Lillian, Pup and I were as predictable as farts after beans.

I let them in.

I hugged Pup and fretted over the big scrape on his forehead that he couldn't remember getting. I let

Bert use our bath because the bedsit he was staying at didn't have one, and boy did ours ever look amazing. The chrome table was too small for the loot, so I rolled up Lillian's beige shag living-room carpet, and we had a picnic on the floor. We had cheese, olives, bread, sausages, peanut butter, Harvest Crunch and vanilla yogurt. And two boxes of red wine.

A quarter into the first box, I let everyone smoke inside.

Three-quarters into the box, Pup started BBQing the sausages in the fireplace. One sausage caught fire and fell onto the hardwood floor, leaving a black stain shaped like a turd or a turtle.

Pup tripped over the phone cord and fell into the counter when we started on the second box, knocking off and breaking Lillian's milk-glass poodle. He spilled red wine all over her wingback chair.

Halfway through the second box, as I opened the window to air out the smoke, I burned a cigarette hole in the Laura Ashley curtains. Roosevelt made a dash for the window and leaped through, and, try as we might, we couldn't lure him back.

As we finished the second box, Bert got lost looking for the bathroom. He ended up in the pickling dungeon, where he started messing around with Lillian's S&M equipment and got his head stuck in her pillory. Pup opened a jar of Lillian's red peppers and poured the olive oil all over the pillory and Bert's head to make it easier for him to slip out. Then he scooped out some of the peppers with his fingers and shoved them in his mouth.

"Wow, Lil sure can pickle!" Pup beamed, olive oil dripping down his chin onto his Hawaiian shirt. "Shit. If I had the cash, I'd invest in her starting a business! We could make a mint off this shit!"

Out of the pillory and sitting on the floor with his legs crossed, Bert ran his hands through his long grey hair. His whole upper body was as slippery as a fish coated in vaseline. "Pickles?" he said. "No way, man! If you got money, you gotta invest in brick. My buddy out west bought a building for a hundred grand and sold it fifteen years later for a million!"

"Unless you're in Cuba!" Pup growled. "I'll never see a penny from the house I built. I can't even put my fucking name on it! They won't even let me live in it. Yolanda moved her fucking boyfriend in there and changed the fucking locks. I got as many legal rights down there as a fucking ninny goat! You'd think I would've learned my lesson after losing my first house to Missy's Mama, right Missy? Well, now I've lost everything! The house *and* Juan-Howard!"

"Only a dog returns to its vomit, man."

"What the fuck did you call me?"

"I mean, a cat won't sit on a hot stove twice."

Pup snarled at Bert. Then he took a swing at him. But he missed and fell on his knees, bursting into big, heaving, messy tears. "I'm sorry, man. Please, just shoot me! Somebody, for the love of God, just shoot me! If I can't have Juan-Howard, I'd rather be dead. Oh, my baby boy!"

That's when Lillian walked through the door.

If you want me to apologize to Lillian, help her get the men out of the apartment and clean up, go to page 8.

If you want me to try to convince Lillian to join in on the fun and games, and we'll clean up later, go to page 33.

If you want me to tackle Lillian, tie her up and gag her to delay the inevitable, go to page 74.

I tried all of those adventures. I apologized while calming Pup down, cleaning up, and looking for Bert's wallet that he'd lost between his bubble bath and pillory adventure. I must have apologized a hundred times. But she wasn't having any of it. "Get out! Get out! Get out!" she kept screaming, at Pup especially, who was curled in a ball on the floor, still begging for a bullet to the head. I don't know where he thought we could get a gun.

Convince her to join in the fun and games? I tried that too. "Come on, Lillian, have a sandwich. Have a glass of wine. We'll clean up later. Seriously, it's all good." But she wasn't having that either.

"Get out! Get out! Get out!" she kept screaming. When she noticed Roosevelt was missing, she alternated "Get out!" with hollering out the window: "Here, kitty kitty kitty. Here, kitty kitty kitty."

Take her down? Even if I were sober, she would've kicked my ass. She had a green belt in karate.

While she was hanging out the window, I quickly packed up some clothes, dragged Pup up off the floor, and left. I didn't wait to see if Roosevelt came back. I didn't take any furniture because I still didn't have any worth taking. I didn't even take my toothbrush.

Looking back, I'm not sure how long I spent with Pup in that dingy motel room on Rothesay Avenue. Three, six, fifteen days? It was like going on a long, long, long road trip where you've taken too much Gravol and you're not sure where you're going anymore or who's driving. You keep waking up either to puke or ask a question that you never ask because you're still sleeping. As unreal as it gets. But here's what I do remember: the full story of what happened to Pup in Cuba. It came out in bits and pieces. Whenever I thought I understood one section, another fell apart.

The house finally got built? *Yes, mostly.*

Is the house yours? *Yes, but I can't live in it.*

Do you pay the bills for the house? *Yes, but I don't own it.*

Who owns the house? *Yolanda.*

Why? *Foreigners aren't allowed to own property in Cuba. The fuckers!*

Why won't Yolanda let you live in the house? *Because her boyfriend moved in.*

I thought you were Yolanda's boyfriend? *No, I am not.*

Does Yolanda have Juan-Howard? *Yes, when he's not living with Marisol, his grandmother.*

The grandmother lives in the house too? *Yes, downstairs.*

What about The Marias? *They're omnipresent.*

Why can't you live downstairs with the grandmother? *I did, but The Marias kicked me out.*

Why did they kick you out? *Because they hate me.*

Why do they hate you? *How the fuck should I know?*

Seriously, Pup, tell me the truth, why do they hate you? *I got drunk and took Juan out for a ride on my bike without telling anyone.*

Was he hurt? *No, but he could have been. That's why The Marias hate me. That's why everyone hates me. They won't let me see him anymore until I sober up and get my own place.*

Why can't you rent somewhere else? *I'm broke. I spent all my savings on the house.*

Are you going to go back? *As soon as I can afford a plane ticket.*

We went through enough wine to kill a bull moose. When we weren't drinking, we were watching movies or sleeping. I tried to figure out how to get Pup back to Cuba and Juan-Howard. I vaguely remember calling Randall. "Just shoot him," he said. Then I called Mama, but I didn't know what to say when she picked up. She couldn't help. Mama wasn't part of the solution. So I hung up.

A scruffy pigeon kept coming to the hotel window to visit, but even he gave up after a while.

Every time I closed my eyes, I had the most gruesome vision of Lillian, dead for over a week in her lavender bath. Her body decomposing and unrecognizable. Roosevelt, with nothing left to drink or eat, forced to survive on slimy bathwater and her avocado mask. A Patsy Cline song on repeat: "Walkin' After Midnight."

Chances were, I knew, that Lillian was alive and kicking just fine. At worst, lonely. Plus, her parents checked in on her regularly. But I couldn't shake the fact that just a few blocks away was someone who desperately wanted to live, love and be loved by me, and I'd just ruined that friendship like a sack of mouldy laundry. Way too close to home after what happened with The Head. Meanwhile I was trying to keep my father, who was begging me to blow his brains out, alive. Since I didn't have a gun, I called Lillian.

Lillian showed up forty-five minutes later with her father in his pickup truck. They tag-teamed us. While Lillian stuck to me like we were playing a shadow game, her father gently coaxed Pup to come with him. I was sure Pup would resist. I was sure he'd tell Lillian and her father they had no business being so self-righteous and to fuck right off. I was sure he'd call me the most selfish, heartless daughter in the whole world because that's how I felt. But he just rolled over and went limp. Like a dog so old no one could decide what was best for him. "Do whatever you want with me," he said. "I don't care anymore."

If you think I should have him euthanized, go to page 42.

When Lillian's father scooped him up in his big arms and carried him from the motel room out to his truck, Pup looked at me as if for the last time. *See? I knew you wouldn't help me. I knew you didn't want me. No one does.*

And he was right. I didn't have what it took to kill or keep him anymore. If you want me to give him up for compassionate adoption to folks who have the will and the way to keep him safe and comfortable, go to page 96.

It was my only option, and the most heartbreaking of them all.

Lillian and I walked home together while her father drove Pup an hour of of town to rehab. The air tasted like I'd been locked in an outhouse for a week and just let out. Glorious.

"I'm sorry I put you through all that," I said.

"Well, if it weren't for *all that*, Roosevelt would never have discovered the great outdoors," she said. "His mood has improved tenfold since becoming an outdoor cat. You'll barely recognize him. He's a different cat altogether."

"Yeah?" I said.

"Oh, yes," she said. "Whoever came up with the idea that it's best to keep your pets imprisoned was a psychopath."

“You’re not worried he’ll get lost or, like, move in with someone else?”

“Not at all. He’s got a perfect sense of direction. And, why would he choose another home? He’s got exactly what he needs chez nous.”

“I’m looking forward to seeing him. I missed the little guy.”

“He missed you too,” she said. “A lot.”

The apartment smelled like banana bread. There was no evidence of the debauched picnic. Lillian had patched up the curtain and bought a cute area rug to cover up the turtle-shaped stain on the floor. Even the poodle was hot-glued back together and sitting all poodle-proud on the counter again. Only the keenest of eyes would be able to tell that his face was a little wonky. Never in a million years would I have thought he could be fixed.

17

Smooshed Gopher

About two years into living with Lillian, round two, I was punched in the gut three times in one day. Technically, only one of the punches was real.

Here's how the day unfolded.

Saturday morning. April Fool's Day, no less. I'd spent the night at Grey's place. We'd been dating five months to the day. Lillian knew him from her Toastmasters Club and had introduced us. He managed his family's small but successful hardware shop, called Ritchie's (their last name). He was of average height and average weight, with brown hair and hazel eyes. Small hands, large feet; large nose, small chin. Polo shirts, white sneakers. Cautious pedestrian, careful driver. Picky eater, fragile digestive system. His favourite pastimes were video games and collecting manga. His two styles of kissing mirrored his two styles of sex: the chicken peck and the dog slobber. He spent way too much time on my tits, which never did anything for me, and no time on my butt which, had he tried, absolutely did. He got hard-ons in his sleep and was always trying to hump me, claiming it was his equivalent of sleepwalking. He had an obsession with all things Asian and his manga collection took up half his living room. He started all of his jokes with "Here's one for ya!" and ended with "Badum-tss!" None of them were ever funny. After one month of dating, he gifted me a synthetic duvet. "So I can spend the night at your place sometimes. I'm allergic to feathers," he said, while bagging up my childhood duck down one I'd brought from Poverty Hill. He gave me a Dustbuster on our two-month anniversary. "I'm sorry to be the bearer of bad news. But ya got some dust bunnies multiplying under your bed. I'm allergic to dust, too." For our fourth, he bought me an alarm clock with a personalized recorded message—*Rise and shine, sunshine! Have a wonderful day!* I immediately deleted it without telling him.

On our fifth anniversary, the morning in question, during a chicken peck session on his couch before we parted ways, he gifted me a pair of fancy insoles. Because it was April first, I thought it was a prank.

"I've noticed you have flat feet," he whispered between pecks. "These should do the trick until you can see Dr. Crowley, a podiatrist over on the West side. He's a family friend, so I got you a deal. Do you have insurance? If not, you can go on mine. I took the liberty of scheduling your first appointment for next Thursday, eleven a.m. That's your day off, right? I can take you for lunch after, if you're available." Then he told me he loved me. That wasn't a prank either.

"Missy, I think this is it."

"It?"

"Yeah, the big L-word."

"Lesbian? Labia? Lemur?"

"L for L-O-V-E, Missy Whynaught. I think I'm in love with you," he said. "I'm a smitten kitten!"

I looked up at the clock: 8:35 a.m. It was one of those black Kit-Cat clocks. The ones with the big rolling eyes and a wagging pendulum tail.

"Uh, um," I finally spoke. "I think your cat's got my tongue."

"I don't have a cat," he replied. "I'm allergic."

"Really?" I don't know why I was surprised. "You never told me that! I thought you were only allergic to feathers and dust! How come you're fine around Lillian's ferocious feline?"

"Lots of Benadryl. And the superpower of the L-word. I considered catnapping the big guy, but I need to stay in Lillian's good books to keep close to you too."

"Oh, dear," I said, wincing. "You said it again."

"Yes, dear, I did, dear. Want me to say it louder this time, dear? Okay, here's one for ya. How 'bout I say it in another language just to be sure you understand? Amour! Amore! Gobble Gobble! That's Turkish if you were wondering. I'm fluent. I'm half turkey, on my mother's side. Turkeys take the L-word very, very seriously. It's in our wings. Badum-tss!"

"Listen," I said, forcing a smile. "I'm really, really sorry. But can you just, like, give me twenty-four hours to gather my thoughts? I am, umm. I mean... It's just... It's still so..."

He took my hand and smiled reassuringly, like a bedside nurse.

"Stop. You have nothing to apologize for," he said. "You don't have to say anything in response. It's still early days. Way too early to say the L-word. It's me who should be apologizing to you. So here you go: I'm sorry, Missy Whynaught, for falling in love with you. I hope you feel the same one day, but even if you don't, even if it'll hurt me like hell, I'm willing to take that risk. I believe you're worth it. I've never met anyone as interesting and kind and silly as you. I've never had so much fun with someone in my whole life. I am the luckiest guy in the world. Take twenty-four hours, or two weeks, or two months. I'll give you whatever time you need. I'll give you my forever, if you want it. Because…" He paused for a few more pecks. "Because I'm a lovesick turkey! And damn proud of it!"

He stood up from the couch and gobbled while flapping his arms as he made his way towards the front door to leave for work. "Please lock up and leave the key under the mat, okay? I'll call you later!" he squawked, using a long shoehorn to put on his white sneakers. "And watch out for them sly foxes. They can smell a fine turkey a mile away! And, you, my L-word, are one fine bird!"

First punch.

Nine-thirtyish a.m. I found myself walking through the Old Loyalist Burial Ground in King's Square, Canada's oldest graveyard and a popular pigeon and junkie hangout. Even though I hadn't been there in close to two years, I knew and loved every inch of it. I'd walked through it hundreds of times since moving downtown. When I lived at the Montague Suites and was so lonely, I would show up with booze and birdfeed. If no one was around or the pigeons got boring, I would hang out with dead folks and wonder how they lived and died. I was particularly drawn to the tombs with heartbreak written all over them.

Mr. Edmund and Mrs. Eloise Hogan, married in 1840, were my favourites. They shared a grave and birthdate: November 22, 1819. They also died on the same day, December 29, but sixty years apart:

Mr. Hogan in 1843 at twenty-four, and Mrs. Hogan in 1912 at eighty-four. I spent countless hours on the bench by their grave, polishing off bottles of red, chatting away.

Eloise (we were on a first-name basis) and I talked a lot about relationships and why she never remarried after Edmund tragically died of Scarlet fever. It's not that she didn't try to love again, but, even with so many handsome, eligible bachelors in Saint John, none could hold a candle to Edmund. And those who did, well, they couldn't handle her feisty, unladylike nature, preferring women who knew how to sew and bake and keep their mouths shut. Despite longing to be a mother, she accepted her spinster fate as a small price to pay for experiencing real, reciprocal love, albeit briefly. She found solace in memories of Edmund and in her conviction that they'd be reunited in heaven. But don't worry, she'd told me (before I met The Head), one day you'll find your Edmund and you'll live happily ever after. Chances of premature death are so much lower these days; you'll have nothing to worry about. Followed by (when The Head and I were together), take it from me, Missy, it's better to have loved and lost than to never have loved at all. Even if your Mama is right, and The Head does kick the bucket, love unites you forever.

I had turned my back on Eloise when The Head died. I wasn't proud of it, but I was jealous that she, if only as worm feed, got to be reunited with the love of her life, whereas I was convinced The Head had put a restraining order on me in the afterworld. I started to hate her. I stopped going to King Square entirely. For almost two years, I made a fifteen-minute detour to work just to avoid her. Fuck forever love and that gloating bitch!

Now there I was again, without even realizing it, mere steps from her grave. The church bells chimed nine times. Far from being heartbroken and jealous, I was torn over breaking Grey's heart, and I couldn't wait to share it all with Eloise. I sat down on the bench, lit a cigarette, apologized for being mean and petty, and let it all out.

I told her everything. How sweet and calm and generous Grey was. How he stocked up on my favourite foods when he knew I was coming over: carrot cake, Ringolos, peanut butter and chocolate ice-cream. How he made a mixtape of all my favourite songs and made sure it was playing when I walked through the door: Blue Rodeo, Patsy Cline, Portishead, the *Pulp Fiction* soundtrack. How he memorized my work schedule and gave me a key to his place and offered to put me on his insurance plan. The thoughtful, though boring, gifts. The long massages he gave without asking for anything in return; the regular six p.m. phone calls; the Valentine's Day card he slipped into my purse after only a few weeks of dating: A cartoon train puffing *I choo-choo choose you.* How he barely noticed my messiness, and seemed to take pleasure in tidying up after me. How he just now told me he loved me and gave me as much time as I needed to feel the same.

"But wait!" I told her. "Don't get too excited! There are downsides!"

His jokes were so painfully corny I was embarrassed to be with him in public. He read self-help books about how to understand and get attention from women, and jerked off to manga women. How he was annoyingly punctual, believed in horoscopes, wouldn't try new foods, used a shoehorn, and humped me in his sleep. And, oh my God, that alarm clock message! How he pecked at my neck like a chicken and slobbered all over my face and unmentionables like a dog. How he washed his hands a hundred times a day because he's a germophobe and allergic to everything. How, if my feelings for The Head were a roller coaster ride, those for Grey were a warm blanket or a bubble bath. And, most importantly, how, just a few days ago, I'd told my new best friend, Lillian, that I was planning on dumping him. I was always planning on dumping him.

"You can teach a man to be a better kisser, Lillian said," I told Eloise. "You can teach him to knock it off with cheesy jokes. But you can't teach a man to be generous, loyal, hygienic, and to pay attention to your likes and dislikes. You compare him to a bubble bath, but have you ever stopped to think how much you love bubble baths? You take them every day. They calm you down. They help you sleep. The exact opposite of a fucking roller coaster! I mean, really, Missy, he doesn't give you orgasms? You could wait a lifetime to find a dude who knows how to solve that man-puzzle. You were lucky to find one in the first place. Do yourself a favour and buy a dildo. I like the rabbit one. It's a two-for-one situation. You get a good cocking while the cute little bunny ears take care of your clit."

"Seriously, Missy, she said," I continued. "Men who are punctual and value dust-free rooms are few and far between. Plus, Grey works, and he has money. Family money. If you look at your track record, Grey comes out way, way on top. He's not homeless. He lives in Canada and speaks English. Maybe French too, I don't know. He doesn't have a creepy foot fetish that he needs to hide behind a phone. Get over your bad-boy, daddy issues and embrace the Greyster. You'll thank me for it one day."

"There you go, Eloise," I concluded. "You've got the whole picture now. What do you think? What should I do about Grey? Please give me a sign."

I lit another smoke and waited a few minutes. But when no sign came, I stood up to leave. It looked like it might rain anyway. Putting out the cigarette, I walked towards the garbage can to throw away my butts because I hadn't wanted to litter near the Hogans' graves. And that's when it happened.

Punch!

All of a sudden, everything—the gravestones, the cars passing by the park, the trees, the pigeons, the squirrels, my hands, the garbage can—were vivid and fuzzy at the same time. Like getting off a roller coaster. Like falling in love, or being in the throes of my *unreals*. But by the time I came to my senses, the culprit was a hundred metres ahead, crossing the road, turning left on King Street. I would have been useless at a lineup. Maybe white, maybe not. Maybe a teen, maybe an old geezer. Maybe three sheets to the wind, maybe sober. It happened so fast: impossible to be sure. My only recollection was that the stranger wore a jean jacket with a blue hood. And that it was a man. But come to think of it, maybe it wasn't even a man. No, who am I kidding? Of course, it was a man. Or was it?

I wanted to chase him down and ask: Why? Tell me, please! What did I do to hurt you? Whatever I did, I didn't do it on purpose! I felt worse than I did when someone gave me a dirty look if I accidentally bumped into them on the street. Memories of Jemima accusing me of trying to steal Bobby away from her and The Head believing I'd hurt him on purpose came to me, and I burst out crying.

There was no way I could have caught up with the stranger. So I continued walking as slowly as possible, holding on to the tenderness in my gut. I wondered if it was a sign from Eloise. If so, what the hell did it mean? For a split second, I thought: I wish Grey was here with me. He'd know what to do. He'd take care of me. A warm feeling came over me like the bubble bath Lillian was on about, but better. It was a feeling I'd never had before for a human being with a penis. Then I remembered the insoles, the turkey, the Dustbuster, and my thoughts about dumping him started all over again.

No, it wasn't a sign, I concluded. Despite my imaginary dead friend, I don't even believe in the afterworld.

Second Punch.

I was eager to tell Lillian about the punch—but also mostly about the L-word and the fleeting, potentially life-changing, warm stirring I'd felt thinking of Grey.

"Missy!" She was in the living room, sitting on the loveseat with Roosevelt on her lap, wearing her lilac housecoat and avocado facemask, drinking from her primrose-print china tea cup. She looked up from her Globe and Mail. "I'm happy you're home! You better sit down; I've got some difficult news for you—"

Then the phone rang.

"I'll get it. Hold that thought," I said.

It was Nadine. "Hey! I'm calling from my parents' yacht, and the phone will probably die any second now, but I've got some wild news. You listening?"

With Nadine, the news was always wild; whether or not it was real was another matter. I could hear the slush slush of the waves and the woosh woosh of the wind in the background, so I knew at least the yacht part of her story was real.

"I'm listening."

"Remember that guy you dated? The one who leached off you?"

"Which one?"

"The tall one who thought he was a tortured genius and left without saying goodbye. The one who drank Tia Marias for breakfast and couldn't get it up."

Those big hands and feet. That dark hair and eyes, the suicidal tendencies that brought me to my knees. The smell of Tia Maria still turned me on.

"Nathaniel."

"Yes, Nathaniel. Well, he tried to kill his ex-girlfriend. Found out she'd been seeing someone else, so he ran her over with a stolen truck. He left her to die like a smooshed gopher. She's in the hospital and expected to survive, thank God. Now he's in jail," she said. "I overheard my dad and his defence-lawyer friend who's representing him talking about it over dinner. What a coincidence, eh? Turns out his parents are loaded. After all that money you spent on him with nothing in return! What a dick! They say he'll be out on bail soon, even though he's a flight risk. His parents own an island or something. And a private jet. Anyway, before the phone dies, I also wanted to tell you about this new guy I'm dating. He's got six fingers—can you believe it? His fingers are magic!"

While Nadine rambled on about her six-fingered lover, I took the phone into the kitchen so I could stuff my face with a bag of cookies I'd bought for Grey but forgotten to bring over the day before. Nathaniel had liked cookies too. I remembered the time I baked him shortbread from scratch even though I hated baking. It was near Christmas, and I'd even bought reindeer cookie cutters and green and red sprinkles. At one point, I was licking the spoon, and he looked up from his word processor and asked me to please try and control my impulses. He reminded me that he preferred Amazonian-type women, like Gwen Stefani. "I know you can't do anything about your height," he'd said. "But your weight is fixable."

I put Nadine on speaker while I climbed on a chair to take the jar of Nutella out of its hiding place. I was only half-listening.

"He has a brother, who also has six fingers. It's a recessive gene. And he's single and looking. You game for a double date when I'm in town next month?"

I didn't respond. I was too busy dipping the last few cookies into the Nutella while remembering the Christmas stocking I'd also made Nathaniel. I stuffed it with his favourite things—a bottle of Tia Maria, a Tom Waits CD, a big chunk of hash, a Rubik's Cube—and gave it to him a week early out of fear he'd been gone by Christmas day.

When she mentioned Nathaniel's name again, I jumped down and took her off speakerphone. There was Nutella all over my hands, my face, now the phone.

"What?" I said.

"You scared?" Nadine asked.

"Of the six-fingered brother?"

"No, dummy. Weren't you listening? About Nathaniel probably getting out on bail soon. Like, what if he comes looking for you? You scared?"

I opened the fridge to look for something else to eat, making a mental note to wipe off the chocolate smudges before Lillian saw them. I was feeling as unreal and shaky as I had after being punched for real.

"Missy, did you hear me? I said: Are you scared he'll come looking for you?"

I was scared, but not because I thought Nathaniel might come looking for me. It scared me how much, despite not having thought much about him over the years, I wanted him to come looking for me. It scared me how much I wanted him in comparison to Grey. It scared me how much I wished that smooshed gopher had been me. It scared me that the only thing I wanted to do was douse myself in Tia Maria, take myself to bed, and fantasize about my fat ass on Nathaniel's disinterested face.

"No," I whispered, "Nathaniel never loved me enough to want me dead."

"Maybe I shouldn't have told you. Hold on a sec, the wind here is crazy." I could hear the scraping of matches as she tried to light a smoke over and over again. "Hey, I just thought of something else. Ya think it might have been Naked Lady—?"

Then the line cut.

Third punch.

I washed away the Nutella evidence and took a container of heavenly hash ice cream into the living room. Lillian was lying down, listening to one of her Toastmasters tapes on her yellow Sony Walkman with her eyes closed. She hadn't noticed my return, which meant she hadn't heard my conversation with Nadine. Lillian had only met Nadine once, but she couldn't stand her. She called her a sociopath and an entitled brat. Whenever Nadine's name came up, no matter the context, she went on a rant about how trust fund kids should be forced to work at McDonald's for a year. Then she'd start on about politics, which would lead to the pros and cons of her running for city councillor. Then whether she'd be able to hold her tongue, because she couldn't abide citizens who complained about issues like parking and minimum wage. She was in it only for the power and the benefits.

I was happy Lillian hadn't heard anything. I wanted her to dump on Nadine and discuss her political aspirations as much as I wanted another punch in the gut. I only wanted to tell her about Nathaniel, the punch from the stranger, and the L-word, in that order. But just as I was thinking of a way to bring up Nathaniel without mentioning Nadine, Lillian took out her earphones and jumped to a sitting position as fast as if someone had just pinched her bum. "You ready?"

"For?"

"My news."

"Yeah, sure Lillian. It's just that I want to—"

"Good," she interrupted. "Brace yourself, Missy, it's a doozy. You better sit down."

"It can't be any worse than the last two hours," I said through a mouthful of ice cream.

She put her hand on my knee, took a deep sigh, and closed her eyes, the only part of her face without avocado mask: "I'm pregnant."

I took a second to process. It wasn't as bad as I thought. "Okay..."

I said: "Well, what do you plan to do about it?"

I said: "I mean, this is a manageable situation whatever you do."

"With Pup's baby," she blurted out. "When he was here two months ago, we fucked like rabbits while you were at work. He's a surprisingly good lay. I was so into it that I forgot to double up on condoms. I've decided to keep the baby. You can call me Mama Lil from now on."

Imagine this in slow motion: I dropped my ice cream. Lillian did a nosedive to catch it in the nick of time. She ended up on the floor beside the coffee table, face up, holding the container high above her head like a live grenade. Meanwhile, I was frozen on the couch, trying to catch the breath that was knocked out of me again. Roosevelt, who'd left her lap when I sat down, waddled by, stopped to check out the action, hissed, then continued on his grumpy, highfalutin, cat way.

Lillian burst out laughing. "April Fool's!"

She sat back beside me and snort-laughed like a Boston terrier. "Jesus, Missy. It was just a joke! Where's your sense of humour? Of *course,* I'm not pregnant. You *know* I always double up on condoms. You *know* I want to be a mother about as much as I want herpes."

I still said nothing.

"Oh, come on, Missy. I've been planning that big boy for days now. Lighten up! Do you *really* think I'd sleep with your dad? Even *I* wouldn't go that far." She winked as she straightened up the pile of *O* magazines that had slipped off the coffee table. "As tempting as it is. *Not!* Now, how about we go and drink mimosas in the park? We can play your weird dog-person matching game. And you can tell me all about your last two hours. I hope it's good. I'm intrigued. Is it about Grey?" she asked. "You up for it? I'll buy you lunch."

"Very funny. Joke's on me. But maybe later, okay? I need a nap. I'm not feeling so hot. I think I might be coming down with something."

Lillian's forehead got all crinkly like when she was stuck on a cryptic crossword. "Really? It's only noon. It'll ruin your circadian rhythm. You won't sleep tonight, and then you'll sleep in tomorrow and waste half the day, and then go to bed too late and be exhausted at work Monday morning."

"Really."

It was mostly true. I knew I wasn't coming down with something. I could have easily joined her. I loved mimosas. I loved going to the park. I loved that she humoured me with my dog-person matching game. I loved spending the day with her, doing anything, anywhere. But I wasn't in the mood to tell her about my day anymore. I was exhausted. And my tummy actually did hurt. A date with Lillian could wait. She wasn't going anywhere, and I loved that too.

"Okay. Well, you go rest," she said. "I'm going to go out for a walk. I'll pick you up some vitamin C and echinacea. That always does the trick."

I took myself to bed and crawled into my new synthetic duvet. It was much more comfortable than the old smelly feather one. It had never occurred to me to replace it. Just as it had never occurred to me to dust my room or wear insoles for flat feet I didn't know I had. I checked the alarm clock Grey gave me: 12:42 pm. I wondered if I should have kept Grey's voice message after all. It was more soothing than the standard beep beep beep. But I didn't bother setting it. It was Saturday and I could sleep as long as I wanted. Lillian would surely wake me up if I slept too long. If not, Grey's punctual six p.m. phone call would.

Falling asleep, my mind kept returning to the smooshed gopher lady and the stranger who punched me in the gut and Eloise and Naked Lady. I felt the four were somehow related. I thought maybe Eloise hadn't spent her life pining over Edmond after all. Maybe I hadn't given her enough credit. Maybe she'd been relieved when he croaked because she was lesbian and was left to finally explore her sexuality and have the time, peace and quiet, without a man underfoot, to write her best-selling lesbian motorcycle romance novels. And perhaps the smooshed gopher lady *was* Naked Lady, who *had* been in a relationship with Nathaniel all these years. She'd briefly died from the attempted murder on the operating table, just enough time to meet up with Eloise in the afterworld that *does* exist, who told her to come and knock some sense into me once she was discharged. "Missy'll come visit my grave around nine a.m. on April Fool's Day. Give her a taste of what she dodged after being left by Nathaniel, and you didn't. Maybe it'll make her think twice about dumping that nice Grey guy who would never hurt a hair on that love-confused head of hers. Tell her that Lillian's right: men who value dust-free rooms and listen to your needs are few and far between. Get the dildo. The rabbit one rocks."

Thinking about it like this made the warm fuzzy feeling about Grey come back and I contemplated calling to tell him. I suddenly felt really lucky that he loved me. But I didn't want to give mixed messages, so I decided against it. He said I had all the time in the world to figure out my feelings. If the warm fuzzy feelings stuck around, maybe I'd tell him about it when called me later. I tried to imagine how I'd feel if he didn't call as usual. I tried to imagine how I'd feel if he changed his mind about the L-word. Would it upset me? But it was so impossible to conceive that I fell asleep before I had an answer. Maybe that was a good thing. Eloise, Mama, Lillian, and possibly even Naked Lady/Smooshed Gopher would be pleased.

18

Eight Ways to Dump Grey

July. It was a Sunday and I'd spent four nights in a row at Grey's. I stayed over so often, he'd bought me a housecoat, slippers, and an expensive electric toothbrush. Neither of us had to work and I was sleeping in. Meanwhile, he'd already run 10 km and made heart-shaped waffles and coffee from beans he roasted and ground himself.

I was on his Japanese-style floor mattress in his manga-fantasy-themed room: orchids and samurais and anime princess warrior posters on the walls. I half-woke to the sound of tinkle, tinkle, tinkle, tinkle. When I eventually opened my eyes, Grey was sitting beside me cross-legged, looking lovesick dopey, wearing a fake kimono and tinkling a fake zen wind chime. He was getting on my last nerve.

"What are we, in a cartoon? A video game?" I said. "I'm not a tinkle-tinkle, orchid-loving morning person. Why don't you just pay some computer whiz to create a fake manga warrior princess online girlfriend for you. I hear they can do that now, you know? I saw it in a movie. You can design her exactly the way you want. With big eyes and big tits and a tiny body that is so out of proportion there's no way in hell she could be real. But being real isn't the priority, is it? The priority is that she looks exactly like the girls you whack off to and, more importantly, doesn't talk back. The only things she'll say are what you program her to say. *Yes, Grey. Of course, Grey. You're so smart and sexy, Grey. Wanna stare at my big tits again while I stare back at you with my huge bug eyes and bat my long lashes and wave my magic samurai sword to the tune of your favourite anime cartoon song? I'll serve you tea afterwards and feed you sushi with my tiny hands*. I mean, come on, Grey, just thinking about your manga warrior princesses makes me feel fatter and clumsier and louder than I already am. And what's with the big tits, anyway? One: I don't have big tits. And, two: neither do most *real* Asian women. And Lillian told me it's racist to have an Asian fetish, and she's never wrong about these things. She has a university degree. Anyways, I'm the complete opposite of your manga princess warrior fantasy and you're gonna realize that one day and regret ever buying me that overpriced toothbrush. So I'm going to do you a favour and just say it: Sayonara!"

August. I sat on the bathroom floor one morning with a mirror between my legs and counted eleven spots. Then I counted three. Then I counted nine. Then there were none, and then there were eleven again. It was hard to get a good look; I was carrying fifteen extra pounds from all the cooking Grey did for me, and I didn't know what I was looking at or for. But there was no doubt in my mind: the STI from the German tourist I'd had sex on the beach with in Cuba was back.

I went to a walk-in clinic. "Nope, no spots," said the first doctor.

"Are you sure?" I said. "This is very, very important. I've got a boyfriend now, and he's a good person. I don't want to infect him."

"I'm sure," he said.

I went to another clinic. "Nope, no spots," said the second doctor.

"Please, look closer," I begged. "There were at least eleven this morning."

"Nope, you're all good to go."

Still, I went to the ER. "Nope, no spots," repeated the third doctor. "But aren't you the one who came here last year with a broken heart? Looks like you're on the mend, eh? Good for you!"

Directly after the ER visit, I got a large Iced Capp and four honey crullers from Tim Hortons. Then I sat down and wrote a letter. *Dear Grey, I'm so sorry I didn't tell you sooner, but I have a chronic STI and it's very, very contagious. You should get yourself checked out asap. Again, I am so, so sorry. I never meant to infect you. Please know this to be true. Regretfully yours, Missy.*

October. We hosted a Thanksgiving party at Grey's for both of our families. Randall bought a case of beer; Grey's sister brought champagne. Mama brought Nanaimo bars from the marked-down section at the Superstore; Grey's mother made two pumpkin pies from scratch with real whipped cream. We played charades, my family versus his. The Whynaughts didn't catch the CBC references; the Ritchies didn't know the game shows. Grey switched up the players halfway through to make it fair. "Here's one for ya! The Richnots versus the Witchies. Ha! Get it? Badum-tss!"

I'd been mixing champagne and beer all night. After everyone left, Grey and I were cleaning up in the kitchen. "You think my family's stupid, don't you?"

"Absolutely not," he said. "I think they're adorable."

"You're lying. You think they're adorable like you think Miss Piggy from the Muppets is adorable, which she isn't. That's why it was my nickname in high school. Because she's repulsive, fat and slutty just like I was. Like I still am. I was hoping you'd never find that out about me, but now you know. Miss Piggy's only cute in the way tourists from Toronto think folks from Milton, Nova Scotia, are adorable, so they take pictures and buy their stupid-ass trinkets and even fuck them, but then joke about how inbred they are in the books they write about them afterwards. Never in their wildest dreams would they marry and reproduce with them. Oh, yes, I've read the books. I *can* read, you know. All the Whynaughts can, which I know must come as a shock to you."

"Missy, I really don't know what you're talking about," he said. "I think your family is great, and I have no idea what books or Toronto tourists you're talking about."

"Yes, you do!" I threw a leftover pumpkin pie in his face. "You treat me like I'm a Miltonian inbred! Like I'm a Muppet! And now that I've thrown a pie in your face and you know about my slutty past, I know it's over. So it's over!"

December. Grey was concerned about my snoring. Not because he couldn't sleep, but because his uncle had a heart attack because of sleep apnea. He was worried that I would have a heart attack, too.

"It's genetic," I said. "Pup snores too. No one dies from snoring. Going to the doctor is a waste of time."

But he came home with his uncle's backup sleep apnea machine and begged me to give it a try. "Please, Missy," he said. "Just for one night to see if it helps. I'll sleep on the couch to give you time to get used to it on your own."

He redid the bedroom to maximize the best sleeping conditions, and set up a lavender mist infuser. He bought blackout shades and a little teddy bear with white noise options: heartbeat, waterfall, and an option to record your voice like that alarm, which, of course, he did: *Sweet dreams, Missy. I love you.* Then he took down the Asian princess warrior posters.

Grudgingly, I tried the machine.

I felt like an elephant with a long, thin trunk. I felt like someone was trying to smother me with ether. I felt like someone had abruptly come into my life and tried to correct flat feet I didn't know I had and triggered the STI spots that had been dormant for ten years and forced me to try sleeping quieter and more daintily like an Asian girl, which Lillian says is definitely a racist thing to say.

So I ripped off my trunk, stuck it on the teddy bear, and recorded a message of my own: *I really appreciate the trouble, Grey. I really do. But I like the way I sleep just fine, so I'm going back to my own bed. For good. Sweet dreams.*

January. One evening after sex, I admitted to Grey that, sometimes, most of the time actually, I never came. That the only person I came with other than myself was The Head. And the only way I *could* cum with Grey is if I imagined him as The Head having sex with Kathleen from rugby. And, while I was being honest, every once in a while, Freddy Krueger joined in for a threesome. To boot, I finally told him that I barely had any nerve endings on my nipples. "I know you're a boob guy, but you might as well be sucking on the end of my nose. Seriously. It does nothing for me. I've been pretending for years. I'm an ass girl, through and through."

"And while the boob stuff probably isn't a deal breaker," I continued, "I'm sure the fantasy stuff is. I hoped it would just go away on its own, but it hasn't. I understand it's just too messed up for you to stick around, and I can't explain why it's happening, only that it's getting worse. I should probably get help, but I'm not sure I even want to know why it's happening, so maybe I'm just doomed to a life without sex, which is fine by me because I don't really like sex. And I know you want kids, and how are we supposed to have kids if we don't have sex. Anyways, just imagine what being conceived out of Freddy Krueger fantasies could do to a kid! On that note, you should also know that I don't think I can ever love anyone as much as The Head."

Grey smiled calmly. "Don't worry about it, Missy. I don't expect you to love me the same as you loved The Head. And fantasies are just that: fantasies. As you know, I'm partial to manga-style women, but I don't *need* to make love to one. I don't *need* titty action, especially now that I know you don't. I'm more than satisfied being with you. As long as you *do* cum, it doesn't matter what's going on in your head. And I love your ass! Why didn't you just tell me it needed more attention? And, hey, here's one for ya: How 'bout I buy myself a Freddy Krueger mask? I've heard that's a real kink, you know? Ha! And I'm wide open to inviting a chick into the mix! I wish I'd known sooner! You're so fucking cute and weird; I love it!"

"That is the worst possible thing to say ever," I said. "Now I can never have sex with you again because, in addition to imagining you as Freddy Krueger, who doesn't turn me on unless Kathleen is around, I'll still be thinking that you imagine me as a warrior princess who's hotter and skinnier than me, and there's no way in hell I can deal with that screwed up double whammy. And saying all of this outloud makes me think I must be part lezzy. It explains everything. Maybe I'd have no problem cuming if you were a woman. But if you were a woman, I wouldn't come near you because, one, being a lezzy scares the shit out of me, which I know is homophobic of me to say, but it's true. And, two, lezzies in Saint John get beaten up, so I'd have to move to Toronto if I wanted to find a way to live my true self, which I don't have the guts to do, not to mention the fact that I could never afford an apartment in Toronto on a vet tech's salary. Now, if you'll kindly excuse me, I'm outta here, because, for sure, we can't move forward now that my perverted cat is out of the bag. Not that lezzies are perverted. I'm not homophobic, I'm really not. But anyone who fantasizes about Freddy Krueger surely is. I'm really sorry for wasting your time."

March. Grey went to a winter spa for a five-day work retreat. Something about improving employee morale and team building. He warned me that there were no phones on the retreat, no electronics at all. He said I could call if there were an emergency, but he truly hoped, for my sake, there wasn't. It would be the first time I wouldn't speak to him in a little over a year. But then I came up with the idea of leaving cute lovey-dovey phone messages every day, like diary entries to document our time apart. "He's always hinting that it would be nice if I showed him more attention," I told Lillian. "But it doesn't come easy for me, so not being able to call is the perfect opportunity. I keep telling him that if he backs off a bit, it'll make me want to chase him more. But he says games like that are unhealthy. A few phone messages can't hurt us, though, right? He'll love it!"

"Hey, Grey," I said on day one, "I hope you're having fun. Me and Lillian went to the movies. Then we cleaned the bathroom. Both activities were boring but helped pass the time, because, well, you'll be happy to know, I miss you. And I think you're great. And, no, this isn't a trick. This is me showing you that you make me happy. Anyways, if you get the chance to call, which I know you can't because there are no phone calls, please do."

Day two: "Hey, it's me again. The weather outside sure is shitty, eh? But I guess you're cozy by a fire, having spent the day in the hot springs, drinking and stuff, right? I hope you're having fun. I'm thinking of you and can't wait to see you again. Please call me if you can, even though you're not going to get this message until you get home, so no worries. Miss you!"

Day three: "Hiya. I had this crazy-weird dream that you were sharing a room with a pretty colleague, even though I know all your colleagues are men, and that she managed to seduce you because she was so pretty and you're so easily seduced, especially in your sleep. Ha, ha. I gotta tell you that I didn't like it, not one little bit. And I also don't like that you're away even though I know you're coming back soon and it's normal for couples to spend time apart. Maybe I shouldn't be telling you this at all, and I probably wouldn't if you'd called. But anyway. I hope you're having fun. Bye."

Day four: "I had another dream about you and your colleague—who, of course, is Asian— sharing a room together, so I tried calling. The receptionist said she'd give you the message but that they were short-staffed so it might not be until tomorrow morning. I thought, isn't it weird that a receptionist wouldn't give a guest the message immediately? And then I thought, maybe you told her that you didn't want messages from me and that the whole emergency-calls-only is just bullshit so you can be alone with your Asian colleague. And then I thought: Missy, you shouldn't tell Grey what's going on in your mind because even nice guys like Grey don't want to hear it. But here I am telling you anyway. I hope you're having a better day than mine. I really, really, really miss you. Please call me back."

Day five: "Okay, so Lillian said I shouldn't be leaving these messages because they are crazy and that women shouldn't waste their time being crazy, especially when it comes to men. And when I told her that you wished I'd make more of an effort to show you affection, and this was my attempt at making an effort, she said: Missy, you don't need to show anything to anyone. He's just trying to save you from something you don't need saving from. And then I said, Yeah, you're probably right. I *don't* need anyone to save me, and I sure don't need to be leaving crazy messages on answering machines to someone I'm not even sure I want to be with. So I asked her: You think I should dump him? And she said, Absolutely not, Grey's great, despite his saviour complex.

But I can't handle you being away, which is messed up because most of the time it annoys me that you want us to spend so much time together and, I'm sorry to say, it's true I'm always thinking of dumping you. So, you should probably go find someone who actually does need saving and doesn't want to dump you all the time. Which means we should break up asap. I'm sorry about this, about everything. And you don't need to call me back. Seriously, it's all good. Have a safe drive home. And a nice life. I'll send your key in the mail."

May. In the middle of the night, I got out of Grey's bed, walked the three blocks back to Lillian's pad, woke her up, and told her that Grey had dumped me. I don't remember anything about it. Apparently, I hadn't grown out of my Complex Nocturnal Visual Hallucinations. Apparently, I was sobbing and as pumped up as a warrior princess.

June. I moved in with Grey. Lillian was on board with it because her dominatrix business was booming, and she wanted to turn my room into a second, operating room-themed, dungeon. Nadine was in town, and we celebrated the move and my birthday. We hit at least five bars and she spent at least two hundred bucks. At the fifth bar, I ran into Dirk the Jerk on the dance floor.

"Looking good, Piggy," he said.

I pushed him away.

He came back. "You're looking good, *Missy.*"

I pushed him away again; he came back again. He pulled me in for a dance. He kissed my neck. He put his hands on my ass cheeks and squeezed them to the beat of "Crazy in Love."

I followed him to a bathroom stall. He put his hands down my pants and groaned. "I've missed you, *Missy.* You're so fucking hot, *Missy.* I want you, *Missy.*"

When the bar closed at one a.m. I called Grey from a payphone.

"I didn't push him away," I whispered.

"Did you like it?" he asked.

"No," I said.

"Are you okay?" he asked.

"Not really," I said.

"Are you going to do it again?" he asked.

"Never," I said.

"Then come home, Missy. Just come home."

19

Little Waves

Pup's funeral fell on an unusually warm day in October. So warm that the wake was relocated from the Fern Hill funeral parlour to Mispec beach. So warm that everyone was overdressed, and the room, despite little bowls of potpourri everywhere, smelt like sweaty frat-boy hangover. So warm that the weather dominated the conversation.

"Even dead," said the funeral director, an old drinking buddy of Pup's whose voice was startlingly similar to Feet Guy's, "Pup Whynaught found a way to follow the sun! That lucky bastard had an invisible umbrella over his head. He left rainbows and little waves wherever he went. If this here building were struck by lightning right now, absolutely everything would go up in flames. Except—" He took a moment to pat the coffin. "Except for this fella right here. Bless his sunny soul." It took everything I had not to stand up and yell, "Then why the fuck is he the one in a pine box and not us?"

Two days before the funeral, it rained. It wasn't unusual rain. It was that cold Maritime, it's-almost-November breakup-song kind of rain that comes every year, reminding us that in five months' time, even the Suzy

Sunshines of the world would rather shove an icepick in their ear than shovel one more dirty pile of snow. The kind of rain that made me want to pull out my winter clothes, take myself back to bed, and binge on cookies and Nutella while I wept over my summer fling. Not that I'd had a fling that summer I'd turned twenty-six. I'd had a baby. With Grey. He was three months old. We'd named him Philbert, after Pup, but called him Puck because he was round and his hair was black. Naming him after Pup was Grey's consolation gift for my finally agreeing that Pup was no longer welcome to stay with us when he was back in Canada or use our address to keep his residency and receive his pension cheques. Fortunately, Lillian stepped up again, but doubled her fee. I couldn't have spent the day in the bed even if I wanted to, I had to feed Puck.

And I certainly couldn't have spent the day weeping in bed because I didn't feel sad. I wished I could cry, but I couldn't. I hadn't shed one tear since I'd received the death call. It didn't make sense. What was wrong with me? I felt like a monster. How could I burst into tears over worrying I'd upset a stranger who punched me in the stomach, but feel not one iota of sadness over Pup's death? Even more monster-like was that I'd had the giggles all day, as if I'd smoked one giant spliff after another. I watched sad videos to try and snap out of it: A woman cradling her stillborn daughter to "In the Arms of an Angel." A fawn trying to suckle her mama who'd just been shot dead by a hunter. The compassionate adoption story of an emaciated Mexican street dog covered in hundreds of swollen, blood-filled ticks. He spent the minuscule amount of energy he had left trying to lift his hind leg to scratch away the mites partying all over his ears, but he didn't stand a chance and the mites knew it. No tears fell, not even one. I found the videos frighteningly funny. Especially the dog one.

And I couldn't have spent the day bingeing on ice cream and Nutella either: I had to go to the mall to buy an outfit for Pup to wear in the coffin. I strapped Puck in a carrier against my chest and headed out.

On the way, I watched an old geezer fall ass-first into a slush puddle. It took me five tries to help him back to his feet because I was laughing so hard.

At the mall, I politely asked a man approximately Pup's size if he could please model the clothes I'd picked out. Amazingly, he agreed. Tan cargo pants, Hawaiian shirt, white crew socks and blue boxer briefs with sharks on them. "The briefs are a bit tight," he said when he came out of the changing room.

"Not an issue," I hooted, slapping my thigh. "He's dead!"

As I was leaving the mall, my rock-hard tits dribbling milk, "Bicycle Race" came over the loudspeaker. All the shoppers stopped where they stood and started singing along to Freddie Mercury. True story. It was hilarious. I knew right away I'd choose it for the funeral. When it finished, I felt compelled to call an old friend from the mall payphone. I hadn't spoken to Candace in seven years. In tenth grade, she found her father in their garage after he'd blown his head off. He was American and had served in Vietnam. Of the half a dozen or so times I'd been to their home, I don't think I ever saw him smile, or sober. The day before his funeral, she invited a bunch of girls from school to her place for a fashion show of the black dresses she was considering wearing. She had loads of them. Each time she came out of her bathroom to model a new dress, she'd added something silly to it. A blue feather boa, a clown nose, green lipstick, a cone bra. By the time she was lip-syncing to "Papa Don't Preach," we were all up on our feet boogying along with her.

"Hey, Candace," I said. "It's Missy. Missy Whynaught."

"Oh, hey, Missy," she said. "Long time no see. What's up?"

"Not much. Just got a quick question for ya."

"Sure. Fire away."

"Did you love your dad?"

"You bet I did."

"Did you like him?"

"Not really." Then she started to laugh, and I did too.

"Thanks, Candace."

"Any time, Missy."

And the day before my excursion to the mall, I sat on the kitchen floor with baby Puck, both of us binge-eating, while I called all the important people in Pup's life. No one was ever home, so I left messages. "Hi, it's Missy. Pup's dead. Please call me back." I spent countless hours dialing, leaving messages, dialing again, leaving more messages, feeding Puck, stuffing my face. Pup had a lot of friends. My nipples were so bloody and chapped I was sure they would never recover. But baby Puck was having the time of his life. He got more milk that week than a dairy farmer. Every once in a while, just for shits and giggles, I let out a moo.

Randall was the first to call me back. He was convinced Pup was murdered. "Good on the Cubans for having the balls to do it. I'm surprised it took as long as it did," he said. But I could hear his voice cracking.

I could hear him chain smoking. I thought of the time when he was five and Pup had called him a sissy for refusing to jump into the twenty-foot water hole with us. And when he was twenty when Pup borrowed his band's van and crashed into a bear. He totalled them both, the van and the bear, then took the first flight he could get out of the country. "Did he leave any money?" he asked. I pretended I didn't hear him.

"Gotta call Mama," I said.

Mama said it was fucking divine retribution. She said it reminded her of a fucking Monty Python episode. Then she said she didn't believe me. "You fuckin' pulling my leg again, Missy? You better not be fuckin' lying, or I'll fuckin' pull all yer hair out!" Her voice was cracking too. She was also chain smoking. She sounded both scared and furious like she did when Pup once got locked up for DUI with me and Randall in the backseat. "Did he leave any money?" she asked.

"Gotta call Jemima," I said.

When Jemima finally returned my phone calls, she only wanted to discuss logistics. "Well," she said. "As I'm the eldest, I'm going to take over from here. We'll have the funeral in Saint John because there's an airport and lots of people will want to fly in. I'll get his body back. I'll make the arrangements. I'll do the paperwork." I didn't call her out for being so businesslike. We hadn't spoken properly since my disastrous visit to Milton when I was fifteen. We barely knew each other; I was still scared of her. All I knew was that she was still married to Bobby, had four teenagers and was recently born again. They lived in Grammy's old home and had added an extension and an in-ground pool.

"What can I do to help?" I asked. She responded

as if she'd been preparing for the conversation her whole life.

"You can buy him something to wear in the coffin. And you and Randall can choose two objects each for the display table and one song each for the funeral."

"Roger. I'll get right on that," I said. "What about Juan-Howard? You want me to get a song and an object for him? I can email his mom and ask—"

"The Cuba chapter is over, Missy," she snapped. "Juan-Howard isn't our brother. Never was. I don't ever want to hear his name again."

"Okay. I'm not sure if he left any money, though."

"Gotta go," she said.

Twenty-four hours before that, I was in the kitchen. Puck was in his bouncy chair, following me with his big baby eyes that were hazel like his Grey's but with the woebegone dazzle of his Grandpa Pup. I was exhausted. I'd barely slept the night before. But I couldn't have taken a nap even if Puck wasn't wide awake. I felt as though I'd just drunk twelve cups of coffee so I could stay awake to complete a life-or-death task made worse because I couldn't for the life of me figure out what the life-or-death task was. Food was my best tranquillizer in these situations. I kept asking Puck whether I should eat a salad or a Costco-size bag of two-bite brownies, but he was pretty useless. I'd gained a lot of weight since the pregnancy, and everyone was on my case about it, except him. He didn't care. Feeding time was feeding time. It was always feeding time. When the phone rang, he looked at me like, *Mama, as long as you get your boobies out for me, I don't give a rat's ass what you stuff your face with.* He was such a sweet baby.

I swallowed my brownie and answered the phone.

"Hello," I said.

"*Hola.*" It was a woman's voice. There was a delay and an echo.

"Hola," I replied.

"Es Pup. Él es—"

And then the line went dead.

The phone rang again two minutes later.

"Hello," I said.

"Pup esta muerto!" yelled the mysterious Latina.

It was hard to hear her over the bad reception and Puck's crying.

"What?"

"Muerto!"

"How?"

"En un agujero."

"Agujero?"

"Sí. Hole. En la playa. Beach."

Then the line went dead again.

I waited for her to call back, but she didn't. I waited for my tears to fall, but that didn't happen either. I felt nothing. The life-or-death task feeling, gone. The caller might as well have been trying to sell me vacuum cleaners. Puck was howling bloody murder, his mouth wide open like an angry demon, but, strangely, I couldn't hear him. The room was eerily silent. I sat down on the floor and stuck him on my boob while I finished the bag of brownies. Then I waited for Grey to come home from work so I could send him out for more.

In the middle of the night before the death call, I was woken up by dogs. I was in our King-size bed with Grey's hungry hard-on poking my butt one end and Puck's hungry lips searching for my tits on the other.

Neither of them woke up. At first, I figured it was the neighbourhood strays doing their thing to the full moon. Maybe a fire had broken out at the SPCA, or some puppy mill had just been busted. I waited for it to stop or for Grey and Puck to finally wake up, but when neither happened, I weaseled my way out of their grip. I grabbed my smokes and went out on the balcony. I didn't see any dogs or a full moon, but the howling continued. The sound was so deep and loud and intense that I got a chest-thumping, jaw-rattling, feel-it-in-your-bones rave feeling. Except it was the opposite of an exciting get-up-and-dance, feel-in-your-bones rave feeling. It was that heart-wrenching, listening-to-someone-sing-In-The-Arms-Of-Angel-acapella-at-a-funeral-for-a-child, feel-it-in-your-bones feeling. It was the saddest thing I'd ever heard.

These dogs don't sound scared or excited or hurt or pissed off, I thought. These dogs sound like they are mourning the death of their beloved master and don't know what the hell to do except howl their furry jaws off. The feeling was contagious. Without realizing it, I was howling along with them, tears streaming down my face. When it stopped as fast as it started, I lit a cigarette, waiting for round two, thinking maybe it was an intermission. But the only sounds were the rustle rustle rustle of the dying autumn leaves and Puck's wailing for milk. Must be another one of my Complex Nocturnal Hallucinations, I concluded. The auditory kind. How bizarre. Better go feed the kid.

When I slipped back in bed, Grey was still sleeping. He'd slept through it all; the dog song and Puck's cry. And Puck fell back to sleep while draining my left tit. Lucky guys. But I was still wide awake. That heart-wrenching, someone-singing-*In-The-Arms-Of-Angel*-acapaela-at-a-funeral-for-a-child feeling suddenly replaced by the life-or-death task feeling made worse because I couldn't for the life of me figure out what the life-or-death task was. I slipped out of bed again to check the stove and the front door and the bathtub and the BBQ that we hadn't used in weeks. Everything was fine; everyone was safe. Still, I couldn't fall back asleep or shake the feeling that, if I did, something awful was about to happen. So I spent the rest of the night on the couch watching *Law & Order* reruns, polishing off a tub of frozen yogurt and leftover Chinese takeout. Until it was Puck's feeding time again.

The week before the dog's requiem, Pup called me in the middle of the night. After a successful five-month stint in rehab, he'd returned to Cuba to complete step eight of his AA program: make amends with The Marias. When they laughed in his face, he fell off the wagon again, but somehow managed to hide it enough to be able to move back in with Marisol, Juan-Howard's grandmother, and keep up the arrangement of taking Juan-Howard out twice a week under supervision. I had access to his bank account and knew his small pension barely covered his bar tab. Still, he bought phone cards and called me almost weekly. Sometimes sober, sometimes not. I think I spoke with him more that year than I had in my whole childhood. I was sure every conversation would be our last. But this one really was.

"Missy! It's so good to hear your voice. You booked your ticket to come visit me yet? Is it the expense you're worried about? You don't have to pretend with me. I know that moneybags boyfriend of yours won't fork out a penny when it comes to me. I just don't get it. I've always liked the guy.

Never harmed a hair on that pretty little head of his. I bet The Marias got to him, didn't they? You tell him that The Marias are nothing but lying, gold-digging Commie spies. You tell him I've got proof they've been sucking Castro cock in exchange for extra meat since they were old enough to suck cock. They won the fucking lottery when I came around! A house, more meat, no more cocksucking. And, worst of all, *my* son who they seem to think is theirs! And what do I get in return? While they sleep soundly under *my* roof, with *my* son, in *my* house, that *I* built, I'm sleeping in a fucking hole on the beach. That's what!

"Now, to tell the truth, Pet, I think my hole is gonna work out just tickety-boo. I can finally get some peace and quiet. You know me. I'm happiest on my own. Never was a people person, me. I'm a loner by nature, born this way. Who needs a fucking home anyway? Homes are overrated if you ask me. Humans didn't always live in homes, you know. We just *think* we need them. Like toilets and microwaves. It's just another capitalist trick to keep everyone in debt. If it weren't for Juan-Howard, I'd stay homeless. But having a roof over my head is the only chance I got to get him back. And living under the same room as The Marias again is no longer an option. So, I'm gonna build another house! Just a small, simple one this time, mind you. More like a hut. It'll be 100 percent organic, like the early humans and the lucky African tribes whose villages haven't been bulldozed over yet by McDonald's to raise their fat, farting cows. I'll use clay and rocks and hay, maybe some scrap metal and glass if push comes to shove, but I can scrounge that up from the dump easily enough. Like a *real* environmentalist. Not like those

David Suzuki and Jane Goodall hypocrites with their AC and three-car garages. The land's gonna cost me a pretty penny though, and, of course, I'll have to pay whoever puts their name on it. It sure won't be someone I've banged before, though, I can promise you that! Learned my lesson the hard way with that sneaky whore, Yolanda! God forbid the fucking Commies actually allow anyone but them to own anything around here. Then they wonder why the Yanks wanna bomb them to smithereens. And maybe they should! Maybe I should call Clinton and tell him what they're up to over here. Oh, yes, I know *all* their dirty secrets. What I could tell the dumb Yanks would make their heads spin right off their thick red necks! Ha! Anyways, I'm just waiting on news from my union rep on some work so I can start getting the cash together. In the meantime, I'll be snug as a bug in my hole.

"But don't you go telling The Marias I'm happy with my hole. That's between me and you, Pet. They'd hunt me down the second they heard I was enjoying any kind of peace. They'd fill it in with concrete. That's what they're like, you know? They've turned everyone else on this island against me too! The favours I'm owed around here could keep me fed for free for the rest of my life. All I'm asking for is a few nights until the hurricanes have passed. But, *oh, no. Sorry, Pup. You can't crash at my place tonight, I'm washing my hair. Sorry, Pup, my kitten's giving birth.* Lying cunts! They're just scared The Marias will put a curse on them if they help me out. And I don't blame them! They're real witches! Seriously, Missy, I'm not just making it up. I've seen 'em in action. I caught them dancing and chanting around a live pig while they slowly sucked the blood right of him. Cackling away, with blood dripping down their ugly, witchy faces, while the poor animal squealed in agony. Took hours for the poor fucker to finally die. Ruthless, I tell ya! The only thing stopping them from murdering me is my next paycheque. So make sure you deposit it, eh? You're still doing that, right? The minute the *dinero* stops, I'm a goner, just like that pig. The Marias' mission is to suck every ounce of *dinero* and joy out of my life. And clearly they've gotten Grey to suck you away from me too! So you tell—"

I finally managed to get a word in edgewise.

"Please stop! That's just not true," I said. "Grey has nothing against you. He *does* like you. He just doesn't want me to travel with the baby. Remember? I have a baby now. He's two months old. His name's Puck. He looks a lot like you."

He always forgot I had a baby, but mention of Puck always calmed him down. And made us both cry.

"How wonderful! When can I come and meet him? That reminds me, I also really need to see a dentist about that front tooth I lost. How the fuck that happened is another mystery. I'm sure The Marias with their witchy curses had something to do with it. Next thing I know my fucking limbs will be falling off! Another reason for me to come visit soon. Make me an appointment, okay, Pet? I can come anytime. Just say the word, and I'll be on the next flight."

"Sure," I lied again, choking back my tears. I remembered the way he looked when Lillian's father picked him up like a baby and took him to rehab. *You don't love me, Missy,* his expression told me. *You're abandoning me just like everyone else.* I blamed Grey for keeping us apart and, in that moment, hated him for it. I wanted to pack my bags and leave on the next flight to Cuba. But then I heard Puck stir in the next room and continued the lie.

"I'll ask Grey tomorrow morning when the best time is for you to come and then I'll look into flights. I'll make sure the guest room is all set up. I don't like the sound of this hole, though—"

"Aww, you're the best. I can't wait to see you. And to meet your little guy. But I know you've got more important things to do than talk to me, so I'll say goodbye now. If you don't hear from me, it means The Marias finally got to me. That's if the hurricanes don't get me first! Those winds will drag me right out to sea! Ha! But don't worry, my hole's a real strong one. I built a roof for it out of an old BBQ grill and palm leaves. It should do the trick. Anyways, you make sure you write to the Canadian embassy in Havana and warn them about The Marias, okay?"

Click.

While we waited for the pallbearers to bring in Pup's coffin, I sat in the front pew, sandwiched between Grey and Mama, Baby Puck strapped to my chest. My eyes were still dry, but the black turtleneck sweater dress I'd stupidly chosen to wear was soaked with sweat. My tits, my neck, my shoulders, my belly—everything was itchy. I felt like the poor dog in the compassionate adoption video, covered in mites. I wanted to scratch scratch scratch, but my right hand was rocking Puck's bum so he wouldn't howl for milk, and Grey was squeezing my left. Every time I tried pulling it away, he held it tighter. It was annoying but yelling at him would have been inappropriate; all eyes were on us. For the millionth time, I wondered why I hadn't dumped him. I'll dump him tomorrow, I thought. Yeah, that's what I'll do.

Directly in front of us, the table displayed the objects that Jemima, Randall and I had chosen to represent Pup's life.

Jemima chose a silver chalice and a bottle of cheap red. She'd had the following poem engraved on it.

Dear God,
I gratefully thank you for giving me
My Dad
You must really love me,
Cause you gave
the best you had.
Watch over him and
Bless him, Lord
And keep him in your care
And may he feel
my love for him is my humble,
Heartfelt Prayer.

Randall deferred choosing objects to Mama, who put her everything into crocheting the most beautiful evil eye amulet the world has ever seen. Her second object was a tuft of Madonna's golden fur that she kept in a heart-shaped Avon jewelry box, alongside me and Randall's baby teeth.

Despite Jemima's clear instructions to keep the Cubans out of it, I made sure to incorporate Juan-Howard into my own objects, which weren't two, but many, all bundled up into a kind of collage/sculpture of things I'd kept over the years. Photographs of Pup with all four of his children. Scribbled on menus and postcards from around the world. A bike lock, court summons, tax returns, BBQ tongs. A petrified Cadbury's fruit and nut chocolate bar, his favourite. A lobster claw. A piece of the deflated donut cushion he used for the angry boil on his ass. Tiny handcuffs from the Guantanamo prison gift shop he'd given me for my nineteenth birthday. When Randall saw my creation, he mouthed *LOSER*. He'd done the same thing when he was carrying Pup's coffin with the other pallbearers and heard "Bicycle Race" playing. We both got a good chuckle out of it.

The ceremony didn't last long. It was too hot. Too smelly. Everyone was literally itching to get the hell out of there. Several of Pup's buddies stood up and told similar drinking stories. Jemima read a prayer about Jesus rising from the dead and how guilty she felt for living her life only for herself rather than for God. She kept repeating: "I am a sinner, I am a sinner."

Mama didn't bother standing up but just shouted from where she was. "Fifty bucks says the fuckin' coffin's empty!" And then: "It's just another insurance scam, I'm sure of it." Then she began to sob until a crow smashed into the window and snapped her out of it.

That's when the funeral director (who I was sure by then *was* Feet Guy) jumped in again and said, "Well, what are we all waiting for? Let's hit the beach! Just as Pup would have wanted!"

Over the years, I've remembered the ceremony in different ways. Did Jemima really allow "Bicycle Race" to blare from the loudspeaker? Was it really Mama who said the coffin was empty? Flash memories of the funeral director/Feet Guy holding me back from prying it open makes me think otherwise. And if anyone would remember a single crow crashing the funeral, it's Mama, but the few times I asked her about it, she said, "Are you on crack? Snap the fuck out of it, Missy; you're a fuckin' mother now."

But that it was an unusually warm October day, there is no doubt. It's documented. Not just in the

Farmers' Almanac, but in a photo album. Big Red by then had built a name for himself as a fine Saint John photographer specializing in candid Polaroids. He didn't attend the ceremony—too sad, he said—but he didn't miss a minute of the twenty-four-hour beach party that followed. He took dozens of photos and made me an album. I regularly show it to Puck. It's our favourite bedtime story.

"There's Uncle Randall, stoking the bonfire," I'd tell him. "He kept that fire alive all night! He took it so darn seriously. Every time someone offered to take over, he was, like, 'No, man, just leave me to it.' It was almost like he was trying to prove something, ya know? Uncle Randall looks so much like your Grandpa Pup in that photo. It could be Grandpa Pup. He was always so scared to be like Grandpa Pup. Still is. That's why he doesn't want children of his own."

"And there's your Grandma Wendy, my mama, combing the beach for treasures she might one day use to summon or keep away ghosts. She's a special one. See her long blonde hair and long black skirt blowing toward the sea? Isn't she lovely? She's so beautiful when she's not shooting her mouth off like a sailor. For sure, she was thinking of a way to forget Grandpa Pup. I don't remember a time when she wasn't. But she never will. She'll wait forever."

"And there's Madonna's old vet, and the funeral director, and Pup's union rep, all sitting on a driftwood log together, sharing a funny story, probably about Pup. Yeah, the funeral director *does* look creepy. I heard he moonlights as a foot masseur. If only you knew the half of it."

"And that's Aunt Jemima cross-legged on the sand, talking to God, pretty as a picture. I don't know what she was saying to God, sweetheart. I've never been able to figure that one out."

"Here's some guests doing the party train around the bonfire. Here's someone building a sandcastle. These two are kissing under a tree. There's Aunt Lillian bossing everyone around. And here's your daddy, cradling you, pointing to something in the ocean."

"Yes! That something in the ocean is *me*! Despite your daddy's best efforts, I stripped down to my bra and undies and started swimming. It felt amazing! My itchy skin began to soothe. My boobs, sore from all your sucking, felt better. My giggles, my anger, all that heavy guilt over not introducing you to your Grandpa Pup all hushed for a moment, too. I kept swimming, leaving a trail of spoilt milk like an oil spill. I kept swimming toward the oil refinery that only a town like Saint John would build off such a magnificent beach. I kept swimming until I could no longer hear you or your father's calling for me to turn back."

"Of course, I eventually stopped swimming! I wouldn't be here if I hadn't, would I? I turned to face the beach. It was so far away. You and daddy were like tiny black bugs wriggling out of the sand. It was kind of scary. I started to panic. I thought: Have I gone too far? Will I make it back? What have I done? But panic's like the tide, Puck. Don't forget that. As soon as I remembered to trust the water, it rolled out again. Plus, I've always been a very strong swimmer. I'm part mermaid, you know."

"Then the wind showed up and blew a few waves around me. It wasn't a dangerous or unusual wind, nothing for anyone to get excited about, nothing to stop the party. But it was enough to get into my bones and send a slight shock up my spine. It was enough for me to listen to its message, which was, word for word, "For goodness sake, Missy, get your big bum back to the beach! It's October, you silly goose!"

The wind spoke to me alright. Moving through the waves, weightless, I turned into the mermaid I was meant to be. Across the water, through the seaweed and the foam and the familiar sea creatures of my dreams. To the sand, where my legs came back, this time more solid than ever. All the way to Grey, who was, as always, a warm blanket after a bubble bath; who was still holding Puck tight as he howled for my milk. And isn't it mind-blowing that never did I once question whether he'd be safe in his father's arms? Or that he'd still be there at all? That wind and its little waves brought me right back to where I'd left them. Then it headed out again, whispering one last time: "Come back when you're ready, Missy. *Mi casa es tu casa.*"

Pup would've seen the funny side of it, and I did, too. It was all such a relief—all of it. Then I finally cried.

Acknowledgements

Thank you to my editor, Leila Marshy, for taking me under her wise and loving wing and for opening up so many doors. Leila believed in me from the get-go, even though I didn't know what the heck I was doing, and continues to put up with me even though I still don't. Thanks also to the rest of my Baraka Books editorial team, including Elise Moser for her meticulous proofreading of my book and to Robin Philpot for taking a chance on me. I am very grateful to be in such good hands.

Thanks to the Conseil des arts et des lettres du Québec and to the Canada Council for the Arts for their financial support.

Thank you to *Riddle Fence, The Missouri Review,* and *Prism International* for publishing some of the short stories-turned-chapters in Missy Whynaught.

Thank you to Heather O'Neill, whose review of the first-ever short story I wrote is tacked to my wall and my go-to antidote when that crippling self-doubt comes knockin'.

Thank you to my beta reader, Tracey Waddleton and to my early writing mentor, Mark Lavorato, who both played an important part in making Missy shine.

Thank you to my valued friend and most loyal fan, Melanie Shatzky, for her impeccable feedback, tireless support, and for "getting" my writing (and always coming to my rescue when I get swayed by those who don't).

Thank you to Rose Gowen, whose editorial expertise on earlier versions, friendship and inspirational commitment to the writing life kept me on track more times than I can count.

Thank you to the one and only Naomi Blenskinsop, for being my nearest and dearest, and to my fantastic mothers-in-crime, Sarah Blumel, Nadine Blumer, Tatiana Gomez, Maia Kapahi, and Kirsty McEachern, who stuck by me through thick and thin (literally).

Thank you to my co-parent, Lune Bellec, for taking the reins of our wildlings while I wrote, and to my wildlings, Louis, Edouard, and Felix Bellec, for keeping it wild (I love you silly).

Thank you to Alex Matteau, whose music and love slow me down in the best kind of way.

Lastly, thank you to my best friend and mother, Judith Gallant—despite her fear that Mama Whynaught is based on her, nothing could be further from the truth; a better parent I could never imagine.

NOTABLE TITLES FROM BARAKA BOOKS

Baraka Books

MY THIEVERY OF THE PEOPLE
Stories by Leila Marshy
Winner, 2026 Danuta Gleed Award for Short Fiction
Finalist, 2025 QWF Paragraphe Hugh Maclennan Award for Fiction

EYES HAVE SEEN, FROM MISSISSIPPI TO MONTREAL
A memoir by Fred Anderson
Finalist, 2025 Concordia First Book Award
Silver Winner, 2025 Foreword Indies Award

NORTHERN GIRLS
True Stories by Michelle Willms

THE GUILT TRIPPERS
A novel by Philippe Mineau

SAINTS REST
A novel by Luke Francis Beirne
2025 Editor's Choice: Maritime Edit Magazine

TUNES FOR DANCING BEARS
A novel by Irena Karafilly

LOOKING FOR HER
A novel by Carolyn Marie Souaid

IN THE SHADOW OF CROWS
Stories by M. V. Feehan
2024 Seaboard Review Book Pick